THE
BRIDGE

by *USA Today* Bestselling Author
SHANNA HATFIELD

The Bridge

St. Johns Bridge interior illustration by Briana Romancier

Cover Design by Shanna Hatfield

Published by Wholesome Hearts Publishing, LLC.

To those who give their all for the greater good.

Books by Shanna Hatfield

Summer Creek
Catching the Cowboy
Rescuing the Rancher
Protecting the Princess
Distracting the Deputy
Guiding the Grouch
Challenging the Chef
Marrying the Mechanic

Christmas Letters
Dear Mister Frost
Dear Mister Silver
Dear Miss Nicholas
Dear Miss Baker

Love on the Beach
Moonlight Cove
Sunset Shore

Winter Wishes
The Snowman's Sweetheart
Sleigh Bell Serenade
Winter Wonderland Romance

CHAPTER 1

"WE HAVE A SITUATION."

The spoonful of Fruity-Ohs halted in mid-air before Portland Police Bureau Sergeant Archer Raines could take a bite. He cringed at his cell phone, wishing he'd ignored it instead of answering when his boss's name had popped up on caller ID.

"Situation, sir?" If Captain Mark Cohen had reached out to him on his day off, the circumstances must be heading toward desperate.

Archer drew in a deep breath, inhaling the scent of the lush noble fir Christmas tree blocking the view out the living room window and the scented wall plug-in that smelled like a combination of cinnamon and fresh winter air. He'd hardly had a chance to enjoy the tree or the other holiday decorations that filled his home. His fingers skimmed over the stack of Christmas cards he'd anticipated reading while he ate his breakfast. In the background, Frank Sinatra sang "Jingle Bells" on the vintage vinyl record Archer had tracked down for his wife's growing collection, adding to what was a festive atmosphere prior to the captain's call.

"I hate to ask, but we need your help."

Archer let the spoon plop into his bowl of cereal, splashing milk on the kitchen counter as he processed what the captain was asking. He'd volunteered to work Easter, the Fourth of July, and Thanksgiving so he could have Christmas Eve and Christmas Day off. All he'd wanted was time away from work to enjoy the holiday with his wife, Lena.

After sleeping in until eight, he'd made his way to the kitchen to indulge in a bowl of the sweetened cereal he rarely ate but had enjoyed as long as he could remember. His intention was to spend the morning lounging on the couch while catching up on all the football news he'd missed the past few weeks. December had been insanely busy. When he wasn't at work, it seemed like he and Lena had attended an endless array of holiday events and gatherings.

"Now, sir?" Archer asked, although he knew the answer. The captain wouldn't have called if the need wasn't immediate.

"Right now." The captain sighed. "Look, Archer, I know I promised you'd have the next few days off, uninterrupted, but this situation requires your expertise."

Archer straightened his slumped posture on the barstool and picked up his phone, mentally shifting into police sergeant mentality instead of a laid-back guy planning a quiet morning to himself. "What's going on?"

"Suicidal and possibly armed man on the St. Johns Bridge. You're the closest person with the necessary skills to talk this guy down. Even if you weren't the closest, I'd still ask you to be there for this one. The bridge is closed, and we're trying to clear multiple wrecks caused by the person in crisis. I need you to get there ASAP and keep this guy from hurting himself or anyone else."

"Any visible weapons?" Archer asked, as he threw away his cereal and quickly wiped up the spilled milk on the counter. Lena didn't need to come home from work and find a mess he'd left behind. He lobbed the dishrag into the sink and turned off the record player before he hastened down the hallway to the bedroom to change. He couldn't exactly leave the house in sweatpants, and the ratty Portland Trail Blazers T-shirt Lena had threatened to banish to the pile of rags they kept in the garage.

"None that we've seen, but he claims to have a gun on him. No one's been able to get close to him to verify." The captain sighed again. "I don't need a jumper off the bridge today."

Archer could picture his boss running a hand through his graying hair in a move he'd seen hundreds of times in the twelve years he'd worked for the Portland Police Bureau. Mark Cohen had dedicated his life to upholding the law and serving the community. It would be a great loss to the bureau when the man got around to retiring.

"I'll get there as soon as I can," Archer said, snagging a clean uniform from the bedroom closet.

"Thanks, Archer. I really am sorry to call you in today. I know you and your wife have plans."

"She'll understand, sir." At least Archer hoped she would. Otherwise, he might spend the holiday sleeping on the couch and watching Santa leave lumps of coal in his stocking.

He sent Lena a text, then tossed the phone on the bed as he pulled on pants and a pair of wool socks. Uncertain how long he might be out in the cold, he layered on a thermal shirt and soft body armor beneath his uniform shirt, gathered his gear into a backpack, then wrote Lena a quick note that he left beneath a snowman magnet on the refrigerator door in case she didn't get his text for some reason. His wife would be home shortly after noon, ready for an afternoon of holiday merriment. They'd decided to enjoy a leisurely lunch at their favorite neighborhood restaurant, then drive over to Pittock Mansion to see the holiday decorations at the historic home. Lena had mentioned tootling around to look at Christmas lights before joining friends for dinner. After that, they'd attend the Christmas Eve service at church.

Now, Archer had no idea if he'd be able to keep any of the plans they'd both been looking forward to for weeks—although, truthfully, he didn't mind missing the mansion tour or driving around to look at lights. Traffic was horrible on a good day, and Christmas Eve was a nightmare with people scurrying everywhere on last-minute errands or visiting family and friends.

Given a choice, Archer would be perfectly content to stay at home, gorge himself on Christmas cookies, and watch sappy, happy-ending holiday movies with Lena until it was time to leave for the Christmas Eve service.

However, it appeared that option was already on the way to being long gone right along with their holiday plans.

Maybe the guy on the bridge would be easy to talk down, and Archer could soon get back to his holly jolly holiday. It was the first time in five years he'd been scheduled to have both Christmas Eve and Christmas Day off, and he'd wanted to make the time they were together special for Lena.

"So much for that," he grumbled as he hurried into his garage, slipped the backpack over his shoulders, then pulled on his helmet and gloves and rolled his motorcycle outside. As he cranked it to life, he glanced back to make sure the garage door was securely shut, then raced down the street. If the bridge was closed, traffic would be in a snarl around it. Days like today made Archer regret buying a house less than two miles away. He couldn't count the number of times he'd been called to help with a wreck or someone acting suspiciously on Portland's tallest bridge.

The steel suspension structure had opened in 1931, and a park had been constructed beneath it on the east side of the Willamette River. As Archer zipped around cars, he could see the Gothic-style towers that were a hallmark of the bridge standing tall and proud against the ashen morning light.

The air felt heavy and damp, as though a storm might roll in at any moment. That was all they needed—to be stuck on the bridge in a drizzling rain or have sleet pounding against them. If the temperature kept dropping as it had the past hour, they might even see some snow. Under other circumstances, Archer would have eagerly welcomed a blizzard on Christmas Eve. Today, though, he'd prefer sunshine and unseasonable warmth to Jack Frost nipping at his nose.

Traffic was heavy and moving at the pace of a snail as Archer zoomed in and out of cars until he reached the barricade that stretched in front of the bridge. Typically, two lanes of traffic flowed in each direction on the Highway 30 Bypass that crossed over the river. With traffic stopped, he drove around the barricade and up the wrong side of the road, past angry-faced drivers sitting in their unmoving vehicles, stuck on the bridge until the wreck ahead could be cleared out of the way. Archer stopped and left his motorcycle on the pedestrian sidewalk near two police cars parked a dozen yards from a multi-car collision in the middle of the bridge.

A vintage pickup hooked to a worn-out camper trailer had stopped sideways across all four lanes, causing the collision and effectively blocking all traffic. The sickly lime-green hue of the pickup matched the rusty cream and green tones of the trailer that appeared to have been held together with duct tape and despair.

The camper trailer currently looked like a misshapen taco with the center caved in from where a maroon car had plowed into it. On the opposite side, the pickup's hood crumpled toward the windshield from the impact of being hit by a minivan.

Archer sent a prayer skyward that no one had been seriously injured as he removed his helmet and left it on the seat of his bike. He took his duty belt from his backpack and fastened it on, then yanked on a stocking cap as he walked over to the police cars parked nearby. Two patrol officers he recognized, Morgan and Garcia, waited for him there.

"Captain Cohen said to check your messages." Morgan handed Archer a police radio.

"Thanks, Morgan." Archer attached the radio to his belt, then quickly glanced at a text from the captain. His cold fingers tapped out a reply, and then he tucked the phone into his pocket. He checked to make sure the radio was working and took the electronic tablet Garcia held out to him. "So, what do we know about our person in crisis?"

"Leon Mumford is forty-two. Divorce was finalized in July. Ex-wife is Tiffany. Two kids—Emma is fifteen, and Aiden is thirteen. He had a job for sixteen years working for the same company in Portland but lost it seven weeks ago. He moved out of his apartment three weeks ago and has no current address except for a post office box in Beaverton." Morgan pointed to the report Archer scanned. "He had a newer sedan that was paid for, but it looks like he traded it in for the old pickup and camper trailer about the time he left the apartment."

"It's likely he's been living in the camper." Archer glanced at Morgan and then at Garcia. "Has anyone gotten any info out of him? Is he talking? Do we know for sure if he has a weapon on him?"

"We were first on the scene, and he told us to stay back or he'd shoot, but we haven't been able to get a visual on a weapon. When he climbed over the railing, he shouted that he was going to jump and wanted to be left alone. He keeps mumbling to himself but won't engage when we speak directly to him. Officer Kennedy is keeping an eye on him. Officer Yeung tried for over an hour to talk him down."

Archer observed the man who sat on the railing in the center of the bridge. At a glance, he might have been sitting on a lakeshore, waiting to catch a fat trout without a care in the world, not precariously balancing between life and death. The tense set of the man's shoulders and the tension in his clamped jaws, however, were hard to miss.

Truthfully, Leon Mumford looked like a powder keg about to explode.

Archer turned back to the two patrol officers. "Where are we with getting the wreck cleared and the rest of the cars off the bridge?"

"The tow truck should be back soon. It's already hauled off two of the wrecked cars. We took down statements from everyone involved in the wreck and those who witnessed it," Garcia said, nodding his head toward the cars stuck on the bridge. "They all said pretty much the same thing. The pickup drove onto the bridge, slammed on the brakes halfway over, and stopped across all four lanes without any warning. Once the vehicles quit plowing into it, the driver hopped out, climbed onto the railing, and he's been there since."

"Injuries?"

"Multiple, but nothing life-threatening. Ambulance crews transported everyone who needed further treatment." Morgan stood with his hands at his sides, apparently ready and waiting for action. "Mumford keeps wiping at his forehead, but we've been unable to get close enough to see if he's injured."

Archer walked over to the pickup and glanced inside. A crack in the windshield smeared with blood and drops of red trailing out of the pickup to the bridge's pedestrian walkway told him Leon Mumford had likely hit his head, either when he'd stopped the pickup or when one of the vehicles had slammed into it. Maybe the guy had hoped to end his life in an accident on the bridge, or, more likely, he hadn't been thinking at all.

"Did you ask if he was hurt? Offer treatment?" Archer asked the two officers.

"We did," Garcia said, "but he refused to speak with us. He won't talk to anyone. If we try to get close, he just threatens to jump or shoot us."

"Okay." Archer sent a text to the captain with an update, offered a silent prayer he'd survive to spend Christmas with Lena, and drew in a calming breath as he walked around the wreck. He strode over to where two officers stood about ten feet from a man huddled in a canvas jacket as he sat on the railing, both hands gripping it with such force his knuckles had turned white.

Archer took a moment to study the person in crisis. Leon Mumford looked like someone whom life had kicked in the teeth. His hair hung in stringy, unkempt strands around his ears. He hadn't shaved in a while and had a full mustache hanging over his lip, based on what Archer could see from his left-side view. The man's coat and lace-up boots were good quality but worn. Leon was thin, probably only five-seven or so, and looked like a strong wind might fell him. Which was not what anyone, with the possible exception of Leon himself, wanted to happen.

The season of hope was upon them, after all, and Archer refused to give up on this man, even if Leon had given up on himself.

He moved closer to Officers Kennedy and Yeung. "Did you get anything out of him?"

"No. He won't talk to us despite every tactic we've tried. He also gets jittery if we try to move any closer," Yeung said, tipping her head toward the railing. "I hope you have better luck than us."

"I'll do my best."

Cautiously, Archer took a step forward, noting bloodstains on Leon's jeans. He watched as the man lifted his right hand to his face, then wiped his fingers on his thigh, leaving behind evidence he'd sustained a head wound.

The fact that Leon was still on the bridge and not already dead from falling more than two hundred feet into the water told Archer two things.

One: Leon wasn't eager to die.

Two: Something made him want to live.

Archer eased back to where the two officers waited. "Get me a first aid kit. Bandages."

Kennedy jogged back to the nearest patrol car. He quickly returned with a first aid kit and held it out to Archer.

"Thanks." Archer nodded once, then walked in a slow, purposeful stride toward Leon. He was five feet away when Leon's head whipped around, and he gave Archer a startled look. With blood running down the right side of his face from a gash on his temple and his eyes glazed from either trauma or possibly drugs, Leon Mumford could have passed for an escapee from a mid-century mental institution.

Archer kept his stance relaxed, his expression open, and tried to take in every detail he could in the moment Leon's gaze connected with his.

Pain. He could read the man's pain as if it were written in bold print.

Archer waited.

Leon continued staring at him while both hands clutched the railing as though the cold metal was a lifeline he refused to relinquish.

"Mr. Mumford, my name is Archer Raines. May I come a little closer?"

"No."

Archer held up the medical kit. "I brought some bandages. Would you like some help with that cut?"

"No." Leon glanced away and then his eyes darted back to the medical kit. He wiped at the blood about to trickle into his eye and smeared it on his jeans. Archer heard a sigh, as though it was offered in resignation as Leon reached out with his left hand.

Rather than give him the whole kit, Archer opened it and tore open a package of gauze and handed it with three large bandages to Leon.

The man dabbed at the blood, then awkwardly pressed one of the bandages to the wound, tucking the others into his coat pocket. The whole time he attempted to treat his wound, he kept one hand gripping the railing.

"Mr. Mumford, I'd like to help you. Would you let me do that, Mr. Mumford?" Archer kept his tone smooth and tranquil, like a disc jockey on an easy-listening radio station winding down the evening playlist.

"No. I don't need help." Leon glowered at him. "I don't like being called Mr. Mumford."

Archer stepped back and handed the medical kit to Yeung, then moved closer to Leon. He leaned against the railing, assuming a casual pose. "Would you prefer to be called Leon?"

A shrug was the only response.

"What brings you out here this morning?"

Leon made a scoffing noise and muttered under his breath.

Archer picked out words that sounded like, "can't even kill myself without causing more trouble." So, Leon did have a death wish. Apparently, he'd hoped to die in a wreck. Of all the places to do that, the bridge had been a terrible choice. Leon could have taken several lives in addition to his own with his recklessness.

Unable to think about how one man's careless choice was impacting hundreds of people, Archer tucked his emotions away. He needed to turn all his focus on getting Leon to come off the railing and allow them to provide the help he obviously needed.

Retaining his casual posture, Archer schooled his expression into one of curiosity. "Did something go wrong with your pickup when you were driving it across the bridge?"

"No."

Archer pointed to the old vehicle that was beyond any hope of repair. "You know, Leon, my grandpa had a pickup like that when I was a kid. Is it 1972?"

Leon turned and stared at him for so long, Archer was able to gather some pertinent information. The man was cold, for one thing. And he kept swallowing as if he was thirsty for another. If Archer wasn't mistaken, Leon had sustained a concussion in the collision.

"Yeah. It's a '72. My folks had one like it when I was a boy."

"When you were a boy?" Archer asked, keeping his tone curious and friendly. "Did you grow up on a farm?"

"No. In town. Roseburg. At the time, my father worked for a mill."

"For a mill? A lumber mill?"

Leon nodded. "I used to go with him sometimes. He drove a lumber truck. I liked to watch them load the logs." Leon blew out a long breath. "I haven't thought of that in years, not since he died."

"Died?"

"His heart stopped when I was in high school." Leon sniffled.

"That must have been hard for you, Leon."

The man nodded but remained silent as he looked out across the water. Archer tapped a quick text message to the team he knew was digging into Leon's life. With his radio on, everyone listening could hear what was said, but he wanted to make sure the team had the pertinent details.

"How about we get you something warm to drink, Leon? Do you want a cup of coffee?"

"No. No coffee."

Archer smiled at him. "What about hot chocolate, or do you prefer hot tea?"

"Chocolate," Leon mumbled, then looked back across the water.

Archer sent a text and waited.

It took less than ten minutes for Morgan to walk up to him with a thermos full of hot chocolate and two disposable foam cups.

"Thanks," Archer said quietly, filling a cup with the steaming liquid, then edging closer to Leon.

"Hey, Leon, I've got that chocolate. It's piping hot." He held out the cup, and Leon took it in his left hand, maintaining his grip on the railing with his right.

Archer poured his cup half full, then screwed the lid back on the thermos and set it near his feet. He took a sip and resumed leaning against the railing.

Leon was paranoid and nervous. He held his cup halfway to his mouth, watching Archer like a hawk. "What if this is drugged?"

Archer took a few more sips. "It isn't, Leon. It's the same stuff in my cup. I promise it's safe to drink."

Leon took a long slurp of the liquid that was hot enough to sear off taste buds, then swallowed.

"How's that taste, Leon?"

The man took another sip, then another. "Good."

"What would you think about a stocking cap, Leon? Maybe some gloves to keep your hands warm? It's getting colder."

Leon eyed him warily, then said, "Sure."

Archer sent another text, and Garcia soon appeared with a green stocking cap and a pair of fuzzy purple mittens.

"It's all they had at the store just up the street," Garcia said quietly, handing the items to Archer.

Archer yanked off the tags and took a step closer to Leon. "Here you go, Leon. This should help. Sorry about the mittens, but they didn't have any gloves. Must be a run on them with this cold weather."

Leon snatched the stocking cap from him and pulled it down over his ears, then struggled to get the mittens on without releasing his hold on the railing. For a guy who claimed to be ready to jump to his death, he was surely keeping a tight grip on that railing.

All Archer needed to do was figure out how to push that advantage and get Leon to step over the railing and back to safety.

"So, Leon, do you enjoy football?" Archer leaned back against the railing, resuming a relaxed posture although he was feeling anything but tranquil.

It was going to be a long, long day.

CHAPTER
2

ROSALEE

"THANK YOU AGAIN FOR stopping in, Betty. I hope you have a wonderful holiday." Rosalee smiled at her client and pushed herself to her feet, trying not to get stuck behind her desk with her protruding, thirty-seven-weeks-pregnant belly.

"Thank you, Rosalee. I hope you and your husband have a lovely Christmas. Just think how special it would be if your little one made a surprise arrival."

Rosalee forced herself not to let the horror summoned by Betty's comment show on her face. The baby wasn't due until the seventeenth of January, and Rosalee needed every day between now and then to finish getting ready for the little one's arrival. She and Rob, her husband, had been so busy with work and holiday festivities that they still had a lot of things they needed to wrap up before she'd feel prepared for their baby's arrival. One of the few things they'd recently completed was the nursery.

They'd transformed what Rob called their junk room into a nursery, painting the walls white and adding décor touches of buttery yellow and soothing green. Last weekend, they'd finally agreed on and purchased a crib with a matching changing table and dresser, and Rob had hauled them into the room with the help of a friend while Rosalee had hung curtains. Together, they'd adorned the walls with prints of adorable little teddy bears that matched the color scheme. Rosalee had ordered a large sign that read "Dream big, little one" to hang on the wall above the crib.

When Rob had hung a mobile that featured a bear sleeping on a moon with stars all around it over the crib and turned it on to play "A Dream Is a Wish Your Heart Makes," Rosalee had cried. Then again, it seemed like tears were always simmering beneath the surface, waiting to erupt at the most inopportune moments.

Like now, with thoughts of all she had left to do before their baby entered the world.

Both family and friends had encouraged Rosalee to wait to buy a lot of what she felt they needed until after her baby shower, which was planned for the first Saturday in January. Her best friend, Mackenzie, had tried to talk her into a shower in November, but Rosalee had resisted. Now, she wished she'd given in to Mac's suggestions. At least then she'd know what else they needed to buy, like blankets, piles of diapers, and cute little outfits.

Neither she nor Rob wanted to know if they were having a boy or a girl, wanting it to be a surprise, which was why they were going with neutral colors. Rob had jokingly said they should go with pink because he was certain Rosalee wanted a girl, and what she wanted, she made happen.

While that wasn't always true, she did work hard to turn dreams into goals and goals into reality.

That was why, when she was twenty-six, she'd been made a partner at the accounting firm where she worked in Portland's Pearl District. Six years later, she had a corner office with a great view of a park, where she liked to eat her lunch on warm, sunny days.

Betty patted Rosalee's hand, bringing her thoughts back to the moment. "Well, even if you have to wait three more weeks, I know you and your husband are going to adore that little one. I do appreciate your time this morning to go through my financials before you take your maternity leave. It's wonderful you'll have four months to enjoy your baby before you return to work."

"It *is* wonderful, Betty." Rosalee handed the older woman an envelope that held a gift certificate to a local bookstore. Her client was an avid reader and would put the gift certificate to good use.

She placed a hand on Betty's thin shoulder. "Thank you for the beautiful blanket you made for the baby. We'll cherish it."

"You're welcome, dear. No one makes handmade items anymore. It's all from the Pottery Barn or Nordstrom's, or so my granddaughters tell me."

"Well, I love it." Rosalee picked up a baby blanket, knit with the softest, airiest pale blue yarn that made it look as though it was spun from clouds. "This truly was so kind of you."

"My pleasure. Now, you enjoy your Christmas. I expect to receive an announcement when the baby arrives."

"I'll be sure to send you one," Rosalee said, adding baby announcements to her growing list of things to which she hadn't given a thought. "Merry Christmas, Betty."

"Merry Christmas, Rosalee." The old woman tucked the envelope into her voluminous bag and shuffled out the door.

Rosalee rubbed an aching spot on her lower back as she walked over to the window and gazed outside at the dreary day. It wasn't raining yet, but it certainly looked like the heavy, gray clouds might start dumping puddles on the city at any moment.

The leaden sky made her feel chilled. She turned from the window and walked over to the coatrack behind her desk. She slipped on the sweater she'd grabbed as she'd rushed out the door earlier that morning. Betty liked to meet at eight on the dot, so Rosalee had left the house at a quarter past seven to make the nine-mile drive to her office. Her husband had been asleep, so she'd kissed his cheek and quietly gone out the door.

She hoped to wrap up with her last client by ten-thirty, then surprise Rob by arriving home early. They could have lunch and enjoy some holiday fun before their evening plans. They were going to Mac's annual Christmas Eve bash, where there'd be an abundance of delicious food and loads of laughs before they attended the Christmas Eve service at church.

Rosalee started to reach for her phone to send Rob a text, only to realize she'd left it on the charger at home. Oh, well. She could live without the phone for a few hours.

With a grunt, she settled into her chair at her desk and was rubbing her belly when Audrey, her assistant, rushed in.

"Here's your tea." Audrey set a china cup and saucer on Rosalee's desk, then placed a red square tin adorned with a scene of winter woodland animals beside it.

"What's this?" Rosalee asked, removing the lid to reveal an assortment of Christmas cookies.

"A little something to tide you over until lunch. Are you still hoping to get out of here early?"

"I am, and you are too. I want you out the door by noon, if not sooner. You should be enjoying the day instead of being stuck in a stuffy office. Aren't you and Kai driving to Seattle this afternoon?"

"That's our plan. He's so nervous about meeting my family, I think he'd be happy if we got snowed in here."

From the tin, Rosalee selected a tree-shaped sugar cookie covered in frosting and green sprinkles and bit into it. "So good. You really should open a bakery."

"Nope. That would take all the fun out of it." Audrey glanced at Rosalee's planner, which rested on the corner of her desk. "Mr. Kolinsky's appointment is the only other meeting you have scheduled this morning, right?"

"Yes. Can you bring me his file? I want to make sure every *i* is dotted and *t* crossed. You know how exacting he is."

Audrey rolled her eyes. "We all know how cranky Mr. Kolinsky gets if things aren't up to his impossible standards. I'll grab his file for you." She hurried out of the office.

Rosalee took another bite of the cookie, then lifted the cup of peppermint tea, her favorite.

Audrey possessed the magical ability to make it with just the right amount of sweetener and steep it until it tasted like minty heaven.

"I can't find his file. Is it in here, by any chance?" Audrey asked, rushing back into the office.

Rosalee looked around her tidy desk. Every evening this week except for the night Rob had taken her to *The Nutcracker*, she'd worked late to make sure she left her office clean and her business finished for the year. She wouldn't return to the office until after New Year's Day, and then only for a few weeks until the baby arrived. She'd done her best to tie up every loose end she could before Christmas.

A sudden recollection of taking the Kolinsky file home with her made her want to kick herself. The image that thought evoked in her mind almost made her laugh. She felt like she had a beach ball strapped to her waist and was as unwieldy as a walrus slogging through a mud bog.

"I took it home to review last night and left it there, along with my cell phone. Good grief! If pregnancy hormones are the reason for my forgetfulness, I'm pretty sure I won't even remember my own name by the time this baby arrives." Rosalee rubbed her hand over the mound of her belly pressing against the desk. "I'll dash home and get it."

"Are you sure?" Audrey gave her a concerned look. "I could go get it for you."

Rosalee took another sip of tea. "No, I'll do it. I'll check on Rob, retrieve my phone and the file, and be back before you know it."

"It's nice your hunky hubby is at home waiting for you. Didn't you say he has time off this week?"

"Yes. It's going to be great. He would have used some vacation time to take a whole week, but with him planning to take two months off when the baby comes, he didn't want to push his luck."

"That's smart." Audrey backed out of the office. "Finish your tea and cookie. I'll have Jimmy bring your car around to the door."

"Thank you." Rosalee ate the last bite of the cookie, drained the cup of tea, and then visited the restroom before she shrugged into her coat, which she could no longer button over her belly. She wrapped a scarf around her neck and then gathered the tin of cookies, the blanket from Betty, and the gift basket of decadent lotions and soaps Audrey had given her when they'd exchanged gifts before Betty had arrived.

Audrey had been pleased with the beautiful leather tote Rosalee had chosen for her, as well as the monetary bonus for another year of a job done well.

"Ready to go?" Audrey asked, taking the things from Rosalee's hands. She picked up the purse

Rosalee had absently left on her desk and walked with her to the elevator.

Together, they rode it down to the lobby, then Audrey set Rosalee's things in the car while Rosalee gave Jimmy, the parking garage attendant, a tip and then forced her belly to fit behind the steering wheel of her SUV.

A glance at the back seat made her smile. She and Rob had been overjoyed to receive two high-end car seats last week; they were Christmas gifts from her parents, who were off on a Mediterranean cruise. Although it had taken the better part of last Sunday afternoon to figure out how to properly install them in their vehicles, Rosalee loved looking in her rearview mirror and seeing the seat there, imagining the beautiful little human who would soon fill it.

"I shouldn't be gone more than forty-five minutes, an hour at the most." Rosalee smiled at Audrey as the young woman set the tin of cookies on the seat beside her. "That gives me enough time when I get back to do a quick review before Mr. Kolinsky arrives."

"And then you can escape until after the holidays."

"*We* can escape. See you soon." Rosalee waved at Audrey and Jimmy, then pulled away from the building, taking Highway 30 toward her home in an effort to avoid the traffic on the freeway. The news reports earlier had warned anyone who was out and about to be careful with the harried holiday drivers rushing around. There were already reports of multiple wrecks on the freeway.

Rosalee tapped her thumb on the steering wheel and sang along to a jazzy rendition of "Up on the Rooftop" as she made her way north. Traffic was heavy but moving along at a steady pace. She turned onto the St. Johns Bridge and glanced at her watch. She'd made good time. It had only taken fifteen minutes to get from the office to the bridge. Another five, and she'd be home. She'd just need a minute to gather the file and her cell phone. If Rob was sleeping in, she wouldn't disturb him. If he was awake, she might have him drive her back to the office and pick her up later. A wave of exhaustion had settled over her about a mile before she reached the bridge. All she wanted was to curl up under a warm blanket and sleep, but she had far too much to do today.

There would be plenty of time for catching up on her rest after Christmas when she had the entire week to do nothing but get ready for the arrival of the baby.

Her stomach clenched as she drove onto the bridge and merged with the inside lane. She breathed through an intense pain that felt like a cramp in her lower abdomen. What if she was coming down with a stomach bug? That would definitely mess with her holiday plans. She could not be sick. She and Rob had too many things to do today for either of them to be ill.

"We're fine. Right, baby?" She rubbed a hand on her belly.

The baby kicked against her hand, and Rosalee smiled. Rob was convinced she wanted a girl, but Rosalee knew she was having a boy. She didn't know how she knew, but in her heart she was certain she was carrying a boy who would have his daddy's blue eyes and warm smile. The last few nights, she'd even dreamed of how he would look when he was born, with dark hair and a perfect little nose. The pale blue blanket Betty had given her would be so perfect for their baby boy.

Rosalee looked ahead as the traffic slowed. Horror filled her as she watched an old pickup with an equally ancient camper trailer swing into oncoming traffic, blocking all four lanes on the bridge. A minivan plowed into the front fender of the pickup, and an SUV hit the passenger door. A small pickup ran into the back of the SUV.

The screech of crunching metal and shattering glass grated on her ears while the smell of rubber assaulted her nose as people slammed on their brakes and tires skidded.

With a quick look in the rearview mirror and a glimpse beside her car, Rosalee whipped into the outside lane, then slammed on her brakes, bracing her arms against the steering wheel in anticipation of an impact. When she failed to feel a jolt as she'd half expected, she opened her eyes and glanced back to see that a small electric car had stopped a few feet behind her. Traffic was no longer moving.

Rosalee watched a man climb over the bridge railing, apparently planning to jump. Even through the closed windows of her vehicle, she could hear people screaming at him to get back to safety. He was ready to jump. She could see it in the way he bent his legs and held his arms out to the sides. He lingered there, precariously balanced on the thin metal bar of the railing. At the last second, he climbed down on the outside of the bridge but reached back and grabbed onto the railing as though he needed a minute to think about his decision.

She reached for her phone to call 9-1-1, only to remember she'd left it at home.

Great. Who knew how long she'd be stuck on the bridge. She needed to let Audrey and Rob know where she was.

Maybe it wouldn't take long to clear the wreck and talk the guy off the bridge. From experience, she knew the bridge remained closed if anyone was trying to jump off of it. They'd even closed it the day the fire department had rescued a stray kitten that had fallen down on one of the braces.

Grateful she wasn't in any of the vehicles that had smashed into the pickup and camper, Rosalee observed as people rushed forward to the wrecked cars and tried to help. She saw a man a few cars ahead of her pull a fleece blanket from his trunk and carry it to the SUV. A woman hurried by dressed in Christmas scrubs. It was good that a nurse was on hand to help until paramedics arrived.

Normally, Rosalee would be one of the first to offer help, but at the moment, she felt weak and lightheaded. If she ever made it home, she might just cancel all her plans for the rest of the day and stay there. Rob wouldn't mind. He was generally someone who liked to stay home and enjoy the quiet, while Rosalee was the social one who loved to be around people.

The sound of sirens cut through the noise around her. She could see lights flashing as patrol cars drove up the bridge on the other side of the wreck. She glanced back to see police blocking the entrance to the bridge behind her.

Another cramping pain in her abdomen stole her breath. Maybe it was Braxton-Hicks contractions. She'd had a few of them last week and asked her doctor about it when she'd gone in for her checkup three days ago. After assuring her they were normal and that everything looked good, the doctor had told her she'd be out of town with her family for ten days for a ski trip to Vail, Colorado. Rosalee might have worried about her doctor being gone, but she'd be back in plenty of time to deliver the baby.

"Everything is fine, sweetie. Mommy's going to just sit here and relax while we wait for the road to clear so we can go home." Rosalee rubbed her belly as another intense cramp declared war on her abdomen. She grasped the steering wheel and squeezed it in an effort to relieve the pain.

What was happening to her? She absolutely, positively could not go into labor on the bridge right now! It was too early to give birth, wasn't it? What had she read? Was it thirty-eight or thirty-seven weeks that marked the safety zone for an early delivery?

Rob would know. He'd absorbed all those details like a sponge while Rosalee had struggled to remember the basics. Did that mean she'd be a terrible mother? Even if she hadn't memorized the "what to expect" books, she loved the child growing in her with a fierceness that both shocked and astounded her.

When the cramp eased, she glanced at her watch. Although it seemed like only a few minutes had passed, it was closer to thirty minutes since the collision had taken place. How much longer would she be trapped on the bridge? She could almost hear crotchety Mr. Kolinsky complaining to Audrey when he showed up for his appointment, and she wasn't there. She tried not to think about what he'd say. It wasn't as if Rosalee was avoiding him on purpose.

Where was her stupid cell phone when she needed it? She could use one of Rob's pep talks right about now, not to mention her need to apprise Audrey of the current situation.

She squeezed the steering wheel again but this time out of anger with herself for being so forgetful.

The sound of an ambulance drew her attention as it drove up the wrong side of the bridge. The paramedics loaded two people out of the SUV and left in a blur of sirens. Rosalee prayed that those who'd been injured would be okay. She could hear sirens approaching on the other side of the bridge.

Rosalee breathed through another siege of pain in her abdomen. When it stopped, she noticed patrol officers from the Portland Police Bureau going from car to car, taking statements.

She rolled down her window and gave her statement, telling the officer who looked like he was fresh from the police academy that she was fine when he asked if she needed help.

"You seem awfully pale, ma'am. Are you sure you don't need assistance?"

"Not unless you can magically make a bathroom appear," she joked, even though she desperately needed to use one. The baby seemed to take great joy in tap dancing on her bladder and left her unable to go more than an hour without making a pit stop in the nearest restroom.

"Sorry, I can't help you with that. If you do feel like you need assistance, wave your hand out the window."

"Thank you, Officer. I'll do that." She smiled and rolled up her window, then took shallow breaths as another pain arced through her abdomen while her lower back began to throb as if someone was prodding it with a searing poker.

She looked at her watch and wrote down the exact time on a notepad she kept in the console. When the next pain hit, she realized it had only been nine minutes since the last one. This wasn't good. Not at all. Despite trying to convince herself otherwise, Rosalee concluded she was, in fact, in labor.

Another ambulance appeared and loaded a woman and her son from the minivan. The little boy, who couldn't have been more than four, was screaming hysterically and clinging to his mother, who appeared to be barely conscious. Rosalee wished she could comfort the child, but she wasn't sure she could even walk the short distance to the ambulance. The mother and boy were in good hands now, anyway. The ambulance was from Lennox Medical Center, where she planned to deliver her baby.

Rosalee timed another contraction, this one at eight minutes. How could they be coming so quickly?

Then again, she'd had a backache since yesterday morning and twinges that felt like cramps off and on since the previous afternoon. She'd just assumed the Mexican food she'd eaten for lunch hadn't agreed with her, but the reality was that she'd likely been in labor all that time.

"How could I be such a ninny?" she moaned after the contraction passed. Suddenly overheated, she peeled off her scarf and held her hand against the cool glass of the window before pressing it to her forehead.

Well, one thing was certain. She would not give birth to her baby in her vehicle on a bridge.

Nope.

She didn't care what had to happen, even if she had to cross her legs and tie her ankles together, but there was no way she was going to be a headline in tomorrow's news. She could picture it now. "Christmas Baby Born on Bridge Next to Suicidal Jumper."

"No, no, no," she chanted as she opened her door and stepped out. After dragging in a deep breath, then another, she took a few steps. She could do this. Maybe she could just walk it off.

Rosalee walked to the front of her SUV, keeping a hand on it for balance, then turned and made it to the back before a particularly strong contraction hit her with such force that she doubled over in pain. Warmth slid down her legs, and she glanced at the puddle forming around her feet as her water broke.

"That can't be good," she said, fighting down the panic bubbling in her chest.

CHAPTER 3

NOVA

A JAW-POPPING YAWN MADE Nova glad she wore a mask to hide it. Exhaustion had tugged at her limbs until they felt as though they weighed twice their normal size as she went through her end-of-shift tasks at Lennox Medical Center. Five minutes later, she finished her work and went to stand at the elevator, too tired to take the stairs down to the locker room.

"Are you finally outta here, girl?" asked Jill, a friend and fellow nurse, as she breezed down the hallway in a set of light blue scrubs with a happy-faced snowman on the front.

"I am. It's been a long night." Nova studied Jill, who was young, fresh-faced, and appeared rested.

Nova held back a sigh. She used to look that way. But after spending thirty years as a registered nurse, almost twenty-two of them at Lennox Medical Center, she was neither young nor fresh-faced. The past few weeks had definitely been anything but restful.

In a game of shuffling schedules to secure four days off starting with Christmas Eve, Nova had worked the night shift the last two weeks. After the second night, she recalled all the reasons she'd hated it and had done everything she could to stay away from working in the ER, particularly at night. People's most terrible traits shoved their way out in the midnight hours. Stabbings. Shootings. Drug overdoses. Suicide attempts. She'd seen it all in the last two weeks. She would happily return to her day shift in the post-anesthesia care unit without a single word of complaint. How fortunate she'd been to secure a nursing position that allowed her to be off evenings and most weekends.

Between her body struggling to adjust to working at night and trying to keep up with the things at home she normally handled during the day before or after work, not to mention preparing for the holidays, she felt as if even her bones were tired.

She couldn't wait to get home, climb into her bed, and sleep for a few hours before she dove into creating a fun family Christmas for her husband and son.

Neither of them expected her to do much, but she wanted to. She *needed* to, for her own sake. It was their first Christmas without her daughter, who was spending the holidays with her fiancé and his family. They were good people and Nova was happy for Macie, but the holiday wouldn't be the same without her oldest child at home.

Nova knew she was going to have to get used to sharing holidays with her kids' future in-laws, but she didn't have to like it. At least her son was still single. Maybe she'd have a few more years with him before he moved on to the next phase of his life that would involve settling down with a wife and starting a family of his own.

Another yawn made her jaw crack, and Nova held a gloved hand in front of her mouth even though she still had a mask on. "Sorry. I'm so ready for a little sleep."

"I hope you get caught up on it. Next week, you're back to regular shifts, right?"

"Yes, thank goodness. I don't think I could take one more shift like the one I had last night."

Jill nodded sympathetically. "I heard it was pretty gruesome with the multiple stabbings and two shootings. Was it gang-related?"

"Sounds that way." Nova glanced down at her blood-spattered clothes. The pink scrubs with little gingerbread characters would never look the same.

"I'd give you a hug, but you don't want this all over you."

Jill smiled. "I won't look much better by the time this shift ends, but it's nice to start the day clean. I will wish you a Merry Christmas, though, Nova. I hope you and your family have a wonderful holiday."

"Same to you, Jill. Happy Christmas Eve!"

The elevator dinged, and the doors opened. Nova waved once to Jill, stepped into the empty elevator, pushed the button for her floor, and slumped against the wall. If she closed her eyes, she figured the janitor would find her snoring while standing up.

"He'd love that," she mumbled to herself, thinking what a character the lead janitor could be. The man prided himself on his harmless pranks and ongoing jokes. "Probably post photos on the cafeteria bulletin board."

Nova shook her head as the elevator reached her floor. In the locker room, she took a quick, cool shower to wake herself up, only to realize she'd forgotten to bring any street clothes to wear. She pulled on a pair of navy scrubs with adorable reindeer faces on them. She'd have to remember to bring an extra set of scrubs to work next week to replace them. She always kept at least one, if not two, spare sets in her locker.

After slipping on her coat, she grabbed her purse and headed to the cafeteria, where she got a to-go cup of the spicy tea they only had during the holiday season. Nova loved all types of tea, but this was one of her favorites. She sipped it as she walked outside to the parking lot. The air felt even colder than she'd anticipated. Between the shower and the frigid breeze, she was now wide-awake. Aware it was only a temporary reprieve from her weariness, she hoped to drive home without worrying about falling asleep at the wheel.

She left the parking lot and started toward the freeway, then changed her mind at the last moment. Today seemed like a great day to avoid being on the freeway in all the traffic. If she went the other way and took the St. Johns Bridge, she could run by the grocery store that was just a few blocks past the bridge, get what she'd need for the next few days, and then head home. Mind made up, Nova removed her phone from her purse's front pocket, tapped a voice recognition app, and started talking, creating a grocery list as she drove north.

She'd turned onto the bridge and had only traveled a short distance when brake lights lit up like a Christmas parade. She slammed on her brakes to keep from rear-ending the car in front of her and watched as vehicles collided into a pickup pulling a ramshackle camper that had stopped across all four lanes of traffic.

Did the idiot driving the pickup have a death wish?

As she watched the man stagger out of the vehicle and climb onto the railing, she knew he most certainly did.

Nova threw her car in park and had her hand on the door handle to see what she could do to help when the man on the railing got down and hovered on the outside edge of the bridge, his hands clutching the railing behind him. It was good he hadn't jumped, but she figured it was going to take considerable effort to convince him to return to safety.

She turned off her car, took her keys, and hurried to check on the people who had smashed into the suicidal man's pickup. The occupants of both an SUV and a minivan would need to be transported to a hospital, and Lennox Medical Center was the nearest.

Nova called 9-1-1, explained who she was and that more than one ambulance was needed, and remained on the line describing the injuries as she went from one vehicle to the next. She walked around the back of what was left of the camper to discover vehicles had slammed into it on the other side of the bridge. Pieces of the camper were scattered all over. There was even a piece of insulation hanging off the bridge railing.

Quickly assessing the injuries, she suggested dispatch have ambulances come from both directions, then went back to the SUV, where a couple seemed to have sustained the worst injuries. Thank goodness none of the wounds appeared to be life-threatening. Concussions. Broken arms and legs. One woman had a dislocated shoulder. It would all heal.

The woman driving the minivan had passed out, and her little boy wouldn't stop screaming but refused to let anyone touch him. The child didn't seem to be harmed, just frightened. His mother had blood gushing from a cut on her arm. Nova wrapped the woman's arm in a roll of gauze she retrieved from her car to help slow the flow of blood. She quickly used the supplies she always kept in her car, wishing she had a box full on hand to help the injured until the ambulances arrived.

A few people brought blankets, while others produced bottles of water. Everyone who gathered around the injured seemed to genuinely want to help. Much to Nova's relief, no one felt the need to heckle the suicidal man. The police were trying to talk to him, and he continued waving them away, shouting threats about shooting them or jumping.

She'd heard the officers discussing the option of bringing in someone trained in negotiation to talk down the man who seemed to waver between wanting to live or die.

Nova wondered if the man in crisis had known when he'd awakened that morning that he'd end up on the bridge, disrupting the Christmas Eve plans of so many people. The way he'd suddenly pulled across traffic, coupled with his tight grasp on the railing, made her think he hadn't strategized any of it. He'd acted on impulse and now battled with himself to decide his next course of action.

Once the ambulances arrived and hauled those who needed further treatment to the hospital, Nova gave her statement to a police officer who looked too young to be a cop and returned to her car. She used a bottle of water and hand sanitizer to wash her hands, then settled in the driver's seat, knowing she could be there a while. While she waited, she sent her husband a text message, letting him know where she was and that she was fine, in case he'd already heard about the crash.

The exhaustion she'd felt earlier had fled as adrenaline flooded her system, but she had no doubt she'd soon be too weary to move. Maybe she could get her husband or son to run by the store so she wouldn't have to. After all this, she just wanted to go home.

Eyes closed, she tilted her head back against the headrest and envisioned their cozy living room, where the stockings waited to be hung by the fireplace, and the Christmas tree took up the whole corner by the television. Unable to focus on thoughts of home for long, she shifted in her seat as restless energy spurted through her.

Nova opened her eyes, picked up her phone and sent her sister a lengthy text, wishing her and her family a Merry Christmas at their home in sunny Arizona. She messaged her brother in Texas, sending him and his big family of six children and twelve grandchildren happy holiday wishes, then set her phone in her cup holder, observing what was going on around her.

The police had cautioned everyone to stay in their vehicles for their own safety. Nova watched a woman a few cars ahead of her get out of her SUV. She looked upset, almost like she was in pain. Something seemed off as the woman walked to the front of her vehicle. Her gait was hesitant, cautious. Then the woman turned, and Nova could see she was expecting.

The miserable days toward the end of her own pregnancies, when she'd felt like a beached whale with bloated clubs for feet, would be forever lodged in her memories. She could easily commiserate with any woman in her last weeks of pregnancy.

The woman walked to the back of her vehicle, then gripped her belly and bent over.

"Oh, no. Not that." Nova hopped out of her car and rushed toward her. When she reached her, the woman was staring down at a puddle around her feet. "Did your water just break?"

"I ... I think so." She lifted her gaze to Nova's. "You're a nurse?"

Nova plucked at the front of her reindeer scrubs. "Did Rudolph give me away?"

The woman smiled in spite of the circumstances and nodded. "He did."

Nova couldn't help switching into caregiver mode. "How far apart are your contractions?"

"I think around seven to eight minutes."

That was definitely not good news. "All right. Do you feel better sitting or standing?"

"Neither," the woman said, then gave her an apologetic look. "This is my first. I have no idea what I'm doing, and the baby isn't due for another three weeks."

Nova could see the desperation in the woman's gaze, and hear the fear in her voice as she spoke. She would do everything she could to ease her worries and help her through what had to be a terrifying situation. "That's good information for me to know. What's your name?"

"Rosalee."

"I'm Nova, Rosalee. I'll try to help you all I can. Do you have someone who can come get you?"

"My husband, but I left my cell phone at home."

Nova returned to her car and grabbed her phone, then hurried back to Rosalee, handing her the cell. "Use mine. See if he answers."

Rosalee punched in numbers and waited, holding the phone to her ear with a look of hope that soon gave way to profound disappointment. She left a voicemail, and then handed the phone to Nova.

The young woman sighed. "He's probably asleep, or maybe in the shower."

"Is he working today?" Nova asked.

"Not that I'm aware, but he's often on call."

"Okay." Nova stuffed her phone in her pocket. "You wait right here. I'll be back in a minute."

Nova jogged around the end of the camper and over to the police officer who had taken her statement. He was speaking with another officer who looked slightly older and far more experienced.

"Ma'am, we appreciate your help with the injured, but we need you to stay in your vehicle." His gaze flicked to the suicidal man. "It's safer for everyone."

"I understand, Officer Morgan, but there's a very pregnant woman back there, and her water just broke. I'm not sure we can wait for an ambulance to get here. If no one objects, I'll volunteer to drive her to the hospital."

"I, um..." Officer Morgan looked at the other officer.

Nova read his nametag. "What do you think, Officer Garcia?"

"I think..."

Before he could finish, a third officer approached them. Nova recognized her from the emergency room.

"Officer Yeung, we met the other night in the ER. I'm Nova."

"Right. You were there when I brought in the guy who accidentally shot himself in the leg." She motioned behind her to the line of cars. "It's going to be a while before this mess is cleared up."

"I realize that, which is why we have a problem. There's a woman on the other side of the wreck who's pregnant. Her water just broke, and she needs to get to the hospital. I don't think we should wait for an ambulance unless one of you wants to help deliver a baby in the back of her vehicle."

All three of the officers paled.

"Not particularly, no." Officer Yeung took a step closer to Nova. "What do you want to do?"

"Drive her myself. Is that something I can do?"

Officer Yeung thought for a moment. "For the record, we're stating it's best to wait for the ambulance, but if the woman wants to go with you, we'll help you get your car off the bridge."

"Okay. Let's do it."

Officer Yeung and Officer Garcia followed her around the back of the camper. The whole time, they both eyed the suicidal man who was engaged in a conversation with an officer who leaned against the railing and gave the impression he had nothing better to do than listen. From the way the negotiating officer was dressed, with a stocking cap pulled down over his ears and thick gloves on his hands, he looked like he knew he'd be on the bridge for a while.

Someone who didn't know better might think he was just shooting the breeze with the man in crisis, but Nova knew enough to realize the officer was building rapport with him. Doing that took talent, skill, patience, and time.

Time was something Rosalee didn't have at the moment. She needed to get to a hospital right away.

Nova prayed she wasn't making a mistake by offering to drive a woman about to deliver a baby to the hospital. Still, with traffic delays and waiting for dispatch, she figured she could get to Lennox far faster than an ambulance could reach the bridge and head back.

She moved next to Rosalee and placed a hand on her shoulder. "You need to get to a hospital. I'm happy to drive you there. Officer Yeung can vouch for the fact that I really am a nurse who works at Lennox Medical Center. What do you think of letting me drive you? Or would you rather wait for an ambulance?"

"Let's go," Rosalee said as she panted through another contraction. "My car or yours?"

"Which vehicle is yours, Nova?" Officer Yeung asked.

Nova pointed to her car which was blocked in by a bakery truck, a boat of a car, and a postal truck.

Officer Yeung shook her head and pointed to the SUV Rosalee had been driving. "It'll be easier to get this out than your car."

"Okay." Nova returned to her car to retrieve her purse and sent her husband a text, made sure the doors were locked, and then rushed back to the SUV. "How are we going to do this?"

"Get behind the wheel and be ready to pull out when we give you an opening. No one's going to be happy about your leaving and might try to follow, but ignore them and any shouts you might hear. As soon as the tow truck gets here, we'll start clearing the bridge, but everyone else will need to wait until then," Officer Yeung said.

"I figured that much." Nova helped Rosalee into the backseat of the SUV, made sure she was buckled in, then got inside and started the vehicle.

Unlike Rosalee, who was a good six inches shorter than she was, Nova had to move the seat back to accommodate her long legs. She adjusted the rearview mirror, turned on the vehicle's hazard lights, and gave Rosalee an encouraging smile. "You hang in there, little mama. I'll do my best to get you safely to Lennox as quickly as possible."

"I trust you, Nova. Thank you. Lennox is where I planned to have the baby. In three weeks. With my husband beside me." Rosalee looked sad and unsettled.

Nova reached into her pocket, pulled out her cell phone, and handed it to the young woman. "Try reaching him again."

"Thank you, thank you." Rosalee tapped out a message, then gasped as another contraction hit.

Nova set the timer on her watch and returned to watching the two officers as they talked to drivers and got them to move out of the way.

Finally, there was an opening large enough for Nova to get through. She nodded to Officer Yeung, then turned and drove down the bridge. At the end of it, an officer stopped traffic so she could make the turn and head south toward the medical center. Nova was just pulling into the road when she saw a big tow truck approaching. She waved to the driver, then focused all her attention on zipping through traffic to the medical center.

She pulled up in front of the emergency room doors eighteen minutes later, during which Rosalee had endured two more contractions.

"Wait here. I'll get a wheelchair," Nova said over her shoulder before she dashed inside and got a chair, then pushed it out to where she'd stopped in front of the sliding glass doors. "In you go, Rosalee."

"Thank you, Nova. Thank you so much for getting me here and letting me borrow your phone." Rosalee handed the phone back to her, and Nova stuffed it in her pocket again. She grabbed Rosalee's purse and hers, then pushed the wheelchair inside.

"Nova! What are you doing here?" a nurse asked as she rushed around the admitting desk.

"We've got a baby coming a little earlier than planned. Her water broke about thirty minutes ago. Contractions are tracking at eight minutes apart." Nova glanced down at Rosalee. "Who's your obstetrician?"

"Dr. Julia Lemond. She's out of town for the holidays." Rosalee panted as another contraction hit her.

Nova gave the nurse a look, then took the handles of the wheelchair. "I'll take her up to the maternity ward. Who's on duty?"

"Dr. Miller and Dr. Stoakes."

Nova blew out a breath of relief. Amanda Stoakes was one of the finest obstetricians in the state, and would take good care of Rosalee. She headed toward the elevator. "Let's get you admitted, Rosalee."

Nova sent one of the orderlies to move the SUV. She stayed beside Rosalee through the admitting process and remained until she was settled in a bed in the maternity ward, hooked up to monitors and awaiting a visit from the doctor.

"I should head out, Rosalee. I hope you'll let me know how things go and share a photo of the baby. I left my cell number on that notepad by the phone." Nova pointed to the phone on the bedside stand.

Rosalee nodded as another contraction hit her. "Thank you," she panted, then reached out a trembling hand to Nova.

Nova set down her purse and coat, took Rosalee's hand in hers, and coached her through the contraction.

"I have no right to ask this," Rosalee said in a desperate voice, clinging to Nova's hand while tears filled her eyes, "but will you stay with me until my husband gets here?"

Nova thought of her Christmas Eve plans, the groceries she needed to buy, the gifts she had yet to wrap, the food she'd intended to cook, but it didn't matter.

What mattered was Rosalee knowing she wasn't alone.

With a tender hand, she brushed the hair away from Rosalee's face. When she'd first seen her on the bridge, the woman's light brown hair had been smooth and straight, not a strand out of place, looking like she'd just stepped out of a salon. Now, it was starting to morph into thick, wild waves. Fear and weariness mingled in Rosalee's expression while pleading filled her sparkling deep brown eyes.

Unable to leave when Rosalee needed her, Nova smiled and nodded her head. "Of course, I'll stay."

CHAPTER 4

CARTER

T ODAY WAS NOT GOING at all as Carter had envisioned. Rather foolishly, he'd hoped it would be a quiet day for his towing company so he could take care of a bunch of last-minute details he should have crossed off his to-do list long before Christmas Eve.

His wife was working, his son was busy with his own problems, his daughter was spending the holiday out of state, and it was on him to make sure there was food in the house when they finally all made it home tonight.

As Carter backed his truck up the wrong side of the St. Johns Bridge, he couldn't help thinking that today had not gone as planned for everyone around him. None of the people stuck on the bridge, or those who'd been involved in the multi-vehicle collision had anticipated what was coming when they'd driven onto the bridge earlier that morning.

Carter wasn't convinced the man on the bridge who'd caused the wreck and then threatened to kill himself had foreseen things going so far off the rails either. The messy situation smacked of an impulsive decision made without thought as to how one bad choice would ripple out like a stone tossed in a calm lake. The ripples kept stretching farther and farther, affecting more and more people.

Although the officers on scene hadn't said anything about it, Carter thought there had to be divine intervention at play, considering the fact that there wasn't a single fatality from the wreck. The guy trying to kill himself had walked away with just a cut on his head. Carter had heard the worst injuries from the collision had included broken ribs, concussions, and a fractured leg.

If someone had died because of the suicidal guy's stupid decision to pull across all four lanes of traffic, would the man already have jumped to his death into the frigid Willamette River? Or would he still be hanging on to the railing, talking to one of the Portland Police Bureau's best negotiators?

Through his work and the many accidents and incidents he'd towed vehicles away from, Carter was familiar with several of the PPB's officers. In his opinion, the dude with the death wish couldn't have a nicer guy trying to talk him down than Sergeant Archer Raines.

Raines was in his mid-thirties, good-looking, funny, and charming. He had a way of putting people at ease without even trying. From what Carter knew, he was one of the best negotiators at the PPB.

However, it was a shame that things had escalated to the point that Raines had been called in to defuse the situation and talk the guy off the bridge and into living to see another day.

"What happened to this being a jolly time of year?" Carter asked himself, glancing in the side mirror as he backed closer to the wreck. Officer Kennedy held up a hand to indicate he should stop.

It wouldn't take long to hook up the wrecked car that had slammed into the middle of a camper that shouldn't have been on the road. Between the duct tape holding on the bumper and the pieces of the camper littered across the bridge, Carter wasn't looking forward to loading the mess onto one of his trucks.

"Hey, man, that was a fast trip," Kennedy said when Carter jumped out of his truck and approached him.

"I tried to hurry with the last load. We need to get these vehicles off the bridge so the rest of the cars can clear out. I have a feeling the guy on the railing isn't going to do anything good or bad until there aren't as many gawkers around."

"Agreed. The drivers who've been stuck here all morning are getting antsy to go." Kennedy gave Carter a hand, helping push the car back so he could hook it to his truck to tow.

Carter had owned Willamette Towing for years. He'd gotten a job there when he was in high school, working as a part-time mechanic. Once he'd graduated, he'd started working full-time while attending night school, eventually earning a degree in business management. A few years later, he'd bought into the business as a partner, and then taken over as the sole owner when old man Levy decided to retire at the ripe old age of eighty-one. Levy had sold his half of the business at such a reduced rate that Carter felt like he was cheating his former employer, but Levy had assured him it was a square deal as far as he was concerned. Carter had been the closest thing to family Levy had, and he'd listed him as his only heir in his will when he'd passed away five years ago. Carter still missed his old friend and mentor hanging around the shop, drinking coffee, and telling back-in-the-day stories to anyone who would listen.

Carter poured himself into upholding the sterling reputation Levy had built with the towing business he'd started from scratch back in 1953 when he had one tow truck, along with a small service station.

But where Levy had been frugal and cautious about expanding, Carter had seen an opportunity to grow and had taken it. He'd doubled the size and tripled the income of the business by implementing smart changes. It might not be a glamorous way to make money, but it paid the bills.

As someone who lacked the intrinsic skills of a natural-born salesman and who actively avoided small talk, Carter never tried to sell someone on his business. However, he was savvy, honest, and hardworking. The police officers who knew him trusted him to do what he said and often a little more.

If a wreck happened in the northern section of the greater Portland area, Carter was usually the first towing service called and did his best to respond quickly.

"You have big holiday plans?" Carter asked Kennedy, an officer he'd known a few years.

"No. I've only been dating my girlfriend a few months, and I didn't want to set the bar too high for our first Christmas."

Carter studied him as the front end of the wrecked car slid between the steel beams of a bracket, and then he secured it with holding pins. The piece of equipment, known as a yoke, made towing cars and pickups a relatively simple task. If everything lined up, he could have a car ready to tow in about a minute.

He glanced up at the officer as he pushed in the last pin securing the car's passenger wheel. "Did you at least get her a gift?"

Kennedy nodded. "A necklace. Not too cheap or too expensive. It has her birthstone on it."

"Great choice. Fairly noncommittal, but shows you paid enough attention to remember her birthday."

Kennedy smiled as though Carter's assessment pleased him. "I'll take that as high praise from you. Haven't you been married somewhere in the vicinity of forever?"

Carter laughed. "My wife might say it feels that way, but it's only been thirty years."

Kennedy whistled softly. "Thirty years, man? That's pretty dang close to forever."

"Time flies when you're having fun, you know." Carter grinned at the younger man and thumped him once on the shoulder. "When you find the woman you can't bear to live without, you'll know she's the one you want to spend your forever with. Don't settle for anything less."

Kennedy followed Carter as he walked around to the driver's side of his truck. "What did you get your wife?"

Carter opened the door and climbed inside. "It's not one thing, but a bunch of things. She works so hard and needs to relax more, so I got her a spa gift certificate, her favorite fragrance in candles and a bottle of lotion, a box of her favorite chocolate truffles, a playlist of soothing songs she likes, as well as slippers and a robe that cost more than we spent on our first rent payment when we were newly married. Her stocking stuffer is a coupon book of things I'll do for her, like a foot rub or a neck massage."

Kennedy laughed and shook his head. "That sounds more like a gift for you, but I'm sure she'll appreciate it all. For a grumpy old dude, I think you just might be a romantic at heart."

Carter feigned a scowl and waggled his index finger in warning at the officer. "Keep that to yourself, would you? I don't need word getting out that I'm a big softy under this dashing exterior."

"You look more like a grouch who wandered in off the frozen tundra, but I won't share what I now know."

Carter smirked and fastened his seat belt. "I'll be back as soon as I can with the big truck. I'll clear the camper and pickup at the same time. My guys should have everything moved on the other side of the bridge shortly."

"Ace just hauled off the last car a few minutes before you arrived." Kennedy waved at him. "The drivers on that side are elated they can finally leave."

"I bet they are." Carter hollered, then shut his door and drove to his towing company.

One of the improvements he'd made was to purchase a ten-acre parcel connected to the original Willamette Towing lot, where he could store wrecked vehicles until owners decided what to do with them. Sometimes, they went to a mechanic; other times Carter's crew worked on them in the garage they had on site. Vehicles the insurance company declared totaled were either sold to salvage yards or to Carter to use for parts.

At any rate, the extra space had made it possible to expand the business in several areas. He was able to sell the used parts and cars left behind as well as sell cars they'd repaired, adding another aspect to his business that hadn't existed when Levy had owned it.

Carter backed the car into a slot next to the other vehicles from the bridge collision, moved the truck he was driving into the parking area for his tow trucks, then climbed into a big wrecker and headed back toward the bridge.

As he sat at a red light, he checked his phone and saw a text from his wife. He sent one back to her, then texted his son before the light turned green.

It took another twenty minutes in the increasingly busy traffic to reach the bridge. The cars that had lined both sides of it were gone, thankfully. It was a smart decision by the PPB to let them all go. If the man on the bridge actually had the weapon on him that he'd threatened was in his possession and started shooting, an innocent bystander could easily be injured or killed.

Slowly driving up the bridge toward the wrecked pickup and trailer, Carter stopped when Kennedy motioned him to wait. Ahead, he could see the suicidal guy motioning toward the pickup and yelling something at Sergeant Raines.

Whatever had riled him had done a good job. Instead of looking like he was about to jump, the man appeared to be on the verge of imploding.

At this rate, Carter knew he'd be the last one home this evening, and they'd all starve since he was in charge of buying groceries. He glanced at his watch, hoping he'd have a chance to go pick up his son's gift before the store closed. Why hadn't he made time last week to run Christmas errands instead of waiting for today, hoping he'd have the afternoon free of responsibility?

The way the crazy guy was waving his arm and shouting, it didn't appear he'd change his mind and surrender peacefully anytime soon.

A sigh rolled out of Carter as he switched off the ignition on the truck and set the brake. This morning, he should have turned off the office phones and given his crew the day off instead of rushing to help when the call came for assistance on the bridge.

CHAPTER 5

IAN

"**N**o! Not today. Are you kidding me!" Ian thumped his hand on the steering wheel of his 1993 Jeep Cherokee which refused, once again, to start. The vehicle that his dad had gotten for him when he was sixteen and had taught him how to keep running was on its last legs.

Which was one of the many reasons Ian needed to get to his job interview on time. A job—a *real* job—in his chosen field would mean he could afford a new vehicle, maybe even a rental house or apartment he wasn't sharing with five other guys, three of whom were still in college.

He could always move back home with his mom and dad, but he hated the thought of it. He'd unfurled his wings of independence when he'd left home and gone to college in Klamath Falls instead of attending one of the schools in Portland, where he could have lived at home. He'd argued, mostly with his father, about going to the school in Southern Oregon, but the scholarship he'd received that covered his tuition had finally swayed them to let him go. Four years and a bachelor's degree in mechanical engineering later, he'd returned to Portland, eager to begin his career. Along with way too many other recent graduates, apparently, because after a year and a half, he was still trying to land a job that would start him along his career path.

Instead of applying his skills and talent to creating what he thought of as cool stuff that could have a global impact, he worked evenings waiting tables at a trendy restaurant, where he made decent tips and got a free dinner, and spent his mornings as a valet at a ritzy hotel downtown dealing with mostly snobby people who had more money than sense.

His mom kept hounding him about applying for a maintenance job where she worked, which he absolutely did not want to even think about. His father repeatedly offered him a job at his business, but Ian refused to consider it. His dad would treat him like his other employees—fairly and with respect—but Ian didn't want to need help from his parents.

If they didn't like his attitude, that was on them. They shouldn't have raised him to be so independent.

With a glance at his watch, he knew he needed to figure something out quickly if he didn't want to miss this interview.

When he'd seen a listing for Magra, a small company with a huge outreach in the engineering and construction fields, he knew he had to apply. The mechanical engineer position was everything he'd been hoping to find. He'd done his homework, researched the company and key staff members, and submitted his application five weeks ago. When he'd called to follow up, he was told the position had already been filled.

Then, magically, Magra had called two days ago and asked him to come in for an interview. Ian had nearly broken into a happy dance right there at the valet stand when he'd finished the call. He'd begged his best friend from college to grill him with potential interview questions in a FaceTime call last night. He felt as prepared as he could be to meet the owner of the company today.

Although he was grateful for the opportunity to interview with the owner, Taylor Jackson, it had shocked him when her assistant had called and asked if he could come in to speak with her on Christmas Eve morning.

Ian didn't know anyone who actually worked on Christmas Eve if they didn't have to. His parents both landed in the have-to-work category, but he knew there were many people who had the day and the following week off from their regular duties.

Regardless, he sure wasn't going to suggest scheduling the interview another time. Not when he felt it was his one chance to make a good impression and hopefully secure his career for the future.

Not surprisingly, the old Jeep would choose such an inopportune time to refuse to start. He would have asked one of his roomies for a ride, but the college kids had gone home for Christmas two weeks ago, and the only other roommate with a vehicle had gone out partying last night and had yet to come home. Unless he wanted to borrow Trenton's bicycle, he was going to have to find alternate transportation.

He wouldn't bother his parents, and he'd rather walk than take the bus, so without other options, he pulled out his phone and made a reservation for a rideshare service to pick him up.

Nerves made his palms sweat in the chilly December air as he waited for the car. According to the app on his phone, the driver was only seven minutes away.

Ian had planned to arrive at least twenty minutes early for his appointment. Even with the unplanned breakdown of the Jeep, he should still arrive on time. He dashed back inside the house to the bathroom, checked his appearance in the mirror, and straightened his tie, then smoothed the sides of his short brown hair.

Everyone always said he looked just like his mom, with the same color hair, the same smile, even the same nose and eyes. From his dad, he'd gotten his stubborn chin with the little cleft in the center, along with his broad shoulders, although he was far leaner than his father. Ian looked more like a runner than a wrestler.

On his way back outside, he snagged a reusable bottle of water and a protein bar, stashing them in his leather messenger bag, a gift from his parents for his college graduation.

He'd just stepped outside when he saw a vehicle roaring up the street. The rideshare logo was clearly visible in the passenger-side corner of the windshield. He hoped the maniac driving the small SUV wouldn't kill him in a fiery crash before they even made it out of the neighborhood.

He lifted a hand as he stepped out to the curb, and the SUV came to a precise stop beside him. All he had to do was open the door and slide into the back seat.

"You're the dude heading to Magra? Ian Alexander?" the driver asked, giving him a glimpse over her shoulder.

Ian nodded, then cleared his throat. "Yes. I'm Ian. Do you have the address?"

"Got it right here," she said, then blew a big pink bubble and popped her gum.

He was in the process of buckling his seat belt when she hit the gas and zipped into the street, barely slowed at the corner, and picked up speed as she headed toward the highway.

Ian prayed he'd survive the trip and wouldn't be so rattled by the experience he'd mess up his interview. He drew in a long breath and inhaled a fragrance reminiscent of spiced cider and warm fires. He didn't see an air freshener hanging up and wondered if it was just the driver. If so, she smelled amazing.

Head in the game.

Now was not the time to check out a girl. Besides, this one certainly wasn't his type even if she appeared to be close to his age. From the quick glance she'd given him, he'd concluded she was into goth with her thick, black eyeliner and dark eye shadow, a nose ring, blood-red lipstick, and a dragon earring that encircled her entire ear. She had on fingerless gloves with leather cuffs and a black leather jacket sporting silver studs around the collar. He had no idea what color her hair might have been because it was all stuffed up under a slouchy black velvet hat.

He wondered what she'd look like if she washed her face and dressed in something less biker chic and more ... feminine.

Ian almost face-palmed himself. Good grief! He was starting to sound like his parents. He didn't care if the woman was dressed as one of Santa's elves as long as she got him to his interview on time, preferably in one piece.

To distract himself from the fact that goth girl seemed to think she was training for the Indy 500 or perhaps to become a New York City cab driver, he rehearsed what he planned to say at the interview. When it felt as though the SUV went around a corner on two wheels, Ian latched onto the handle above the door and held on for dear life. What kind of crazy person was about to get him killed?

"Ever think about becoming a race car driver?" he asked as she barely slowed at a stop sign and took a right onto the highway.

She glanced back at him and smirked. "Only every other day. Unfortunately for you, today is an even day, and I'm practicing."

Ian wasn't sure if she was teasing or serious, and decided she was most likely messing with him. "What's your name?" he asked. He should at least know who to blame when he ended up in the hospital's emergency room from the wreck he was certain her driving was likely to cause.

"K."

"Kay, like..." He paused, trying to think of an example and realized he didn't know of anyone famous named Kay.

She rolled her blue eyes in the rearview mirror. "Just the letter K."

"Like in *Men in Black*?" He leaned forward slightly. "And K is short for?"

"None of your business."

Ian took her curt tone as an obvious dismissal and looked out the window at the scenery passing by in a blur as the vehicle flew down the road. His driver zoomed in and out of traffic as if her life depended on reaching Magra in as few minutes as possible. One time, Ian was sure they were going to rear-end the car in front of them, but she managed to change lanes and continue onward without incident.

They were almost at the St. Johns Bridge when she glanced back at him again. "I didn't mean to sound snippy. I just get a lot of guys who seem to think that because I'm giving them a ride, it gives them permission to hit on me or expect things they shouldn't."

"Oh." Ian didn't know what to say to that. He wondered if the tough girl persona was part of a defense mechanism or if she really was into the whole dark and brooding scene. The upbeat Christmas music playing on the radio led him to believe otherwise, but he didn't comment on it. "I promise all I want is to get to Magra. I'm sorry some people are that way."

"Me, too. I have a can of pepper spray and a stun gun, and I'll use them to protect myself if necessary."

Ian could easily imagine her spinning around in her seat and spraying some smart aleck guy in the face with pepper spray. She didn't seem like the type to cower in fear and wait to be rescued.

"Have you used either of them before?" he asked, curious how far she'd actually go.

"A few times. I don't particularly enjoy having to defend myself." She turned onto the bridge just as a horrendous noise reached them. Ian bent down so he could better see out of the windshield. Vehicles slammed on their brakes as others plowed into a pickup and camper that rocked to a stop, blocking the entire bridge.

Without missing a beat, K swung a U-turn and sped off the bridge.

"Hey! Shouldn't we have stayed behind to see if we could help? The police might need us to report what happened, won't they?" Ian shifted so he could look out the back window at what had turned into a major collision.

K shook her head. "Only if you want to be stuck on the bridge for hours. They'll have to close the bridge, and then no one will be allowed to move until the wreck's been cleared away and statements taken. It could take a good part of the day. I assume you need to get to Magra or you wouldn't have scheduled a ride."

Part of Ian wanted to tell her to turn around and go back. That would be the right thing to do, wouldn't it?

The other part of him, the one utterly desperate to land this job, was glad she'd engaged her alarming driving skills and gotten off the bridge before someone hit or detained them.

He blew out a long breath. "I do need to get to Magra before nine-thirty. I have a job interview."

She shook her head. "What kind of sicko schedules interviews on Christmas Eve? Is this a satanic cult or something?"

Ian chuckled at the irony of her question in light of the way she was dressed. He caught a glimpse of a skull on the front of her T-shirt. "No cults that I'm aware of, but the owner is leaving for the holiday and won't be back in the office for three weeks. The opportunity to interview with her popped up out of the blue."

K grinned. "Sometimes unexpected things have the most profound effect on us. I hope your interview goes well."

"Thanks. I do too. I really, really need some new wheels, and a solid job will help me make that happen."

"I wondered why you called me when you had that great old Jeep in your driveway. Wouldn't it start?"

"No. My dad taught me how to keep it running, but I didn't want to get all dirty messing with it this morning, not to mention I didn't have time to figure out what was wrong with it and still make it to my interview."

"That's smart. The last thing you want when trying to impress those billionaires is grease under your fingernails and the smell of blue-collar labor clinging to you."

Ian scowled. "I never said anything about a billionaire."

"I read a lot of magazines and watch the local news." She shrugged. "Magra is on track to become one of the most influential businesses in the country when it comes to engineering. Taylor Jackson took over after her father retired, and she's been making impactful changes that have moved Magra from a small local company to one everyone's talking about. She's totally into sustainability and innovative energy options."

"You seem informed about Magra. You know anyone who works there?" Ian asked, eager for any connection that might help get his foot in the door.

"Not a soul. *Women's Truth* featured Taylor in the October issue. That's how I know about her."

"I think my mom reads that magazine sometimes. It's about women in business, right?"

K nodded her head. "That's right. This month's magazine featured Stacy Allison. She was the first American woman to reach the summit of Mount Everest. I think it would be so neat to do something like that."

"Climb a freezing mountain while the wind tries to blow you into a different time zone?"

K laughed as she stopped for a red light and looked at him. "Not that exact thing, but some trailblazing thing no other woman has done."

"Is that why you drive like you're planning to audition for a stunt role in the next *Fast and Furious* movie?"

"No." She laughed again, then hit the accelerator as the light turned green. "I drive like this because it's fun."

Ian figured by the time she left him at Magra, he'd either be dead from heart failure, have a permanent seat belt impression across his chest, or be so badly frightened he'd forget his own name, let alone the reason he was at the company.

"Do you terrorize passengers in your car full-time or is this a side hustle for you?"

"It's a second job thing I do when I'm not working. I have two weeks off from my regular job. You wouldn't believe how many people need a ride during the holiday season. It's a great way to make extra money, as long as you don't mind listening to arguing relatives and shuttling drunks from one celebration to another."

"What about your family? Won't they miss spending time with you today?" What Ian really wanted to ask was if she was married or seeing someone, not that it mattered. After K dropped him off, he'd never see her again. Which was good, because as wrong as she seemed for him, he liked her. He thought she was funny and smart. Although he couldn't tell what she really looked like, she had a lovely profile, as his mom would say.

K sighed and glanced out the side window before she returned her focus to the road. "No family. No close friends. No one but me and Jazzy."

"Jazzy?" Ian tensed. Who was Jazzy? A girlfriend? A kid? A misplaced musical instrument?

"My dog."

Relief washed over him, and he relaxed against the seat. "What kind of dog is she?"

"An Appenzeller Sennenhund."

"Bless you."

K giggled, and Ian pondered what he could say to get her to do it again.

"I didn't sneeze," she said, grinning at him in the rearview mirror. "That's the name of the breed. It originated in Switzerland. The dogs were bred as working dogs. They like to herd and are good in the mountains. They're known for having energy, brains, and confidence. They're not a low-maintenance dog, but Jazzy is worth the extra effort."

"How did you end up with her? Was she a puppy when you got her?"

K zoomed around a car going so slowly Ian wasn't even sure it was moving. "Someone I'm acquainted with through work needed to find a home for the dog when her mother-in-law moved in. Jazzy hates her."

"Smart dog," Ian quipped, and they both laughed. "Does she like to go for walks?"

"More like high-speed runs, but she's a sweet girl. Thankfully, the house where I live has a big yard, so it gives her room to play when I'm not there, and we aren't far from a park."

"A big yard sounds wonderful. I share the house where you picked me up with five other guys, and our backyard is the size of a postage stamp. Then again, that might not be a bad thing since none of us are into lawn maintenance."

She glanced back at him and smirked. "You're probably too busy breaking hearts to concern yourself with mowing the lawn. A sort of not entirely ugly guy like you probably has girls following him everywhere."

Ian wasn't vain, but he liked to think he was somewhat attractive. From K's comment, he hoped she thought he was too. "Wrong. I work two jobs and help my dad when I need extra money. My last girlfriend always wanted me to take her out to eat at expensive places and entertain her with tickets to even more expensive events. I couldn't afford the lifestyle to which she wanted to become accustomed, so I broke up with her in September."

K didn't comment, but from his view of her profile, he thought she might have smiled.

"Footloose and fancy-free, are you?" she glanced back at him, then slipped between a UPS truck and an Amazon delivery van before changing lanes again.

"Something like that." He so badly wanted to ask her questions about what she did for a living. Where she'd grown up. If she had weighty thoughts about hot cocoa versus hot chocolate. But he refrained.

K stepped hard on the accelerator and whooshed through a yellow light. He had visions of vehicles slamming into them from both sides as he held his breath and closed his eyes. When he dared to breathe and open his eyes again, they were continuing down the street, unharmed.

"I promise to get you to Magra in one piece," K said, changing lanes and whipping around a corner.

Ian still had his doubts, but if he had to die listening to her enchanting voice, he could think of worse ways to go.

"What kind of job are you hoping to get?" she asked. "Is it something you went to college for?"

"Yeah. Mechanical Engineer. I even have a bachelor's degree to go with my skills."

She grinned over her shoulder at him after stopping for another red light. "I have no idea what a mechanical engineer does."

"It's a branch of engineering that combines physics and math with science to design, analyze, and create mechanical systems that use force and movement."

"All righty, that's a ..." She shook her head. "That sounded like a spiel from a college recruitment brochure. I still have no idea what mechanical engineer means. Give me some examples."

Ian grinned. "Steam engines. Internal combustion. Springs. Screws. Axles. Pulleys. Pistons. Even robotics. They were once something dreamed up by a mechanical engineer."

"Wow, Ian. That really is cool. So, you're interviewing for a mechanical engineer position?"

"That's the plan. I've been trying to find a job since I graduated last year. Well, I mean, an engineering job. I work, just not in something I want to keep doing forever."

She turned on her blinker and pulled into the Magra parking lot. Ian was almost sad she'd gotten him there in such a short time. He glanced at his watch. It was only ten minutes past nine. He wouldn't be late for the interview.

"I hope you get the job, Ian. You seem smart enough for a dorky dude." She smirked at him as she stopped in front of the main entry. "Good luck to you, and Merry Christmas."

"Thanks, K. I hope you have a good day."

She turned in the seat as he opened the door. Her beautiful blue-eyed gaze connected with his. "My name is Kate."

"Kate. Okay, Kate. Merry Christmas to you and Jazzy." Before Ian made a fool of himself and asked her on a date, he got out of the vehicle, shut the door, and strode into what he hoped would be his future.

If that was the case, why did he desperately want to jump back in the car with Kate and learn everything about her there was to know?

CHAPTER 6

ARCHER

"**W**HAT ARE THEY DOING? Are they gonna move my stuff? They can't touch my stuff!" Leon shouted, pointing to the wrecker that had driven up the bridge to haul off the mangled camper and pickup. Other than two cars that had been left by owners who gave up waiting, the bridge had been cleared.

Archer took a step closer to Leon, who had one hand around the railing while the other waved frantically in the direction of his destroyed pickup. The sight of the fuzzy purple mitten thrust above the man's head might have made Archer laugh under far different conditions. Right now, there was nothing humorous about the circumstances.

Cautiously, Archer moved his hands in front of him in a placating stance. With his fingers outstretched, palms down, he spoke in a soothing, reassuring tone. "It's okay, Leon. It's nothing to worry about. They just need to move it off the bridge. If there's anything you need out of either vehicle, you can get it before they haul them to the towing yard."

Leon started to climb over the railing. Silently, Archer cheered him on. All he had to do was get on the right side of the railing and they could end this situation. Breath held, Archer watched as Leon lifted one leg in the air and swung it over the railing, then he made a guttural noise that didn't even sound like it came from a human and flung his leg back, resuming his post on the narrow edge of the bridge.

The small amount of progress Archer had made in the past several hours felt like it melted away in that moment. He was cold. Hungry. Annoyed. And starting to wish he'd slept in until noon and forgotten to charge his phone.

Not only was he beyond exasperated with Leon, but he was also concerned about Lena. He hoped she'd received his message and wasn't wondering why he wasn't at home, ready for an afternoon of holiday fun. Something, though, didn't feel right. What if she'd needed him and he was stuck with Leon the loon out in the cold for goodness only knew how long? He couldn't let his thoughts dwell on his wife, or he'd lose his ability to focus on the task at hand.

Part of Archer wanted to grab Leon by the back of his coat, haul him over the railing, shove him into a squad car, and go home. But the rational part of his brain knew Leon would jump if he tried to get close enough to touch him.

Something he'd learned years ago floated into his thoughts. *Don't worry about where the situation is going. Worry about where you are in the moment.* Archer needed to stop thinking about where he wanted to be and concentrate on this moment.

All morning, he'd done his best to build a rapport with Leon. They'd talked about sports teams, the weather, the price of fuel, the best time of year to visit the coast, and inconsequential details Archer had no interest in, but Leon seemed to want to discuss. Archer had been making progress, or so he thought, until the man caught sight of the wrecker.

"Are we going to have a problem, Leon, or can we get your pickup and camper loaded?" Archer asked in a friendly tone.

"I don't care." Leon scoffed and made a dismissive gesture before he turned so his back was to Archer.

The urge to shout at Leon to stop acting like a pouty child was strong, but it would only tear away the rapport he'd worked so hard to establish with the man. Leon had clearly suffered from a mental break and was in a bad place. Patience was the best tool Archer had to bring about a peaceful resolution to what was becoming a drawn-out issue.

If Archer were in the same circumstance—divorced, losing custody of his kids, jobless and friendless—he wondered how he'd handle it. He took his phone from his pocket and checked the messages. The captain wanted to talk to him, but he'd wait to call until Leon settled down.

"Before the truck drove up, Leon, you were telling me about your kids. How old are they again?" Archer knew their names, ages, the schools they attended, and even their favorite foods, but as long as he kept Leon talking, the man wasn't plummeting to his death in the water.

"Emma is fifteen. Her birthday is in August. She's so pretty and smart. She wants to be a financial manager when she grows up. She gets the smarts from me, you know. My wife is a looker but not the brightest crayon in the box."

"Brightest crayon in the box?" Archer asked, knowing Leon would talk more about the woman who'd divorced him.

"We met in college. I think her major was beer and boys. I don't know why she ever gave me a second look, but I helped her with her homework, you know. Tiffany has a degree in fashion something or other, but her sorority sisters all left her in the dust when we graduated. She quit partying and wanted to spend time with me. I don't know what made her change, but I certainly wasn't going to turn her down. A guy like me with a girl like her? No way. We dated all that summer, got engaged in November, and married in March. Tiffany was a beautiful bride. She took my breath away when she walked down the aisle."

"It sounds like you really loved her, Leon."

The man nodded, shivering as he turned his gaze to meet Archer's. "I still do. If it hadn't been for that traitorous, no-good, lying—" Leon abruptly stopped his rant and focused on the river beneath him.

Archer wanted to nudge him. They'd covered this topic multiple times, and each time, right before Leon would name the person he viewed as a traitor, he'd clam up. Unless Archer was mistaken, he had a feeling that whoever it was played a part in why Leon was standing on the bridge, trying to decide if he wanted to continue living.

"Your son, Aiden, is thirteen, isn't he?" Archer asked, hoping to redirect Leon's attention.

Leon nodded. "He wants to be a cyber security specialist when he grows up. He's great at that kind of stuff." The hard line of the man's jaw softened. "He's a good boy and deserves better than a loser for a dad, someone who can't even keep a job or his family." Leon scowled, and his expression changed to one of anger. "No boy should have to live with an adulteress for a mother."

"Adulteress?"

"Tiffany. See, she was cheating on me. She thought she was so clever, but I found out. Then she got mad and kicked me out of the house. Divorced me. Kept all my money. Kept my kids. Kept everything. I got nothing. Nothing!" Leon spat and then wiped the fuzzy mitten across his mouth. "I got nothing," he muttered softly. "Nothing."

"What happened when she divorced you?"

"She took everything from me. Everything. So I wanted to take everything from her. I wanted to see her pain. See her suffer like I've had to. See her face when I took the kids from her. But he stepped in. He keeps her safe. I don't care what he thinks. He's not in charge. I am!" Leon pounded a fist on his chest, and his left foot slipped.

For a moment, Archer thought Leon might actually fall and reached out for him, but before he dropped to his death, the man wrapped an arm around the railing and pulled himself up against it.

"Who is *he*, Leon? Are you talking about Jason?"

Archer already knew Leon's ex-wife was dating a manager at a downtown investment firm. The man had money to burn, and apparently, he didn't mind spending it on Tiffany and her kids. The four of them had booked two luxury rooms at a lodge up on Mount Hood for the whole holiday week. From the information Archer had received, Jason Bixby's only crime was a speeding ticket twenty years ago when he was in college. The guy volunteered on one of the hospital boards, donated to several charities, and had never been married. He also didn't seem like the type to get involved in messy domestic disputes. Jason must truly love Tiffany to be involved with her, considering Leon's state of mind and recent actions.

Leon was fully aware of Tiffany's relationship with the investment manager, but the look in his eyes told Archer the guy protecting Tiffany wasn't Jason. Thus far, no one had unearthed any details about her having an affair or any men hanging around prior to the divorce. In fact, she and Jason had met a month after the divorce papers had been finalized.

Archer had unearthed the information from Leon that he was supposed to have the kids for Christmas, but when Tiffany found out he was living in the camper, she refused to let him keep them overnight. Then Jason had offered to take them skiing, and the kids had, as Leon put it, dropped him like a hot potato.

"Jason?" Leon spat, like the name left a bad aftertaste in his mouth. "He's so worried about scuffing the polish on his fancy shoes, what would he know about anything? Drives that stupid car the kids won't even fit in. Acts like he's Daddy Warbucks."

A Lamborghini wasn't what Archer would call a stupid car, but he did see Leon's point. It wasn't exactly a family car meant to transport children back and forth to school or haul their equipment to sporting events.

"And that makes you upset with Tiffany?"

"With her. With Jason. With *him*."

"With him? What did he do?"

"He meddles. He interferes." Leon yanked off the stocking cap and slapped his leg with it. "He lies!"

Archer wasn't going to get anywhere with Leon worked up again. He motioned to Officer Kennedy to keep an eye on him and backed toward the patrol car. "Are you getting hungry, Leon? Maybe I can see about having someone bring lunch."

Leon nodded once, then pulled the stocking cap back on his head. "I like turkey sandwiches."

Archer hurried to the patrol car, started it, and absorbed the heat that spilled through the vents as he called Captain Cohen.

"Any progress?" the captain asked when he answered the phone.

"Not really. You probably heard on the police radio, but he keeps ranting about someone he refers to as *he*, but won't give me a name. I don't think it's Jason. There's someone else involved in this. What do we know about Leon's friends, if he has any? Or maybe Tiffany's? Her family members? Anyone who might try to protect her? Have you dug into Leon's family? His childhood? Something triggered him this morning, and I think it involves more than Tiffany taking the kids skiing with Jason instead of letting Leon have them for Christmas."

"Her parents live in San Diego, and they make an annual trip to visit in the summer. She had a brother, but he died when they were in high school. I'll have the team keep digging. If it isn't Jason who's pushing Leon's buttons, we need to figure out who is. So far, we haven't turned up anything unusual with Leon's family. He was an only child. Mom stayed at home. Dad worked several different jobs over the years."

"He acts so squirrelly and hostile when he mentions this *he* person. There has to be someone somewhere who knows the man's identity." Archer could hear the captain's fingers rapidly typing on his keyboard, as though he was taking notes.

"What else?" Captain Cohen asked.

"I told him I'd see about getting something to eat. He's got to be colder than I am. He's just wearing a T-shirt under his coat, which isn't something meant to be worn for prolonged exposure to the elements. If it gets any colder out, I'm concerned hypothermia might set in."

"For you or him?"

"Both!" Archer knew humor could be heard in his tone, but he'd lost feeling in his toes ten minutes ago. He held up his hands to the vent and warmed his chilled fingers.

"Do you need me to send someone else in, Arch? Say the word, and I'll get you out of there. You've already been at this for what, four hours?"

"Closer to five, but who's counting?" Archer leaned back in the seat. "I'll stick with it, but some food might be a good way to coax him to come over the railing. He won't be able to eat one-handed, and I know he's hungry. I'd offer him a blanket, but I still haven't been able to tell if he's got a weapon on him or not. I'm leaning toward not, but he started acting cagey when the wrecker came to haul off the pickup and camper."

"We should have a warrant to search them shortly. If the towing company isn't in a rush, hold off on moving them until we can look inside."

"Leon isn't going to like that." Archer could see Leon's reaction playing out in his mind. It wasn't going to go well. The man would rant and rave, but perhaps it would be enough to get him on the safe side of the railing. At this point, Archer was willing to give almost anything a try if it would end the stalemate and let everyone go home in time for Christmas Eve celebrations.

"Let's feed him first and see if that mellows him at all."

"Will do, Captain." Archer adjusted the vent so it blew on his face, warming his chilled cheeks and ears.

"You want a hot or cold sandwich, Raines?"

"A patty melt would sure hit the spot. Leon informed me he likes turkey sandwiches."

"You got it. Oh, and I have those audio files you wanted. They'll be sent to you shortly."

"I'll watch for them."

"Hang in there, Arch. You've done the work, and you have the skills. Trust yourself and your gut. You can drive this situation where it needs to go. Don't feel rushed just because it's Christmas Eve. We'll take as long as necessary to make sure everyone leaves that bridge safely."

"Thanks, sir. I needed that. Leon isn't an easy one to build rapport with. It's testing everything I've ever learned to get anything out of him."

"You're doing great."

Archer blew out a long breath. "I'll get back to it. Oh, and sir, can you let my wife know I'm gonna be late?"

"We'll see to it."

Archer removed his boots and changed into a pair of dry wool socks he pulled from his backpack, which he'd left in the patrol car. Although it wasn't raining, the air was so damp it might as well have been.

He relished being able to sit and relax for a minute while his feet and fingers warmed. He wished he could take out his personal cell phone and call Lena, but he couldn't let himself get distracted. If she sounded the least bit disappointed about the fact that he was stuck at work, he'd start worrying about her instead of directing his attention to getting Leon off the bridge.

Archer gave himself a few more minutes of warmth and quiet before he laced up his boots, pulled on his gloves, and glanced at the phone as the audio files arrived from the captain.

He'd save them for when the search warrant came through. Leon would need a distraction from watching the team sort through his belongings. The camper might fall completely apart if they opened the door. Archer could see clothes hanging out the back end and a sofa cushion poking through the broken window. Where the car had wedged into the center of it, insulation, broken braces, and twisted metal were visible in the gaping hole.

Leon had something hidden in either the camper or pickup he didn't want them to find. Something incriminating. Something that drove him to consider jumping off the bridge.

Archer knew it in his gut. Just like he knew Leon was going to hate it when the warrant arrived.

He turned off the patrol car and got out. Cold air slapped him across the face as he tugged on his stocking cap and gloves, then made his way over to where the guy who owned Willamette Towing stood talking to Officer Yeung.

"Hey, Carter. Nice to see you, although it seems like it's never under good circumstances." Archer held his hand out to the man who seemed to tower over everyone, but despite his naturally gruff appearance, Carter was always full of jokes and funny stories.

"Quite a way to spend Christmas Eve." Carter returned his handshake. "Are you ready for me to load this mess?"

"Not quite. The captain's waiting for a search warrant. We should have it soon. He wants a search executed before the pickup and camper are moved. I'm afraid that camper will be a pile of rubble a mile down the road."

"Likely, but I hope it holds together until I get it to the junkyard." Carter glanced at his watch and then his phone. "If it's okay to leave the wrecker here while you do the search, I have something I can take care of in the meantime. It'll probably take me about an hour, maybe an hour and a half."

"That ought to work," Archer said, looking at Officer Yeung. "Can you give Carter a ride?"

Carter held out a hand. "There's a car I need to pick up on the other side of the bridge. I'll drop it off and have one of my guys bring me back."

"Sounds like a plan." Archer shook the man's hand again, then watched as he walked with Yeung behind the end of the camper to the other side of the bridge.

Wishing he could escape instead of returning to talk to a man who made him want to bang his head against a wall, Archer shifted his perspective. He was here to help Leon, and he wouldn't leave until that man was safely off the bridge. He shoved his hands into his pockets and walked over to where Leon held onto the railing, circling it with his fuzzy purple mittens.

"Sandwiches will be here soon, Leon," Archer said, forcing himself to sound cheerful. "What was it you said you did for work?"

They'd already covered the topic twice, but Archer hoped to glean some detail he'd missed earlier that might help unravel the mysterious identity of the man Leon referred to only as *he*.

CHAPTER 7

ROSALEE

"**S**TILL NOTHING?" ROSALEE ASKED as Nova checked her cell phone again.

"I'm sorry, but your husband hasn't texted or called." Nova offered her a sympathetic smile. "Does he often disappear like this?"

"No. Not really. I usually know where he is. I'm sure he left a message on my phone or at home if he's on call and unreachable." Rosalee gripped the sheet in her fists and squeezed as another contraction hit her.

"Just breathe through it. That's right. Breathe." Nova stood beside Rosalee, a hand on her shoulder, providing the encouragement and coaching support she needed.

Except that Rosalee didn't want a stranger there. She wanted Rob. They'd taken all the classes. Practiced breathing techniques. Packed her hospital bag and had it all ready to go, even if it was tucked in the back of their closet, waiting for January to move it to a spot by the garage door.

Rosalee should have left the bag in her vehicle once she'd finished packing it. Now, she had nothing. Well, not exactly nothing. The orderly who'd parked her car had brought back the things Audrey had set on the seat when Rosalee left the office what seemed like eons ago but had, in reality, only been hours.

She had a tin of Christmas cookies, a basket of lotions and soap, and a beautiful hand-crafted blanket for her baby.

Rosalee sighed. She didn't even have an outfit to take her baby home in. What kind of mother was she? Why had she thought attending all those holiday engagements was more important than preparing for the arrival of her child? Rob would have been perfectly happy missing the parties and events. They could have stocked the nursery, finished choosing baby names, and gone over the details of what would happen if she went into labor prematurely.

The thought that the baby might arrive early had never entered Rosalee's mind. The doctor had assured her of the due date in mid-January, and Rosalee, who liked everything to be planned out, had structured her schedule for the upcoming months around that date. Nowhere in her detailed plans had she anticipated the baby's unexpected Christmas Eve arrival.

Angry with herself for being caught unawares and at Rob for not returning her calls, she battled the urge to pound something. She might have if the contraction hadn't stolen her breath.

"You're doing great," Nova assured her when the contraction passed.

"She *is* doing great," Dr. Stoakes said as she sailed into the room with a sunny smile. "Let's just check your progress, Rosalee."

The doctor looked at the monitors and the charts, then did a quick examination. "Everything is progressing right on track. Your baby is just fine, and so are you. I'm thinking it will be a few more hours, though, before that little one decides to greet the world."

"Hours?" Rosalee repeated, not sure she had enough strength left to endure minutes. She took the cup of ice chips Nova held out to her and slid one in her mouth, holding it on her tongue as it melted. She felt as if someone had shoved her body inside a furnace, yet her hands and feet were icy to the touch.

Nova had disappeared a while ago and returned with a thick pair of hideous tan socks Rosalee eagerly allowed her to slide onto her cold feet.

This was not how she'd planned to deliver her child. She and Rob had decided to use a hypnotherapy birthing technique. She'd been fascinated when she'd first learned about relaxation and self-hypnosis techniques that helped the body and mind relax so the birthing process could happen more quickly and painlessly.

Nova helped her with the breathing techniques, but the visuals and sounds Rosalee had collected to help get into the relaxed state she needed were packed in her bag at home in the closet. She'd spent hours choosing the perfect visuals, sounds, and songs and adding it all to her bag, which held clothes, lotions, and everything she'd thought she might possibly need when their baby arrived.

What good was that stupid bag doing her now?

The urge to turn her face into her pillow and cry nearly overwhelmed Rosalee. When Rob finally did arrive, she intended to give him an earful for leaving her on her own on what was one of the most important days of their lives. The rational part of her brain knew if he could be there, he would be, which just made her worry that something had happened to him, or he'd been called in to work. If his boss had called him in, Rob wasn't going to be happy about that.

What if he'd been in a wreck? If not on the St. Johns Bridge, then in one of the many other accidents that had been reported throughout the day. She'd overheard two nurses talking about a massive wreck near one of the shopping malls that had resulted in two fatalities and several injuries.

She took another ice chip and tried to relax, for her sake and the baby's.

"That sound okay, Rosalee?" Dr. Stoakes asked as she patted Rosalee's shoulder.

Rosalee hadn't even realized the doctor was speaking, let alone expecting her to listen. She gave Nova a helpless look, and the woman nodded.

"Sure. Thanks," Rosalee said, with no idea what had been discussed while her mind had wandered to places it was better not to go.

Once Dr. Stoakes left the room, Nova smiled. "She said if you needed something to help manage the pain, to let her know."

"Oh, okay." Rosalee stuck another ice chip in her mouth, then pushed the hair from her face. It felt heavy and damp with perspiration. She could only imagine how frightening she looked. Her hair tended to wave with no particular direction in mind and could get full and bushy, especially on humid days, which was why she usually straightened it. She could almost feel the strands plumping up by the second.

As though she could read her mind, Nova smiled. "You look fine. Is your hair bothering you? I could pull it back out of your way if you like."

"That would be great. I have a brush and hair band in my purse."

Nova retrieved Rosalee's purse and handed it to her. She opened the compartment where she kept toiletries and extracted a travel-size hairbrush and a thick hair band. When she lifted her arms to try to comb back her hair, another contraction hit, and she almost tossed the brush across the room.

"Here we go. Breathe. Breathe. That's great, Rosalee." Nova smiled at her as the contraction ended, then she took the brush, combed Rosalee's hair back, braided it with a practiced hand, and then fastened the end. When she tucked Rosalee's purse back in the closet, Rosalee looked at her, feeling guilty for what she'd done.

She'd been so selfish, not giving a thought to Nova's day or her plans.

Nova likely had a family at home. What if she had a little girl who was anxiously awaiting her arrival? Maybe they'd planned to bake cookies or go to a Christmas movie or were supposed to spend the evening at a church service. What if by being here, offering the comfort Rosalee sorely needed, Nova was missing her child's performance in a Christmas program or taking a little boy for one last visit to see Santa?

"Nova, you should go. You probably have all kinds of holiday plans I'm keeping you from. I'm so sorry. I've been terrible. Please, go home and enjoy what's left of your holiday."

"Don't worry about it, Rosalee," Nova said, moving to adjust the pillows behind her. "It's all fine. Let's just focus on you and getting this baby safely delivered."

Rosalee shook her head. "No. I mean it. You don't have to stay. I'll be okay. Rob will eventually show up. Your family must be so disappointed you aren't with them."

"I'm not leaving you, Rosalee, so just get whatever guilty thoughts that have invaded your head right out of there."

Tears pricked Rosalee's eyes as she stared at Nova, then slowly nodded her head. "Thank you." Rosalee gave Nova's hand a gentle squeeze when the woman finished fluffing the pillows.

She studied the nurse who'd become her unwitting guardian angel. Nova was tall and lithe, with what Rosalee would describe as a dancer's body—graceful and elegant. She was also gorgeous with sculpted cheekbones and skin that looked flawless and ageless. Her eyes were gray and kind, and her hair was a rich mink-brown worn pulled back in a French twist fastened with a large claw clip. Her hands were gentle, and her long fingers felt comforting as they brushed a stray strand of hair from Rosalee's cheek.

The gentle kindness Nova offered left Rosalee perplexed. This nurse she barely knew had offered more affection and concern in the few hours she'd known her than her own mother had shown Rosalee her entire life. Rosalee's mother was a woman who had always been busy with her career in real estate. Early on, before she even knew what it meant, Rosalee had recognized her mom was a detached person who didn't enjoy cuddles or hugs from anyone. What might it have been like to grow up with a mother like Nova, who exuded love and caring? Far different from the home life Rosalee had experienced as a child, that was for certain.

"Is there anyone else you want to call?" Nova asked, as she straightened the covers, then took her cell phone from the pocket of the reindeer scrubs she wore. "I heard back from Audrey. She said she'd obey your orders to go have fun, but she'll be thinking of you the whole time, and not to worry about the cranky client. Also, your friend Mac just sent a message that she'd cancel the party and come right over."

"Please text Mac and tell her absolutely not. Everyone enjoys her Christmas Eve bash, and there isn't a thing she can do to help me now. I'd feel terrible if she canceled because of me, and everyone missed out on something they look forward to all year."

Nova sent the text and pocketed her phone, then looked around the room. "Do you need a distraction?" she asked, lifting the remote and turning on the TV.

A news reporter talked about the wreck on the St. Johns Bridge. Rosalee contemplated how horrible it would have been if her baby had been born there on the bridge with that deranged man.

A video clip someone had captured with a cell phone showed the wreck. When the video zoomed in on the man the reporter said was suicidal and refusing to come off the bridge with police officers surrounding him, Rosalee felt panic grip her by the throat. She gave the screen one more glance, then grabbed the remote away from Nova, turned off the TV, and expelled a ragged breath.

With another ice chip melting on her tongue, she looked to her new friend. "Tell me about your family."

CHAPTER 8

NOVA

"MY FAMILY?" NOVA STUDIED Rosalee. Something about the news report and the person in crisis on the bridge had rattled her. She didn't know if it was because they'd been there and Rosalee had been terrified her baby would be born on the bridge or if she recognized someone.

Rosalee was upset enough without anyone asking questions.

Nova had hoped to distract her with a Christmas movie, but of course, the first thing that popped onto the screen had been the news report from the debacle on the bridge.

Unsettled by thoughts of what was happening there, Nova took a drink from the bottle of soda she'd purchased from the vending machine earlier.

She rarely drank sugary beverages, but she needed the caffeine boost.

After another long drink, she decided maybe walking would help both her and Rosalee.

"How would you like to get up and walk for a bit?" she asked. Before Rosalee could voice her opinion, Nova turned back the covers and picked up a thin cotton robe the hospital furnished.

"I'd like that," Rosalee said, allowing Nova to help her out of the bed and settle the robe around her shoulders.

No one enjoyed traipsing through the halls in the hospital gowns that flapped open in the back. Nova tied the strings of the robe in front and slid the IV pole around the bed, positioning it so Rosalee could hold onto it as she shuffled out of the room.

When they were in the hallway, Nova pointed to the right, and Rosalee began walking, her brow furrowed in concern.

Nova knew Rosalee needed something to divert her attention away from her fears. "You asked about my family. What would you like to know?"

Rosalee stopped and deep breathed her way through a contraction, then began walking again. "Everything. How many kids do you have?"

"Two. My daughter used to ask me to comb and braid her hair. I think I did that thousands of times over the years. Macie played tennis and hated having her hair in her face. Now, she's a computer genius. She lives in Seattle, has a great job, and got engaged in September. She's spending Christmas with her fiancé's family, and I'm hating it. It's our first Christmas without her, but I know it's just the beginning of having to share my kids with their in-laws on holidays. Thank goodness my son hasn't met a girl he likes enough to get serious about—or not yet, anyway. He can build anything. The way his mind works has always fascinated me. He lives here in the Portland area and will be coming over this evening to spend the night. It'll be fun to have him home again, although he's repeatedly warned me that I shouldn't get used to it."

Rosalee smiled, and Nova was glad she was helping the young woman forget her pain and worry, at least for a minute or two.

"Your husband?" Rosalee asked as another contraction hit and they stopped while Nova coached her through it with counted breaths in and out.

"He's amazing," Nova said when they were once again walking. "We've been together for what seems like forever. I almost pepper-sprayed him the first time we met, though."

"Really?" Rosalee's eyes widened in surprise. "How come?"

Nova let the memories of that night wash over her. "It was late. I'd recently finished the nursing program and had a new job at a hospital in the Nob

Hill area working the graveyard shift. On my way to work that night, I hit a rock or something on the freeway, and it blew out my tire. It was one of those eerie, creepy nights when it's both foggy and the moon is shining. It sort of sets the mood to think every shadow is a serial killer coming for you."

Rosalee rested, leaning against the wall, when they reached the end of the hallway. "What happened?"

"A pickup pulled up behind me and stopped. It was one of those great big jacked-up things that sounds like it needs a new muffler and would be better suited for off-road racing or a demolition derby than posing as a road-worthy vehicle. I was convinced I was about to be the next murder-victim report on the morning news when the driver opened the door and stepped down behind my car. I took out my can of pepper spray, rolled down the window an inch, and waited. When the guy tapped on the window, I screamed so hard I somehow accidentally sprayed myself."

Rosalee tried to hide her laugh and failed miserably, making Nova smile. "Oh my gosh. That sounds awful."

"It was awful. My eyes were watering, and I couldn't see, and the whole time, the guy calmly asked me to unlock the door. To this day, I have no clue how I found the button or why I did it, but as soon as I unlocked the door, he helped me out of my car, gave me a bottle of water to rinse my face, and changed my tire while I gathered my composure."

"What about him made you scream?"

"In that terrible murky light, that late at night, with my overactive imagination conjuring up every worst-case scenario you could think of, he looked like a sasquatch. His hair was too long, and a thick, bushy beard covered most of his face. It was like he was channeling the original *Teen Wolf*, only super-sized. Did I mention he's tall? He's almost six-six and a brawny guy. If he hadn't broken his leg in high school, he might have had a professional football career."

"Wow. So, your husband looked like a marauding bear?"

Nova grinned. "A little. He appeared so big and frightening that night, but honestly, he is such a softy and just a really great guy. He's always been more like a teddy bear to me. Underneath his don't-mess-with-me exterior, he's a smooshy marshmallow. Our daughter used that to her advantage far too often in her growing up years."

Rosalee smiled. "He does sound like a terrific guy."

"He is. I can't envision my world without him or the kids as a big part of it. They've enriched my life in ways I never imagined possible. It seemed like a big risk that night we met to give him my name and number, but I've never once regretted it. My husband and kids are everything to me."

"Rob has this thing he says—that everyone has to decide what risks in life are worth taking. What risks are worth running into headlong. Those are the things we should pursue with unflagging faith, passion, and determination. He also says life is all about choices, and one choice can alter our entire future."

"Wow! That is both profound and meaningful and so true. I see it all the time at the hospital, how one choice can alter everything." Nova could hear the love in Rosalee's voice when she mentioned her husband. She just hoped Rob felt the same. She couldn't fathom why he hadn't returned Rosalee's calls or text messages, unless, as Rosalee feared, he was among those who'd suffered injuries today and was in a hospital.

When the doctor had given Rosalee an examination earlier, Nova had left the room to check to see if any patients named Rob had been admitted, but none had. If he was injured, he wasn't at Lennox.

Nova felt her phone vibrate in her pocket and took it out. A message from her son made her smile, and she texted him back, letting him know she was proud he'd persevered through a challenge and come out victorious on the other end. She then sent a text to her husband, apologizing for the change to their holiday plans.

She hadn't even gotten the phone back in her pocket when it buzzed again. She glanced at the caller and immediately answered. "Hi, honey. Did you see our brilliant son's text?"

"I did, babe. Great news, for sure. It's about time the kid caught a break. We'll celebrate tonight once we all make it home. From your text, it looks like you'll be at work a while longer."

"Yes. Unavoidable delays," Nova said, not wanting to say anything that would cause Rosalee to feel more guilt for asking her to stay. Nova could have turned her over to the capable nursing staff on duty, but for reasons she couldn't explain, she felt compelled to be with Rosalee until the baby arrived. Perhaps it was because a Christmas Eve birth was such a beautiful reminder of another precious baby born in a manger all those years ago.

"Sorry to hear that, babe. I've had a few unforeseen glitches pop up today as well. Don't worry about tonight. We'll just play it by ear. If I can find somewhere open, I'll get takeout for dinner."

Nova felt relief that she wouldn't have to come up with something for dinner after such a long, tiring day. She'd been up for almost twenty-four hours straight, but instead of dragging, she felt energized. Helping a new life enter the world would do that for a person. She smiled at Rosalee, then shifted the phone to her other ear.

"I can't begin to tell you how much I appreciate that, honey. Thank you, thank you for taking care of things. Were you able to get my car off the bridge without any trouble?"

"I know a guy," he said with a chuckle that made Nova grin.

"You do know a great guy to handle the job," she said with a laugh.

Her husband knew a lot of people, and it was one of his favorite lines to use whenever something needed to be repaired, ordered, or built. Regardless of the circumstance, he always seemed to know someone who could help if it wasn't something he could handle himself.

"Your car's safe at home, parked in the garage."

Nova felt relief that at least that task was checked off her ever-lengthening to-do list. "Perfect. I am truly so grateful for you, dear husband, and appreciate you more than you can ever know."

"Right back at ya, babe." She could hear the love in his voice, and it filled her heart with joy. No matter what happened, she could go home to a good man who loved her, and that was what really mattered most.

Nova heard a noise in the background, then her husband came back on the line. "Listen, babe, I need to go. When I wrap things up, I'll swing by the hospital. Just text me if you're able to leave sooner, and I'll send the kid to get you."

"Will do. Love you, honey."

"Love you more."

Rosalee was grinning broadly when Nova tucked the phone into her pocket and turned to her. "You two sound like the cutest couple. I hope Rob and I are still so crazy in love when we've been together as long as you have."

Nova was glad she hadn't said, "at your age." Determined to fight growing older as much as possible, Nova did everything she could—from eating healthy and exercising to slathering on face creams and serums—to try to slow the aging process. Yet despite her best efforts, lately, it seemed that every time she looked in the mirror, really looked, she could see the crow's feet around her eyes and the wrinkles digging deeper trenches on her neck. She might have despised each line that tattled about her age if her husband hadn't assured her the wrinkles gave her appearance more character. He still thought she was beautiful and told her that often. Showed her that in his touch and voice and the admiring looks he sent her way. Why should she care what anyone else thought?

She shouldn't, but those pesky wrinkles still annoyed her.

Rosalee placed her hand on Nova's arm. "Seriously, Nova, you should go be with your family. It's not fair of me to keep you here."

"You aren't keeping me here. I'm here because I want to be. I haven't worked in the maternity ward for a long time. It's wonderful to experience it again without having to dash from room to room, assisting patients."

Rosalee gave her a sly look. "I bet you have all kinds of momzilla stories to share. Give me at least one really juicy story."

"I'll consider it if you let me try one of the Christmas cookies you offered me earlier."

"Take however many you like." Rosalee continued waddling back toward her room when a particularly painful contraction made her brace herself against the wall as she breathed through it.

"I think sitting down would be good now," she said, panting from the exertion.

"Just a few more steps, and you'll be back in your room," Nova coaxed as she kept an arm around Rosalee for support.

It felt like the distance of a football field, even though it was only a few feet to get Rosalee back to her room.

"Chair or bed?" Nova asked as they made their way inside.

"Chair?" Rosalee said, sounding uncertain.

"Sitting might feel good. At least it's a different position than the bed." Nova helped her get settled, trying to ignore the rumbles of hunger in her stomach. She hadn't eaten anything since the apple and cheese slices she'd had during her break at four that morning.

"You must be starving, Nova. I never even thought about you missing lunch because of you being here with me. Is the cafeteria still open? Can you go find something to eat?"

"The cafeteria is still open. I will admit I'm hungry, but I don't want to leave you alone."

With a shooing motion, Rosalee gestured toward the door. "Go on, Nova. Please? I already feel like I've commandeered your entire holiday and held you captive by being so pathetic and needy. Please? Go eat something and take some time for yourself."

"You haven't hijacked my holiday, and you aren't pathetic or needy, so don't say that again," Nova chided. She handed Rosalee the nurse call button. "I won't be long. If you need anything, press this button. I'll bring more ice chips when I come back."

"That'll be great. Thanks."

Nova patted Rosalee's arm, grabbed her purse, and rushed from the room. She stopped at the nurses' station to let them know she was going to the cafeteria, then hurried to the elevator.

There were only a few people in the cafeteria, so it didn't take long before she was seated at a table eating a roast turkey sandwich filled with cranberry sauce and cream cheese. She indulged in a slice of pear pie and a cup of spicy tea before she filled a tray with cups of hot chocolate for the nurses in the maternity ward and a large cup with ice for Rosalee, then hastened back upstairs. After leaving the hot chocolate with her fellow nurses, Nova returned to Rosalee's room to find her watching the original black and white version of *Miracle on 34th Street.*

"That's one of my favorite holiday movies," Nova said, adding more ice chips to the cup Rosalee held.

"Mine, too," Rosalee said, slipping another piece of ice in her mouth. "I'm usually so busy with work and social obligations I don't get a chance to watch it. It's been years since I got to see the whole thing. Rob's idea of a great Christmas movie is—"

"*Die Hard*!" they said in unison, laughing.

"My husband and our son also like that movie." Nova tucked her purse out of the way in the corner, then turned to study Rosalee. She didn't look quite as anxious as she had earlier. Maybe the walk and sitting in a chair had done her good.

From what Rosalee had shared, Nova figured she'd been in labor since sometime yesterday but hadn't realized it until the contractions began coming with frequency and increasing pain. She had to be exhausted. Rosalee thought she was weak and needy, but Nova saw her as strong and resilient.

If she'd been the one going through labor alone or with a stranger as her coach, she wouldn't have handled it with the grace Rosalee had exhibited. The soon-to-be mother had managed to keep her sense of humor and shared several witty thoughts throughout the day that had made Nova laugh.

Nova recalled some of the worst cases she'd helped with in the maternity ward, including one young woman who'd been rude and condescending, thrown things at the nurses and the doctor, then screamed for what seemed like four hours straight before her baby arrived. Nova shouldn't have thought it, but that baby had been one of the homeliest she'd ever seen, and she was someone who generally thought all babies were beautiful.

If Rosalee's baby resembled her, the little one would have sparkling eyes, a beautiful smile, a head full of hair, and a good heart.

"How do you feel about dancing?" Nova asked when the movie ended.

"Dancing?" Rosalee gave her a questioning glance. "Like at a party? Swing dancing? Line dancing? Drunken girls on the table dancing? What are we talking about?"

Nova laughed. "Here. Right now. I've heard that some women have found that dancing to a fast beat can help get the baby to shift downward and come sooner."

Rosalee's mouth fell open. "You're kidding me. Look at me, Nova! I'm like an enormous puffer fish with legs sticking out. Nobody, and I mean nobody, wants to see all this bust a move."

"Come on." Nova held out a hand, refusing to take no for an answer. "It'll make you laugh if nothing else."

Rosalee sighed in resignation as Nova took her hands and helped her to her feet. She moved the IV pole out of the way, pushed back a chair, then took her phone from her pocket and found the perfect song. As the opening notes of "You Make My Dreams Come True" by Hall & Oates filled the room, Rosalee rolled her eyes, standing as stiff as a board.

"You do know how to dance, don't you?" Nova asked, wiggling her shoulders and moving her feet back and forth. "You strike me as a cheerleader, homecoming queen type."

"It was prom queen, and yes, I know how to dance. But I never said I wanted to."

Nova nudged Rosalee with her elbow as she danced around her. "Let's see those mad dance skills, Miss Prom Queen."

"You are the cruelest woman on the planet," Rosalee huffed, then broke into a dance routine that would have made Cyndi Lauper proud.

Nova danced with her, and by the time the song ended, they were both laughing, even as Rosalee worked through another intense contraction.

The young woman sank onto the edge of the bed and shook her head while rubbing her belly. "I can't believe I just did that."

Nova grinned. "It felt good, though, didn't it?"

"It sure did." Rosalee pushed herself to her feet. "Now I need to use the bathroom again."

"Yes, my dancing queen. Whatever you need," Nova teased.

Rosalee grinned and tugged the IV pole into the bathroom.

Even if dancing didn't help the baby come sooner, it had put Rosalee in a better frame of mind. That was what Nova had hoped it would accomplish all along.

CHAPTER 9

CARTER

"**C**OME ON, MAN. YOU can do this. You can do this." Carter gave himself a pep talk as he stood outside a huge warehouse-type grocery store. He'd had to park in the far reaches of the parking lot by the trash bins, but at least he'd found a spot that was in the same zip code. His wife was putting in a long day at work, and the last thing she needed was to have to run to the store or worry about fixing a meal that evening.

How hard could it be to walk into a crowded grocery store on Christmas Eve afternoon and hope to find everything he'd need for a ready-made meal? Impossible, probably, but he was going to give it a shot.

A cart rolled unattended through the parking lot, so Carter jogged over and grabbed the handle before it could slam into a parked car. He spun the cart around, then charged into the store as though he was about to storm a castle by wading through a leech-infested moat.

Inside, the place was chaos. Complete and utter chaos.

So many kids were screaming that he winced at the unsettling decibels of the high-pitched wails. Carts clanked into each other. Tempers ran short. Anyone who was supposed to help customers appeared to be in hiding because one determined older man used his cane to thump a pallet while yelling, "Hey! Some help over here! I have money and want to spend it! Hey! Anybody? Somebody?"

Carter sped by the man and his flailing cane, wondering how long it would take for someone to help the old guy. He could see the shelves were nearly bare and didn't hold out a lot of hope of finding anything his family would eat, but he pushed his cart to the produce section and dug through what remained to unearth enough ingredients to put together a green salad—pre-washed lettuce, a cucumber and a tomato that didn't look entirely rotten. In the bakery, he picked up a tray of sliced quick breads for their breakfast tomorrow, then chose pumpkin pie and a chocolate raspberry cheesecake for dessert.

After tossing a bag of dinner rolls and a box of croissants into the cart, he headed straight for the deli, where he loaded up on a veggie tray, a fruit tray, a cheese and meat tray, and two roasted chickens, along with a big tray of barbecued ribs, which he and his son would definitely enjoy. A tub of mashed potatoes and a can of cranberry sauce went into the cart along with a box of assorted crackers, milk, eggs, butter, and two pounds of bacon. He started toward the registers but remembered they needed juice. On the way there, he added two boxes of candy he knew his wife and son would enjoy, snatched the last bottle of orange juice, and raced to the cash register.

By the time he checked out, sweat rolled down his back, and he felt like he'd run a marathon in his work boots.

"If I never have to do *that* again, that would be fine with me," he muttered as he pushed the cart across the parking lot and loaded the groceries in his pickup.

It took twice as long as it should have to get home, where he hustled to put away the food and carry in the mail. He glanced at his watch. He needed to get back to work soon. Ace, his assistant manager, would be swinging by any minute to pick him up, but he stopped long enough to place the gifts he'd kept hidden in the garage under the tree in the living room.

While he waited for Ace to arrive, he picked up a picture of the woman who'd made his life so rich and full and beautiful. He didn't know why, but the first time they'd met, he'd thought she was the most incredible woman he'd ever seen.

He wandered down the hallway, looking at the images that showed little glimpses into the happy moments of their life together. There'd been plenty of hard times. Even a few times when he or his wife—or both of them—had wanted to walk away, but they'd stuck it out. Each time they had, their relationship had deepened, and their bonds had strengthened.

Carter had watched a news report about the suicidal man on the bridge. The reporter made it sound like a recent divorce had caused the guy to spiral out of control.

Unable to picture his life without his wife or kids, Carter wondered what he'd do if he were in the man's shoes. Not a day went by that he didn't feel soul-deep gratitude for his family, for the life they'd built together and the love that filled their home.

To have that all suddenly go away would devastate him. He could almost feel sorry for that guy, or he would have if the man hadn't chosen to cause such a big wreck on the St. Johns Bridge on one of the busiest days of the year.

Carter realized Leon Mumford—that name was hard to forget—wasn't thinking rationally or with any sense, but still. Someone could have been killed when he pulled across all four lanes of traffic. The footage on the news that showed a video clip of the wreck as it happened had been hard for Carter to watch.

What if his wife or their son or some of their many friends had been in the wreck?

The inconvenience of having to run to the store because his wife was tied up at work no longer seemed like such a big deal. He'd survived the unpleasant experience, and now they had food in the fridge.

Inspired by an idea for their dinner that didn't involve cooking or eating grocery store chicken, Carter rushed to the small room they used as a home office and turned on the computer. He looked up the menu at one of their favorite restaurants, placed an online order for delivery, and hoped they'd all be home before it arrived later that evening.

A horn tooted from the driveway, letting him know Ace was there to give him a ride back to the wreck on the bridge. On his way out the door, he flipped the switch to turn on the twinkling white lights he and his son had spent far too much time draping across the front of the house, through the bushes, and around the trees in the front yard. His wife would love coming home to find the lights glowing through the winter darkness. Admittedly, so would he.

CHAPTER 10

IAN

"**G**OOD MORNING. I HAVE an appointment with Taylor Jackson at nine-thirty." Ian smiled politely at the scowling receptionist who had to be well past sixty, as he entered Magra's glass-encased lobby. The woman put him in mind of his third-grade teacher, who had a disposition as sour as the lemons he was sure she sucked dry before class every morning.

He wanted to gape with interest at his surroundings but kept his focus on the woman who glared with cool disdain as she pushed her glasses up on her thin nose.

"You're early. Name, please?" she asked in a monotone that made him send up a plea that she had no influence with Taylor Jackson.

Ian gave her his name and waited as she tapped the keys on her computer's keyboard. A brass nameplate on the desk read Ms. Tipton.

The woman looked up at him and shook her head. "Ms. Jackson is tied up at the moment. If you don't mind waiting, she'll see you as quickly as she can." Ms. Tipton pointed to her right.

Ian took in a large waiting area with two leather couches facing each other and a coffee table between them loaded with magazines. Sleek chrome chairs placed between the ends of the couches completed the seating arrangement. Chrome floor lamps stood behind the couches, while end tables held smaller lamps. Overall, the space looked modern, sleek, and flooded with light from the plethora of windows.

"I'll wait. Thank you."

Ian walked over to the couch that faced the reception area, removed his coat, then took a seat. He kept his bag beside him and gazed out the windows, but the only thing of any interest out there was a squirrel scurrying up and down a big maple tree. Ian wondered if the animal had found a spilled bag of sunflower seeds or something along those lines and was carrying the food up to a nest to save for later.

Thirty minutes had passed by when he looked up to see Ms. Tipton standing in front of him. "Ms. Jackson is unexpectedly occupied, but she did say she wants to speak with you. Do you mind continuing to wait?"

"No. Not at all." Ian would camp out on the couch all day if that was what it took to make his interview happen.

"I'll let her know." She took a few steps toward her desk, then stopped. "Would you care for a cup of coffee?"

"No, thank you. I have water." Ian pulled the water bottle from his bag, glad he'd grabbed it from the fridge at the last minute. He took a long drink and decided he'd likely lose his mind if he spent all day watching the skittering squirrel race up and down the tree.

He dug into his bag and took out a small resealable bag full of paper clips and a little pair of needle-nose pliers he always carried with him. Unable to sit idle, especially when he was nervous, he needed something to keep his hands and mind busy while he waited for Ms. Jackson.

With thoughts of his spunky rideshare driver in mind, Ian began twisting paper clips into delicate little swirls. When he had eight swirls that matched, he used additional paper clips twisted into tiny loops to hold them together. He fashioned a fastener out of another clip, then held it up to examine his handiwork, pleased with how the bracelet had turned out. It didn't look bad, if he did say so himself.

"Did you just make that?" the receptionist asked, standing on the other side of the coffee table with a thick stoneware mug in her hand.

"Yeah. I don't like to sit with nothing to do."

Both of her eyebrows hiked upward, but Ms. Tipton gave him an approving look. "I thought you might like some hot chocolate since coffee didn't seem to appeal to you."

"Thank you," he said, accepting the cup from her and taking a sip. It was hot, not too sweet, and creamy. "It's delicious."

"My own secret recipe," she said with the barest hint of a smile before she returned to her desk.

Ian tucked the paper clip bracelet into a pocket in his bag. If he ever ran into Kate again, he'd give it to her. If he didn't, it would be a reminder of a woman who'd made him think love might be waiting for him somewhere in his future.

Suddenly, he recalled a saying of his mother's. "Whatever will be, will be, and no amount of worrying or trying to alter it will change a thing." For the first time, her words of wisdom really sank into his thick skull.

If he was meant to get this job, he would. If he was meant to ask Kate for a date, he'd run into her again. If not, then he'd accept the unspoken "no" and move on.

In the meantime, he could keep boredom at bay and perhaps make points with the receptionist. He placed several paper clips on the coffee table and started twisting them into tiny little curls of metal. He sipped the hot chocolate until the cup was empty, then focused all his attention on his project. Another hour had passed, and he was starving, but he'd finished what he'd started.

He stood and carried his paper clip masterpiece, along with his empty mug, to the receptionist's desk. "Thank you again for the hot chocolate. It was some of the best I've ever tasted."

"You're welcome, young man." She lifted her chin as though trying to deduce what he held in his hand. "I saw you were working on something. Did you finish?"

"I did." He set a filigree snowflake made entirely from paper clips in the center of her desk. He'd twisted one into a loop for a hanger at the top so Ms. Tipton could use it as an ornament if she chose.

"Oh, my," Ms. Tipton said, reverently lifting it up and holding it by the loop. "You are a creative one, aren't you? Who taught you how to make things like this?"

Ian shrugged. "It's just something I've always liked to do. Take ordinary objects and make them into something different."

"You didn't just take an ordinary object and turn it into something else. You created an extraordinary piece."

"Thank you, ma'am." Ian started to back away from the desk. She held the snowflake out to him, intending to return it. He shook his head. "You keep it."

"Really? Are you sure?" she asked, gazing at the snowflake as though it was encrusted with diamonds.

"Absolutely sure, Ms. Tipton. Enjoy, and Merry Christmas."

"Thank you," she said, then set the snowflake on her desk. She gave him a studying glance, then hurried down a hallway, leaving him alone in the waiting area.

Ms. Tipton returned ten minutes later with a tray in her hands. She set it on the coffee table in front of Ian. It held a stoneware plate with a ham sandwich, a shiny red apple, and three sugar cookies shaped like bells and stars with red sprinkles on top. A bottle of cranberry juice sat next to the plate, along with a vending machine bag of wavy potato chips.

"Since you've been waiting so long, you should eat something." Ms. Tipton nudged the tray closer to him. "And before you refuse or offer to pay for it, it's food we keep in the breakroom. With the office closed all next week, the meat would've been tossed out at the end of the day anyway. Eat up. Growing young men need sustenance."

Ian smiled and nodded at her. "Thank you so much, Ms. Tipton. I was too nervous to eat breakfast, and now I'm starving. Is there somewhere I can wash up?"

"The little boy's room is right over there," she said, pointing to a door around the corner behind her desk.

"Thank you."

Ian used the facilities and washed his hands, then eagerly returned to the couch and the lunch Ms. Tipton had prepared. She might look like a mean ol' biddy at first glance, but underneath that judgmental exterior was a nice woman. He was glad he'd spent all that time making a snowflake for her, especially since she'd brought him lunch.

He was so famished, he would have wolfed down the sandwich even if he'd been following a strict vegan regimen. The ham in it wasn't thinly sliced lunch meat, but a thick slab of smoky baked ham, the kind his mom always served for Easter. The wheat bread tasted home baked, and the cheese and pickle were far better than the generic brands he purchased at a discount grocery store.

Ian wasn't broke or destitute, but his parents had taught him to be frugal. He'd been careful with his money after college, spending as little as he could and saving as much as possible. He had enough set aside for a down payment on a vehicle and what he thought it might take to get into an improved housing situation, but he'd been hesitant to spend the money. He wanted to wait until his finances were on a secure footing with a full-time job that hopefully offered benefits. One of his nightmares was upgrading both his rig and his digs and then losing one of his part-time jobs, which relied heavily on tips to make up a good part of his wages. He could endure a few more months of living in what felt like a tacky frat house and driving his old, increasingly unreliable Jeep.

But the Jeep wasn't all bad if it had led him to meet a woman like Kate.

As he considered her age and what she might do for a living when she wasn't giving passengers heart palpitations with her driving, he opened the juice and took a deep drink. He ate the salty chips, then bit into the apple that was crispy, crunchy, and sweet, just the way he liked them. It had a different flavor than any apple he'd tasted. He glanced over at Ms. Tipton who was taking dainty bites of her own lunch. He assumed his presence was the reason she wasn't on a lunch break instead of keeping watch over him.

"What kind of apple is this, Ms. Tipton?" he asked, holding it up so she could see it. "It's really good."

"A Cosmic Crisp. Isn't it divine?"

Ian nodded and took another bite. "I've never tasted one before. I'll have to tell my mom about them. She loves apples."

"I just happened to notice them the other day when I went to the store and decided to give them a try. I'm so glad I did." The woman took a small bite of her sandwich. "Are you enjoying your lunch?"

"Yes, ma'am. It's wonderful. Did you bake the ham and the bread?"

Her cheeks pinked slightly. "I did, and the cookies. I so enjoy cooking. It's just me now, and I can't quite seem to cut back on the amount I make, so I end up bringing the extras here. No one complains."

Ian chuckled. "I'm sure they don't. You're an excellent cook, Ms. Tipton." He finished the apple, then looked at her again. "Did your husband recently pass?"

"Yes. Three years ago. Our two girls live across the country. One is in Virginia and the other is in Alabama. They come home every other year for Christmas. This is the off year when I'm on my own. I'm actually glad Ms. Jackson needed me to work today. It gives me something to do beyond sitting around moping over a lonely holiday."

"I'm sorry for your loss and that you're alone for Christmas." Ian considered what he was about to do but let the words tumble out before he changed his mind. "My folks and I will also be alone. If you'd like to come over this evening, you'd be welcome to join us. It would be casual, just some old Christmas movies and popcorn. I have no idea what Mom has planned for dinner, but I know you'd be welcome."

"That's very sweet of you, Ian, but I don't want to intrude."

"You wouldn't be. Honest. My folks are always happy to set one more place at the table. If you'd like to join us, we'd love to have you."

She studied him for a moment, then nodded her head. "I'll give it some consideration."

Ian took a notepad and a pen from his bag, wrote his parents' address and phone number on it, and carried it over to Ms. Tipton's desk. "If you decide to come, you'll at least know where it is. Last I heard, Mom wants to eat at seven."

"Thank you, Ian." She folded the paper and slipped it into the pocket of her green and navy plaid blazer.

Her phone buzzed, and she hurried to answer it. Ian returned to his unexpected and tasty lunch. He saw Ms. Tipton look at him and nod as she listened to whatever the person on the other end of the call was saying. She spoke quietly, and he couldn't hear her response to what must have been a question, but he felt the need to hurry and finish his food. He gobbled the last two cookies, drained the bottle of juice, then wiped his hands on a red paper napkin with holly leaves and gilded bells in the corner that Ms. Tipton had included on the tray.

The elder woman got up and walked over to him. "That was Ms. Jackson. She needs to head to the airport and wondered if you'd like to ride along with her. She said she'd conduct the interview in the car if you're up for it."

"Of course. I'll do whatever is necessary for this interview to take place."

"Good. She'll be leaving in about ten minutes. I suggest you get ready to go." She walked back over to her desk and resumed her seat.

"Yes, ma'am. Thank you." Ian tossed the trash from his lunch into a nearby garbage can, then carried the tray over to Ms. Tipton's desk. "Is there somewhere I can take this?"

"Just leave it with me, Ian. Now, go wash up." She jabbed her thumb in the direction of the restrooms.

"Yes, ma'am." Ian felt he'd made an ally of the receptionist. Or at least someone who felt like a stand-in grandparent. Both sets of his grandparents were deceased, and he didn't remember much about any of them. It was nice to have an older person take an interest in him.

He washed his hands, smoothed his hair, straightened his tie, brushed cookie crumbs from the lapel of his navy-blue suit jacket, then rushed back to the waiting area. He gathered his things and stood, waiting for the legendary Taylor Jackson to appear.

The woman rushed into the room like a miniature hurricane. Even wearing a three-inch pair of heels, Ian wasn't sure she was five feet tall. Two people walked behind her, appearing to take frantic notes as she barked out orders.

"That's all. Have a Merry Christmas, and I'll see you in January." She smiled at the two employees, then looked at Ms. Tipton. Although she didn't say anything, Ian caught the two women exchanging looks in what appeared to be a cryptic, unspoken language. He saw Ms. Tipton show Ms. Jackson the snowflake he'd made. Ms. Jackson gave it a thorough study before she whispered something to Ms. Tipton, took a file folder from her, and headed toward him.

"Ian. I am profoundly sorry for making you wait all morning. I've been on the phone with the authorities about a delicate matter and trying to wrap up loose ends before I fly out." She glanced at her watch, then motioned to the door. "If you don't mind riding with me to the airport, my driver can drop you off back here or wherever you like."

"Thank you, Ms. Jackson. That's fine." When he noticed her stopping to pull on a coat she carried over her arm, he set down his things, took the coat from her, and held it as she slid her arms in the sleeves.

"Nice manners. That's a point in your favor. Although we're a growing company, it's also a family company. We want all our employees to treat each other with respect, dignity, and kindness."

"That's one of the reasons I'd like to work for Magra, Ms. Jackson."

She gave him a quick glance as they stepped outside. Ian yanked on his coat as a black luxury SUV pulled up. He opened the back door for Ms. Jackson, then jogged around to the other side and slid onto the seat. He inhaled the rich scent of the leather as he fastened his seat belt and turned slightly so he could look at Ms. Jackson.

She had opened the file Ms. Tipton had handed to her, and he saw her reading a handwritten note. She tucked it into the back of the file, then he realized she was reviewing his resume.

"I feel I should explain why I called you to come in for an interview. When the position opened weeks ago, I made a decision—a bad one—to hire a friend's niece. I took my friend's word that the girl had the required skills and capabilities to fill the position. Sadly, she did not, and I had to let her go last week. I brought in a team to review the applications we'd received from the original job posting. Unanimously, they selected you as one of the top three applicants." Ms. Jackson leaned back in the seat and studied him. "You look good on paper, Ian, but why should I hire you? What sets you apart from a thousand other applicants?"

"Because I'll work harder and smarter for you than the others. I don't just need this job, Ms. Jackson. I *want* it because doing this type of work is what fuels my passion. It's what I've always wanted to do, and Magra is where I want to do it. Everyone talks about sustainability and carbon footprints, going green, and all that. I don't just want to talk about it. I want to create things that make a huge difference, that impact lives and the environment in a positive, sustainable way."

"Tell me more," Ms. Jackson said, writing notes on the back of his resume as he spoke about his skills, his interests, his triumphs, and his failures. He believed in being honest and transparent because his potential employer deserved to know exactly what she was getting if she welcomed him to her team.

"Let's circle back to my original questions. Why should I hire you, Ian? What sets you apart from the other applicants?"

Ian was starting to panic. He thought he'd given her twenty reasons why she should hire him, why he was not just the best choice but the only choice for this job. He reached into his bag, extracted a small box, and removed the lid. He lifted out an AA battery, a small magnet, and a piece of copper wire he'd twisted into the shape of a Christmas tree. He connected the magnet to the battery and stood it in the little box, then set the copper wire on top.

Immediately, the wire began to turn, making it look as if the Christmas tree spun in circles.

"You should hire me, Ms. Jackson, because I'm someone who realizes that sometimes the best options aren't extravagant or complex but simple and elegant. I will give one hundred and ten percent to Magra while seeking successful, creative solutions—even to problems we don't yet know exist."

"May I?" Ms. Jackson asked, pointing to the box Ian held in his palm.

"Of course." Ian extended his hand toward her, and she lifted the little box, watching the tree move around.

"What do you think is a fair wage to pay someone fresh out of college with no prior work experience in this field?"

Ian gave her a questioning look, wondering if this was a test question and how badly he was about to bungle it, but could read nothing from her expression. "The current range for entry-level positions runs from the mid-forties to the upper fifties. Also, Magra offers great benefits, and that plays into the overall compensation package."

Ms. Jackson gave him a studying glance. "You may begin the tenth of January. I'll pay you fifty-six thousand a year. After ninety days, full benefits kick in. If you do your job well, we'll evaluate at three months and see about bumping you up on the pay scale by ten percent, with another increase at six months and then at a year. Sound fair?"

"Yes, ma'am, it does. Thank you." Ian tried not to smile too broadly. He felt his Christmas wish had just come true.

Ms. Jackson looked at the box in her hand and Ian saw something almost wistful on her face. "Would you like to keep that, Ms. Jackson?"

"I would. Thank you, Ian." She removed the copper wire and tucked everything back into the box, then put the lid on it and set it inside her purse. "Tell me more about the snowflake you made for Teresa Tipton. She was quite taken with it. What got you started with paper clip art?"

"One afternoon, when I was about seven, I was with my dad at work and bored out of my mind. He gave me a box of paper clips and told me to entertain myself. So I did. I started twisting paper clips together and have been doing it ever since. I always keep some with me, along with needle-nose pliers. They've come in handy far more often than you might think."

"Interesting," she said, giving him a pleased smile. "You won over Ms. Tipton, and that's not an easy task, young man. Also, you should know I'm impressed that you waited all morning for this interview and were willing to accommodate my request to come with me to the airport. I hope I didn't keep you from anything too important."

"No. I have the day off work today, so it wasn't any trouble to wait to speak with you. I'm very grateful for your time, Ms. Jackson, and for the opportunity to work at Magra. I won't let you down."

She offered him a knowing look as the driver pulled up at the airport. "I have a feeling you will do great things for our company, Ian. I look forward to seeing you at the office in January."

"Yes, ma'am. Thank you."

When the SUV stopped outside her terminal, Ian rushed around the vehicle, opening Ms. Jackson's door while her driver set out her suitcase.

"May I help you with your bag, Ms. Jackson?" Ian asked, eyeing the large case that was nearly as big as the diminutive middle-aged woman who owned a mammoth personality.

"That won't be necessary, Ian, but it's kind of you to offer. My husband and sons are waiting inside for me. Enjoy your holidays, and Merry Christmas."

"Merry Christmas to you, ma'am. Thanks again."

She reached out and shook his hand, then grabbed the suitcase handle and shoved it toward the door.

Ian looked to the driver, who offered him a questioning look. "Where to, sir?"

"It would be great if you..." Ian's voice trailed off. He didn't believe in coincidence or karma. Some things were just meant to be. The fact that the vehicle pulling up behind him was none other than

Kate affirmed his mother's words of *what will be, will be*. Or, as his sister liked to say, perhaps God Winks were in play. Divine intervention seemed like a fantastic reason why Kate would suddenly appear. Or maybe Santa was just granting all his Christmas wishes today.

Ian watched as Kate helped an elderly man get his suitcase onto the sidewalk, then started back toward the driver's door of her SUV.

"Mind waiting a moment?" Ian asked the driver.

"Nope, but don't take too long."

"I won't. Thanks." Ian dashed around the front of Kate's car and stepped next to her vehicle as she slid behind the wheel. She reached for the door, then did a double take. A happy grin lifted the corners of her lips.

"Hey. Fancy seeing you again, Ian. What in the world are you doing at the airport?" Her grin broadened. "Don't tell me you're running away from home."

He laughed and shook his head. "No. My interview was conducted in Taylor Jackson's vehicle." He motioned to the SUV. "If you don't have someone else you're picking up, I'd really like to ride with you again. If you're busy, though, Ms. Jackson's driver will take me home."

"As a matter of fact, I'm about to go on a much-needed break, so I'd be happy to have you ride along."

"Thanks! I'll be right back." Ian hustled to the SUV, retrieved his bag, and nodded to the driver. "I've got a ride, but thank you. Merry Christmas."

"Same to you. Have a nice holiday and enjoy time with your girl."

Ian could have set him straight that Kate wasn't his girl. At least not yet. But he had every intention of doing whatever he could to change that. He turned back to Kate's vehicle to see she'd opened the front passenger door.

He was already making progress if she wasn't relegating him to the back seat. He hoped there was a handle above the door for him to hold onto, though, when she took the corners on two wheels.

"Do you think you got the job?" she asked as he slid onto the seat and fastened his seat belt. He glanced up at the handle above the window, relieved to know it was there in case he needed it. "As a matter of fact, I know I did."

"Congrats, Ian!" Kate high-fived him, then pulled away from the terminal. Much to his surprise, she drove like a normal person as they left the airport and merged into traffic heading west.

"Have you had lunch?" Kate asked as she changed lanes to avoid getting trapped in an exit-only lane.

"Surprisingly, yes." Ian told her about Ms. Tipton and how he felt he'd made an ally in the woman. "Actually, I invited her to come to dinner tonight at my mom and dad's house."

"You what?" Kate gaped at him.

He shrugged. "I felt bad about her being all alone for Christmas. In fact, if you don't have anything better to do this evening, you're welcome to join us too."

"I'll give it some thought, but only if you're sure your parents won't mind."

Ian shook his head. "They won't. My dad invited one of the neighbors who's also spending the holiday all alone."

"Do your parents frequently open their home to strangers?"

"More often than you'd think." Ian thought of all the times his dad or mom had invited someone to join their family for a meal. They'd never complained when he'd brought home friends without asking. His mom had always made it seem easy to stretch the food they had and add another plate, or three, to the table. He realized with her job, it was probably challenging for her to do that, but she'd always been gracious and welcoming.

Just like she'd be if they had extra people join them tonight. He sent his mom a quick text to let her know there would be one more seat needed at their dinner table.

"What about you?" Ian studied Kate's nose ring, the dragon encircling her ear, and the heavy, dark makeup. He was trying to envision her as a carefree child with her hair in pigtails and freckles on her nose, but the image wouldn't quite gel with her studded coat collar or the black jeans she wore that were full of tears along both legs. He could see black fishnet stockings through a particularly large hole above her knee. A T-shirt with a skull on the front and Dr. Martens boots with blue flowers against a black background completed the look, but something about it, something about *her*, made him think it was more of a costume than a fashion statement.

When she glanced at him, Ian could see a softness, almost an innocence, in her gaze that her clothes and attitude belied. He could feel himself getting lost in those pretty blue eyes. His thoughts shifted from her eyes to studying her red lips, wondering what it would be like to kiss her. Would the taste of her kiss be even sweeter than he imagined? Intently focused on her mouth, on kissing her, he couldn't think of anything else.

Suddenly aware he'd been leaning toward her, he sat back and glanced out the window, hoping she didn't notice he'd almost kissed her.

"What about me do you want to know?" Kate asked, breaking the silence that had fallen between them.

"Everything," he blurted, then blushed. He hadn't meant to seem too eager or interested. Perhaps he shouldn't have given up dating to save money. He was obviously out of practice.

Kate raised her right eyebrow as she passed another slow-moving car. "*Everything* is a bit much, don't you think? However, based on your earlier good behavior as my passenger, I'll let you ask ten questions."

Ian gave her a thoughtful study as he nodded his head in agreement. "Before I start asking those ten questions, you never said if you'd eaten lunch."

"I had a sandwich between pick-ups and drop-offs." She looked over at him. "Do you like movies?"

"Sure. You have something in mind?" Fragile wings of hope fluttered in Ian's chest that Kate wasn't anxious to be rid of him. Her question even made it sound like a date sort of thing. Maybe. Didn't movies fall into that category?

"You know the pub and theater on Ivanhoe Street?" she asked.

Ian nodded. "Yeah. The one with the domed roof?"

"That's the one. They're showing old Christmas movies. Want to go watch one with me?"

"I'd love that, but I don't want to take you away from your work."

"Like I said, I'm ready for a break. The last guy I gave a ride to smelled like his menthol had gone rancid." Kate pointed to the back window she'd left open a crack to air out the vehicle. "Go on. You're dying to ask those ten questions."

"True. When you aren't terrorizing your rideshare customers with your driving, what do you do for a living?"

"Teach. I'm a first-grade teacher at the school over by Pier Park."

Ian couldn't help it when his mouth fell open in shock. Of all the careers he could imagine for Kate, teaching wasn't anywhere on the list. Guitarist for a grunge rock band, tattoo artist, and a salesperson at the Harley Davidson dealership had crossed his mind, but not a teacher.

"I see that came as a surprise." She smirked at him. "What else have you got?"

Ian scrambled to corral his thoughts that seemed to have splintered in a multitude of directions. "Do you have a boyfriend or husband?"

"No. When I told you it was just me and Jazzy, it was the absolute truth. I don't have a boyfriend. I've never been married. To answer what will surely be your next questions, I have no siblings, parents, or relatives I'm aware of. My mom left us when I was two. My dad raised me and my older sister by himself. When I was ten, I was at school for soccer practice. Dad and Lauren were coming to pick me up when a drunk driver hit their car. Killed them both instantly. The authorities found my mother. She'd died a year earlier and was buried in a cemetery in St. Louis. Without a single relative to care for me, I went into the foster system."

Ian reached across the seat and placed his hand over hers as it rested on the console between them. "I'm so sorry, Kate. I can't even begin to imagine how hard that would be. My parents drive me crazy sometimes, but they're both incredible, and I can't picture life without them. It must have been terrible to lose both your dad and sister at the same time."

"It wasn't easy, but I survived."

She turned her hand over and laced their fingers together.

Ian smiled and studied her for so long, she finally squeezed the hand that held hers, prompting him. "Next question."

"Where did you grow up?"

"Eugene, mostly. I'd lived in five foster homes by the time I was thirteen, then I ended up with a nice couple. They had two little boys and occasionally took in foster kids. I enjoyed living with them, and they were good to me. When I was seventeen, my social worker decided to move me to a group home that was horrible. I begged to go back to Nate and Ginny's place, but everyone I asked refused to listen. I only had a few weeks left before graduation, so I tried to stick it out, but the night one of the high school boys at the home tried to sneak into my bed, I knew I couldn't stay. I ran away and stayed with a friend until graduation. I applied for financial assistance and ended up with a partial scholarship to attend Willamette University in Salem. I got a job as a dog walker and pet sitter. Through the pet sitting gig, I got jobs in house-sitting and made my way through college without having to pay anything for housing because I always had a house-sitting job to go to. Which is what I'm doing now."

"Now? I thought you rented a house with a big yard?"

Kate smirked again, and Ian fought down the urge to lean over and kiss her enticing red lips.

She gave him what could only be described as a knowing look as they entered the St. Johns neighborhood. "I never said I rented a house. I said I lived in a house with a big yard. The uncle of one of my coworkers is a techie guy for some fancy-pants company. He frequently gets sent overseas to set up systems for clients, but they live here. He and his family left for two years in Germany back in September. I do a quick video chat with them every six weeks so they can see that Jazzy and I are taking good care of the place."

"And you get to live there rent-free?"

"Yep. Completely rent-free, and they pay the utilities. It's an excellent arrangement. I'm saving up to buy my own house, hence the side hustle when I'm not teaching."

"Wow. How did I not know anything about house-sitting? That would be far better than living in a dump that smells like a high school locker room with a bunch of guys who haven't learned how to pick up after themselves. They're pigs."

Kate laughed and turned onto a side street and was soon parking by the pub. Ian hopped out and ran around the vehicle, opening her door for her.

"Thanks," she said, giving him another smile as she took the hand he held out to her and stepped out of the vehicle. She was taller than he'd expected, and he liked that he wouldn't have to bend over far to kiss her—when the opportunity arose. He should probably figure out a way to ask her out first. Then again, did a Christmas movie at the pub count as a date? Surely, it did. He hoped it would be the first of many, many dates he and Kate enjoyed together.

"Did you know this place was built in 1905 as part of the Lewis and Clark Exposition?" she asked. "It was part of the National Cash Register Company's exhibit hall."

Ian kept in step with her as they crossed the parking lot. "I did not know that. The Exposition wasn't held in this area. How did the building get here?"

"It was barged down the river after the expo and set up here. It's been a Lutheran church, an American Legion Post, a bingo parlor, and even a place where Gypsy wakes were held before someone decided to turn it into a pub."

"Wow. Gypsy wakes, huh?" Ian grinned at her. "Do you think it's haunted?"

"Probably. The ghosts just belly up to the bar for peanuts and beer, and it keeps them happy."

Ian shook his head. "What other fascinating tidbits do you know about the area?"

Kate shrugged as Ian held the door for her. "I know the St. Johns neighborhood was named after a man named James John who gave away land and helped people when they needed it. This neighborhood has been around for more than a hundred years and was once just a sleepy little town on the banks of the Willamette River. Thankfully, it retained most of that charm. I think a big part of that comes from the locally owned businesses."

"Agreed." Ian paid for their movie tickets, but Kate insisted on buying the popcorn and drinks. When she ordered his favorite soda, he couldn't explain it, but he felt, in his heart, he'd found the woman he would marry, dragon earring and all.

The fact that they were about to sit down to watch *It's a Wonderful Life* wasn't lost on him. At the moment, he felt like he was living a wonderful life.

CHAPTER 11

ARCHER

"**D**ADDY! PLEASE? WHATEVER IT is you're thinking of doing, don't! We need you. Aiden and I need you, Daddy. Please? Please come see us. Mom said you can even spend Christmas with us if you just come back. We love you, Daddy."

The desperate tone of Leon's daughter's voice made the man's eyes well with tears. Archer waited to play the recording until Officer Yeung let him know the search warrant had come through. She had two officers ready to search the camper while she and Officer Kennedy went through the pickup.

To keep Leon distracted, Archer had played the audio files the captain had sent to him. Leon's ex-wife and two children were aware he was on the bridge, contemplating suicide. The daughter had been willing to do or say whatever was necessary to help her father. The boy, Aiden, also recorded a message, but it lacked the sound of urgency and sincerity of Emma's recording. Even Tiffany, Leon's ex, had sent a message apologizing for keeping the kids from him for Christmas and inviting him to come to her place to see them if he'd just come off the bridge.

Archer didn't think listening to the ex-wife would help Leon, but the man seemed quite moved by his daughter's voice.

"Emma was always a daddy's girl. She and I had some great adventures together." Leon's voice sounded reflective as he spoke.

"You can come off the bridge and make new memories together, Leon. It's not too late. You can still be part of their lives. Part of their future."

"No." Leon shook his head, then looked back out over the water.

Archer glanced down at his phone as a message arrived from the captain. He shared his report from speaking with Leon's former employer.

It seemed Leon had worked for the same company for years and had been a valued employee during that time. After the divorce, he began making mistakes in his work. Being rude to coworkers. Paranoid. Angry. Then he started showing up late or not at all. He was drinking at work, leaving early. The last straw was when he threatened a coworker with a knife when the man accidentally knocked a file off Leon's desk. He was fired and escorted from the building with a directive never to return. From the details shared, it appeared that Leon had once been brilliant in his field of work.

Archer could hardly reconcile the man wiping his nose on his coat sleeve with the one who'd invented an airborne turbine that might someday provide a way to harness wind power above the earth and turn it into clean energy.

He saw Officer Yeung hold up what looked like a knife in the pickup cab and examine it. So far, Leon was unaware that they were going through his belongings. Archer wanted to keep it that way.

"Would you like some more hot chocolate, Leon? Maybe some coffee?"

"Chocolate," he said without even turning to look at Archer.

He'd been almost shocked earlier by the way Leon had managed to scarf down his lunch with one hand. The other one remained firmly grasping the railing the whole time. The hope had been that Leon would need two hands to eat a messy sandwich and would come back onto the bridge instead of lingering on the edge.

Somehow, he'd peeled back the wrapper and eaten the sandwich in huge ravenous bites, then used his coat sleeve as a napkin. It was like observing a starving animal rip into its prey. Archer had left Officer Kennedy overseeing Leon while he retreated to the warmth of a police vehicle, where he could spend five minutes eating in peace.

He hated to get out of the warm car and back to the business of coaxing Leon off the bridge, but he felt his own sense of urgency to get the man to climb over the railing and surrender.

The temperature had dipped below freezing, and they had less than an hour of daylight left before dusk settled. Archer was tired of Leon's game. Part of him couldn't help feeling that the man was toying with the entire police department just to see what they'd do.

Archer glanced over and saw the two officers who were supposed to be searching the camper step out of the back end of it and motion to him.

"Officer Morgan!" Archer called and waited as the young man approached him.

"Yes, sir?"

"Keep watch over Leon for a minute," he said in a whisper.

"I'll try," Morgan said, going to stand where Archer had been, a few feet away from Leon.

Archer hurried to the back of the camper. "What did you find?"

"Blood. A lot of blood. I think there was writing in blood, but part of what was written is busted out from the wreck."

Archer wasn't surprised by the news. The more time he spent with Leon, the more he knew the man was lying about something. He also knew Leon was obsessed with the person he continued to refer to as *he*. When the conversation turned to the mystery man, Leon got such a look of hate in his eyes that it was hard to witness. What had the unknown man done to cause such a violent rage in Leon, who, from all accounts prior to his divorce, was a quiet-spoken, mild-mannered guy?

"Let's see it." Archer followed one of the officers into the mangled mess of the camper. There wasn't room for the three of them to squeeze inside, especially with the wall on one side partially caved in from the wreck.

Blood soaked a rag in the sink and was, as they said, smeared everywhere. What appeared to be a warning had been written in blood on the cabinets in the kitchen area.

"What does it say?" the officer with Archer asked, as he tried to decipher the words.

"*You* is the first word. That's a *W*," Archer said, digging through the rubble, then pointing to what looked to be a cabinet door. "There. What's on that one?"

The officer picked up the door. "*Ill.*"

"No, it spells out *will. You will* ..." Archer kicked aside pieces of insulation and twisted metal. He yanked out another door and turned it over, sucking in a breath. "*Die*. The message is *You will die*. The question is if Leon wrote the message or received it."

Expecting to find a body, or at least parts of one, Archer looked through the camper, picturing what it looked like before the wreck. There was a bedroom at the back where they'd entered. The end had broken off during the collision. A lumpy, stained mattress leaned against the wall. The tiny bathroom next to the bedroom was oddly clean.

Archer sniffed and could smell bleach. Had Leon hacked someone to pieces in the shower, dumped the body, and then cleaned up the evidence with bleach?

"Spray luminol in here. I want to know if there was a lot of blood and who it belongs to."

Archer tugged the warped door off the small refrigerator to find it was empty except for a carton of expired milk and a hunk of smelly cheese.

He envisioned Leon sitting at the small fold-up table, eating a meager breakfast, then rising from the table and deciding today was the day he was going to end his life right after he killed the mystery man.

Turning to leave the camper, he spied a framed photograph beneath broken dishes. He picked it up, removed the photo from the broken frame, and took it with him. The image showed Leon with his children, sitting in a pool of sunshine, the three of them laughing.

Somewhere in the wounded, angry man outside was a guy who loved his kids. Archer just needed to find him.

Outside, he could hear Leon shouting. He ran around the wreck to the front of the pickup, where Officer Kennedy looked ready to leap and grab Leon if he tried anything. Leon stood facing the pickup, one fist drawn back as if he'd slug anyone who tried to touch him while screaming at Officer Yeung to leave his things alone as she bagged a bloody knife.

"Leon!" Archer yelled to be heard above the noise the man was making. "It's okay, Leon. Everything is okay." He shifted his tone back into one that was calming, tranquil, and reassuring.

"No, it isn't! Nothing is okay! Nothing is good. Nothing is right. It's all bad. So bad." Leon glowered at Archer, and the hate emanating from him was almost palpable, like an evil, living thing. "Don't touch my stuff!"

"We have to touch your stuff, Leon," Archer said, keeping his voice even. "You wouldn't talk to us, so we had to get a judge's approval to touch your stuff. Why is there blood in your camper, Leon? Is it yours? Is it his?"

"Oh, it's his, all right. I showed him a thing or two. I showed him!" Leon cackled, and Archer wasn't sure he'd ever seen anything more frightening in his life than the look of pure evil on the man's face.

"Whose blood is on the knife, Leon? Is it his, too?" Archer pointed to the knife Officer Yeung held.

"His blood. So much blood." Leon cackled again and turned away.

Archer got a text from one of the officers in the camper that confirmed there was blood, followed by a video showing the spots in the shower the luminol highlighted. The blood had apparently dripped across the floor to the sink, then into the kitchen, where it was obvious.

He sent a quick text back for them to gather all the evidence they could, then get out of the camper before it caved in on them.

"Leon. You heard your daughter. She just wants her daddy to come home. Safely. To spend Christmas with her. Don't you want to give Emma her Christmas wish? Don't you want to be there for her and Aiden?" Archer held the photo out to him. Something wet touched his cheek, and he glanced up as sleet began to fall. Tiny little pellets of ice felt like they'd cut through his exposed skin. Perfect. This day just kept getting better and better. Archer tamped down everything he was feeling and offered Leon an encouraging look. "They love you, Leon, and you love them. Let's figure this thing out so you can be there for them. Come with me, and we'll see about connecting you with Emma and Aiden. What do you say?"

Leon took the photo and stared at it for a long moment before he slid it into his pocket. He stuck his hand inside his coat and pulled out a semi-automatic pistol, then pointed it at Officer Yeung. "I say you should have stayed out of my stuff."

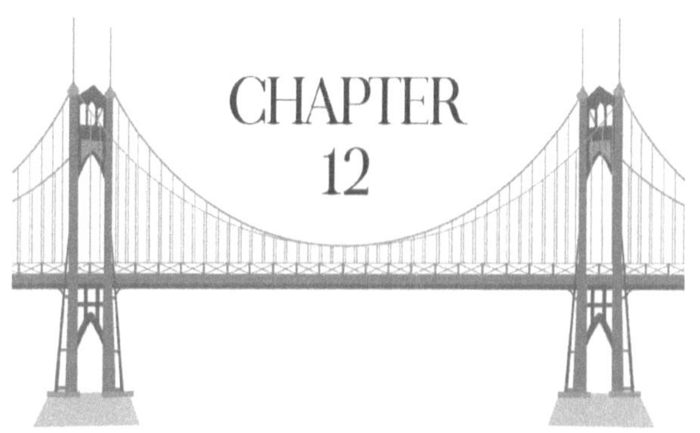

CHAPTER 12

ROSALEE

"I'M READY TO GO. All done. Let's call it a day and try this again another time. A couple more weeks sounds good to me," Rosalee said as she caught her breath after another painful contraction. "Think I can reserve the same room for mid-January? I'll be sure to pack my wool socks and a big robe."

"Leaving now is not an option, Rosalee." Nova grinned at her. "I'm trying to picture you engaging in covert maneuvers to get out of here."

"Ha! My fastest pace right now is a slow waddle. You really think I could sneak out of here?" Rosalee asked, trying to sound serious, although she couldn't. If she wasn't in so much pain, she might have giggled at the vision of trying to sneak out in the ugly hospital socks and gown.

"Your sweet baby has decided today is the day to greet you, and nothing's going to change those plans," Nova said, sponging Rosalee's face, then giving her another ice chip to suck on. "You're doing great."

Rosalee sighed. It felt like she'd been at the hospital for weeks instead of hours. A glance at the clock confirmed it had been more than six hours. In terms of delivering a baby, she knew that wasn't a lot of time, but she was exhausted.

And she missed Rob. From the moment she'd arrived at Lennox Medical Center, she'd prayed he would be there soon.

This milestone in their life, welcoming their first child, was not something she'd ever considered doing alone. She and Rob had made so many plans. Talked about so many dreams. Not a single one of them included her being by herself, at the mercy of strangers, while Rob was elsewhere. It wasn't like him to be this disconnected. Even when he couldn't talk to her on the phone, he usually texted to let her know everything was fine.

Something had to be wrong. She couldn't explain it, but she felt it all the way down to her bones that something had happened with Rob.

Without her phone and with her not being home, no one would know where or how to contact her, even if he was injured. What if Rob was …

"That's enough!" Rosalee snapped, unaware she'd spoken aloud until she saw the look of shock on Nova's face. She grabbed Nova's hand, keeping her from moving back from the bed, and clasped it between both of hers. "I'm so sorry, Nova. I didn't mean you. I was listing in my head all the reasons Rob isn't here, wondering if he's hurt or maybe he was …" She couldn't bring herself to say the words echoing in her thoughts. "I told myself that's enough of the terrible what-ifs."

"I agree. You can't let your mind drag you down a dark path. When Rob arrives, he'll have a very good reason as to why he was delayed. You're such a lovely person, Rosalee. I imagine your husband as someone who's equally wonderful, or you wouldn't be having a child with him. Just focus on positive thoughts. It won't do you or the baby any good to get upset. Bringing a child into this world under ideal circumstances is hard enough, but if you're plagued with worry, it's only going to make things harder. Something my husband does when I'm stressing is to remind me of all the good things in my life. The things I can be grateful for, like my health, our home, and our kids, as well as the life we have together."

"I'm deeply grateful you just happened to be on the bridge this morning and offered to give up your entire Christmas Eve to help me, Nova. I can't even begin to tell you how thankful that makes me." Rosalee felt tears burning her eyes and tried to blink them away, but they spilled down her cheeks. "I'm grateful to be here in the hospital where I planned to deliver my baby, in the care of an excellent doctor." Rosalee brushed at her tears and sniffled. "I'm thankful for my home and my health. For a career I enjoy. For good friends. For my husband, wherever he may be at the moment. For hope. For good, caring people who show me what sacrifice and love truly mean. People like you, Nova. Thank you for staying with me when I know you'd rather be with your family."

"You're stuck with me until this baby arrives, Rosalee. It's my pleasure and honor to be here with you. It's been a long time since I've had the opportunity to assist with a delivery, so think of it in terms of you doing me a favor by allowing me to be here."

Rosalee scoffed. "If you hadn't realized what was going on and gotten me off the bridge, I have no doubt at all my baby would have been born in the back seat of my SUV right there by that suicidal lunatic who caused the wreck." She squeezed Nova's hand again. "Truly, I am so incredibly grateful for your help and your friendship, Nova. I know we just met, but I feel like I've known you forever. Gosh, that sounds like some hokey cliché, even if it's true. I've never been close to my mother and, in fact, wouldn't want her here. You have been a lovely, unexpected blessing to me today as you stepped into a role I didn't even know I'd always longed for someone to fill."

"You are such a sweetheart, Rosalee. I know exactly what you mean. I feel like we've been friends for ages, not just hours. I hope after this is all said and done, you'll keep in touch."

"I would love that. In fact, if it isn't presumptuous of me to assume, I'd love for you to attend my baby shower. It's in a few weeks."

Nova's eyes widened in surprise. "You haven't even had your baby shower yet?"

"No. My friend, Mac, the one who's holding the Christmas Eve party tonight, wanted to do it last month, but I told her I was too busy with work and getting ready for the holidays. I asked her to wait until after Christmas. I'm currently rethinking that decision, even though it's way too late to change it."

"What do you have for the baby?" Nova asked as she fluffed Rosalee's pillows. "What do you need?"

"My parents sent two car seats for Christmas. They're on a cruise and won't be back until February."

Nova gave her a high-eyebrow look that made Rosalee smile.

"Yep. They're *that* kind of parents." Rosalee thought of how uninvolved in her life her parents had always been and likely always would be. "Rob and I have the nursery painted. We set up a crib, dresser, and changing table, and Rob bought a super soft, really cute teddy bear that's in the crib. I've purchased zero outfits because we were waiting to see what we got at the shower and also to find out if this impatient baby is a boy or a girl."

"Don't forget, you have this gorgeous blanket from your client." Nova brushed her hand over the soft blanket Betty had made.

"I think the blanket will be what our little bundle of joy goes home in since I don't have any clothes for our baby."

"It'll all be fine, Rosalee. You'll see. Once you hold your baby in your arms, everything else will cease to be important. What a special joy to have a Christmas Eve baby."

Rosalee sighed. "I've been thinking of Mary and Joseph a lot lately. The kind of people they must have been to be given Jesus to raise. It's more than my mind can fathom."

"Mine, too. There were days when my kids were growing up when I felt like the worst, most incapable mother on the planet. But to be entrusted with the Christ child? God knew what he was doing when he chose Mary because I would've failed at it so spectacularly."

Rosalee pictured Nova as a younger version of herself with two children underfoot, working long hours as a nurse and building a life with her husband. She couldn't imagine her being any different than she was now—a kind, considerate, generous person.

"You were probably one of those spectacular mothers who somehow managed to balance everything, keeping all the balls in the air all the time."

"Ha! I was more like the crazy mom dropping at least one, if not more, balls a day. The kind who always showed up with snacks from the store because I didn't have time to bake. One time, my son's class was raising money for a field trip and held a bake sale. He forgot to tell me until that morning, and I didn't have time to even run to the store. I opened a can of chocolate frosting, smeared it between graham crackers, then dipped them in melted chocolate candy. You know, the kind you use to make peppermint bark."

"Yeah, I know those little dipping wafers well."

Nova grinned. "I was so embarrassed to give them to him for the bake sale, but they sold out, and he asked me to make them the next time he needed to take treats to school."

"Now, that's funny. And creative. Mom for the win!" Rosalee said, then grunted as a horribly painful contraction nearly stole her breath away.

"How's our little mama doing in here?" Dr. Stoakes asked as she breezed into the room.

"I think she's getting close," Nova said, winking at Rosalee.

The doctor gave Rosalee an exam and smiled when she finished. "I don't think it'll take too much longer. Soon, we can welcome this little baby just in time for Christmas. Isn't it a glorious day for bringing a new life into the world?"

The doctor sailed out of the room before Rosalee could gather enough breath and strength to answer.

"Want more ice?" Nova asked, holding out a plastic spoon with a piece of ice on it.

Rosalee opened her mouth, then rested back against the pillows.

"What happens next?" she asked as she sucked on the ice chip.

"You're about to head into the transitional stage, and it can be painful. After that, you'll move into the delivery segment of this adventure."

"Okay," Rosalee said, feeling another contraction hit her. "I'm definitely experiencing the pain portion of the program. My lower back feels like it's throbbing in time to the beat of my heart."

"Let's try and focus on the hypnotherapy details you remember. I think I have your playlist pulled together, and we'll just envision those images you chose to relax you. Close your eyes, Rosalee. Visualize those swaying palm trees. Fluffy clouds floating overhead. Sunlight reflecting on the surface of a crystal-clear lake. Tulips reaching up toward an endless blue sky. Listen to the soothing sound of waves lapping against the shore."

Rosalee couldn't hear anything except the pounding in her head and the nagging thought that something had happened to Rob. Before she delivered this baby, her husband had better magically appear.

When he did, she was going to kill him.

CHAPTER 13

NOVA

"D R. STOAKES?" NOVA CAUGHT up with the doctor as she came out of another delivery room down the hall from Rosalee. While Rosalee was in the bathroom, Nova had darted out to find the doctor.

"Is something wrong, Nova?" Amanda Stoakes asked, looking concerned as she tossed a pair of blue nitrile gloves in a garbage can and took a step toward Rosalee's room.

Nova moved in front of her and shook her head.

"No. Nothing seems wrong. I just wanted to touch base and make sure you thought everything looked normal for her. She's stressing quite a bit about her husband not being here, and I have no idea how to find him."

Dr. Stoakes nodded and motioned for Nova to follow her to the end of the hall where they wouldn't be overheard. "She's doing great, Nova. All her vital signs are good, and the baby's vitals are strong. I don't expect any complications at all, but I know how hard it is when a soon-to-be-mother wants someone to be here who isn't. It makes it harder on her. We'll just hope and pray her husband shows up." The doctor patted Nova on the back. "How are you holding up?"

"I'm okay. Once this baby arrives, though, I may go home and sleep right through Christmas."

The doctor grinned. "Been there and done that, my friend. I'll be in to check on Rosalee in about fifteen minutes. If anything changes, come get me."

"I will."

The doctor nodded and hurried away to see her next patient. Nova rushed back to Rosalee's room, walking inside just as the young woman opened the bathroom door and stepped out. Rosalee made a ridiculous face that caused them both to laugh and shuffled back toward the bed.

"Would you like to walk? Or stand? Sit in the chair?" Nova asked. "I could bring in a ball for you to sit on if you'd rather."

Rosalee nodded. "I'll walk a little if that's okay. As for those balls, keep them away from me, please. When they were the new thing to have instead of office chairs, I used one for a day before I gave up. I kept falling off, feet in the air, in front of my clients. Thank goodness I had pants on that day. It was mortifying, not to mention I went home with bruises all over my bum. Once I assured my husband someone hadn't beaten me, he thought it was pretty funny. I passed the ball off to one of our interns and retrieved my office chair the next morning."

Nova grinned. "I don't sit on a ball at work, but I do like to use one for stretching."

Rosalee gave her a studying glance as Nova helped her slip on the thin robe. "You look like you keep in great shape. What's your exercise routine?"

As they slowly meandered down the hall, the two women shared fitness tips as well as exercises they loved and hated.

When they reached the end of the hall, Rosalee stopped for a moment to catch her breath.

"You mentioned your parents are uninvolved in your life. What about Rob's?" Nova asked, wanting to learn more about Rosalee's absentee husband and his family.

"His parents are great. They live in Santa Barbara. His dad sells insurance, and his mom manages an assisted living facility. We usually try to visit them in the spring, and they come to see us in the fall. They're planning to come for a week at the end of January to help with the baby. Rick and Marilyn have always been so kind to me and made me feel like part of the family. They shipped a big box of gifts for Christmas, but we were waiting to open it until tomorrow. Fingers crossed it has some baby stuff in it."

"Does your husband have siblings? Do you?" Nova asked as Rosalee once again began walking in a slow waddle back toward her room.

"Nope. We're both only children. I think that's part of the reason why we'd like to have a few more kids. It wasn't all that great growing up without a sibling. Although, I'm also rethinking that decision right now. I'm not sure I want to go through this again." Rosalee bent over, hands braced on her thighs, as she breathed through another contraction.

Nova rubbed her back and coached her through the contraction. When the young woman straightened, Nova brushed a few damp tendrils of hair away from her cheeks. The braid she'd fashioned earlier was a mess, but neither of them cared at the moment.

"That was a tough one," Rosalee said as they continued back toward her room. She glanced at Nova. "What about you? Do you have a bunch of siblings? Where do your parents live?"

"My parents died several years ago. So did my husband's. Our kids have never really had grandparents." Nova knew her son, especially, had missed having grandparents like his friends did. "As for siblings, I have a sister and brother. We stay in touch, although we don't see each other often. My sister lives in Arizona, and my brother is in Texas. They both have such nice families, but my brother and his wife have six kids and several grandbabies to dote on."

"Wow. That's a big family." Rosalee stopped as another contraction hit her before they moseyed along the hallway. "What about your husband?"

"He has one sister, two years younger. They look a lot alike but have nothing in common. They don't fight or argue but prefer not to see each other, which is fine with me. I shouldn't think it, let alone say it, but my sister-in-law is not a person I enjoy spending time with. She's bossy, overbearing, conceited, selfish, and downright rude most of the time. Thankfully, she lives in Wisconsin, and visits are rare."

"If you don't like her, Nova, she must be a terror." Rosalee grinned. "From what I've observed, you seem to like almost everyone."

"I generally do, and she *is* a terror. That's a great way to describe her. I'll have to show you some recent pictures she sent from a trip to Spain. She took her cat with her."

Rosalee's eyes widened. "You're kidding."

"Nope. She hauled her seventeen-pound cat with her. I'm sure that was fun for everyone." Nova had felt sorry for the cat but not for her sister-in-law.

It was a good thing the woman was single because Nova couldn't think of anyone who'd put up with all the nonsense she dished out.

Rosalee laughed, then sucked in a breath as another contraction hit her with such force, Nova had to support her, holding her upright with both arms wrapped around her, until it passed.

"Let's get you back to your room," Nova said, eyeing Dr. Stoakes as she approached them from the end of the hall.

"Is the baby ready to make a debut?" the doctor asked as she helped Nova get Rosalee settled back into the bed.

"I sure hope so," Rosalee said, panting through another strong contraction.

A quick examination resulted in Dr. Stoakes nodding to Nova. "The baby is going to make an appearance soon. We'll just get ready for the arrival."

Nova smiled at Rosalee as she quickly sent a text message to her son and one to her husband. She pulled up a playlist of mellow music and set her phone by the bed, lifted up the rails on the side of it, and sponged the young woman's flushed face.

Was this what it would be like when her children had children of their own? This feeling of anticipation and excitement, coupled with worry over the pain of giving birth and concern over all the things that could go wrong?

Nova could picture herself with her daughter, holding Macie's delicate hand as she gave birth to a baby girl who would be just as beautiful as her mother. That thought filled her with joy as she smiled down at Rosalee. "Focus on staying calm, visualizing the things that help you relax, and before you know it, you'll be holding your sweet baby in your arms."

Rosalee expelled a sigh through her pursed lips that seemed to come all the way from her soul as she worked through another contraction. "I just hope my husband's here by then."

For Rosalee's sake, Nova hoped he was too.

CHAPTER 14

"DO YOU THINK WE'LL be able to load the wreck now?" asked Ace, Carter's assistant manager and long-time employee, as they headed back to the St. Johns Bridge. Like old man Levy had done for him, Carter had taken Ace under his wing when the boy was a sophomore in high school and taught him all he knew about mechanic work, running a business, and being a good person.

Ace used to walk by the towing yard on his way home from school. A few things had disappeared over the course of a month. Carter had figured the kid sold the parts to a chop shop. One afternoon, Carter had watched Ace slink over to a wrecked Camaro, pry off a hubcap, and try to hide it beneath his threadbare shirt.

Carter had made his way out a side door and sneaked up behind the boy, grabbing him by the collar. After he'd made it clear he would not tolerate someone stealing from him, he'd offered the felon in the making a job.

Ace had started working for him the next day. A year later, the boy proudly drove off to pick up his prom date in the Camaro that Carter had helped him repair and restore. Occasionally, when the weather was nice, Ace still drove the Camaro. He and his pretty wife enjoyed taking it to car shows in the region.

Carter glanced across the cab of one of their service trucks at Ace. He'd gone from being a scrawny kid no one could trust to a respectable, responsible man on whom Carter depended. It was hard to believe it had been ten years ago when Ace had tried to steal that hubcap. Since then, he'd become important to Carter, like another son to him.

Not once had Carter regretted giving Ace a chance. Second chances were something he believed in wholeheartedly. Goodness knew Levy had given him plenty of chances even though he'd had every right to toss him out on his ear when he'd been a stupid kid full of bravado and attitude.

Carter wanted to pay forward what had been given to him, so he looked for opportunities to live his life in a way that he hoped would make Levy proud. The old man had been more of a parent to him than his own, who'd rarely paid him any mind. Most of the time, that hadn't bothered him.

There were times, though, when he stopped and evaluated his life to make sure he never treated his children the way his parents had treated him. Then again, if he acted like a jerk, his wife wouldn't hesitate to let him know exactly what he'd done wrong. She was good that way—pointing out his flaws.

He grinned; she was also the first to sing his praises and tell him how proud she was of him and all he'd accomplished. Life with her was never boring but almost always sweet. They'd had so many wonderful years together, and he prayed they'd have many more.

What was it about the holidays that made him so nostalgic and sappy? At the moment, he felt like he could write greeting card verses or maybe a script for a Hallmark movie. He wished there was a way to bottle up the joy his memories gave him and preserve it forever.

He and his wife had always loved the holiday season and did all they could to make it special for each other and their children. If there was a button he could hit that would make his kids little again, with their excitement for Santa's arrival filling every crevice of their home, he'd push it in a blink. He'd give anything to go back, for just an hour, and enjoy them at that age one more time. Maybe that meant he'd be ready to spoil grandkids when they came along, although he wasn't in a rush for anyone to refer to him as Gramps. Maybe he could be Pop-Pop or something snazzier rather than a name that made it seem as though he was one step away from a need for geriatric care.

"The wreck, boss? Do you think they'll be ready for us now?" Ace asked again, tugging Carter from his musings.

Carter shrugged. "I sure hope so. This has been quite a day, hasn't it?"

Ace nodded. "For sure." He rubbed a hand along a darkening bruise on his jaw. "It's not every day I end up in the middle of a fistfight when all I'm trying to do is tow a car."

"Maddie won't like seeing that bruise," Carter said, referring to Ace's wife. "I'm sorry that guy decked you."

Ace scowled. "I would have gladly returned the favor, but with the police right there, I figured it was better to keep my hands to myself while the cops put cuffs on him."

"You did the right thing, Ace. Still, the idea of people brawling over a parking space isn't something you'd think about finding on a service call, especially on Christmas Eve."

"I'm telling you, people have lost their minds, boss. Completely lost their minds. If I had my druthers, I'd stay home and not leave from the day before Thanksgiving until the third of January. By then, the drunks have all made it home, and the weirdos have crawled back in their holes."

"That would be something, wouldn't it? To hibernate from the world and enjoy a peaceful December and holiday season. Too bad that'll never happen for either of us," he scoffed. "Your Maddie is a social butterfly, so you'd better get used to the notion that you're never going to be staying at home if there's an event she wants to attend."

"Don't I know it. We've been to so many Christmas parties the past few weeks, I don't care if I never taste eggnog again." Ace made a disgusted face that caused Carter to chuckle. "Laugh all you want, but I'm telling you, there's only so much of that stuff a man can stomach."

"I'll take your word for it. I'm not a huge fan of it myself unless someone's baking it into cookies or doughnuts."

"You're lucky your wife is a good cook. Maddie is still in the learning stage." Ace glanced at Carter. "How long does that last, exactly? You know, before they start making food that's actually edible?"

"Depends on how much they still had to learn when you met them." Carter smirked. "If I recall correctly, you told me that when you met Maddie, she was so pretty, you didn't care that she couldn't make toast without setting off a smoke alarm. Am I hearing that you've now changed your mind?"

"Maddie is so pretty and sweet, it's easy to overlook certain ... challenges," Ace said with a broad grin, "but just one meal that didn't give me indigestion wouldn't be too much to ask, would it? I've started buying antacid tablets by the gallon. If her cooking doesn't improve soon, I might be forced to take cooking classes."

Laughter burst out of Carter, and he shook his head. "You should do that, Ace, because it's just as much your responsibility as hers to cook. Besides, I have zero sympathy for you. You've got it tough, kid. A beautiful wife who adores you. A nice starter home in a good neighborhood. Three vehicles, all paid for. A good job that pays you well. A great boss who puts up with you. What more could you ask for?"

"Eggs without pieces of shell in them or bacon that isn't incinerated beyond recognition," Ace deadpanned, making Carter laugh again. "Besides, who said I had a great boss? He can be kind of demanding sometimes, expecting his staff to work at least half as hard as he does."

"I know, I know. He's awful. Well aware of the fact." Carter stopped teasing and sobered. "Thanks for sticking with me today, though. I honestly thought we'd be wrapped up and on our way home hours ago. What is it about this Christmas Eve that's turned people into maniacs?"

"Must be something in the air." Ace bent his neck at an angle and looked up at the sky. "Those clouds seriously look like snow. Wouldn't that be the cherry on top of the disastrous cake that's been our day? If it snows, we'll be out until the wee hours of the morning towing wrecked cars."

"Or maybe the snow will make them all stay home, and we'll have a quiet, peaceful night." Carter hoped that was the case. He absolutely didn't want to have to work tonight. Not on Christmas Eve.

Ace started singing an off-key version of "Silent Night."

Carter hummed a few bars of the song, then stopped as he saw a woman on the side of the freeway walking around to the back of her minivan.

"Looks like a flat," Ace said, as Carter turned on his hazard lights and pulled up behind her.

"Let's help her with it. The wreck will still be there ten minutes from now." Carter got out of the truck and walked over to the woman who'd opened the back of the minivan and was trying to wrestle a plastic panel loose on the left side of the cargo area.

"May we help you with that?" Carter asked, pointing to the panel, trying not to grin at the two little faces peering over the back seat at him. The little girls, with red bows in their curly brown hair, looked like they were dressed for a Christmas program.

"Oh, I ..." She glanced from him to Ace, then over at the service truck. "I didn't call anyone for help. Yet."

"We just happened to see you. We're on our way to another call," Carter explained, trying to put the woman at ease. "I can grab my tools, and we can get that changed for you in a jiffy."

"Seriously? You'd do that?" she asked, stepping back while Ace loosened the panel and started removing the nuts that held the tire in place.

"Happy to do it, ma'am." Carter retrieved a full-size jack and a cordless impact wrench. The woman watched as he and Ace quickly changed the tire, then set the flat in the back of the van's cargo area.

Ace put the tools away while Carter retrieved a few miniature candy canes from a plastic tub he kept in the cab during the holiday season. A little treat went a long way in making some people happy—especially kids.

"For the little ones," he said, handing the candy to the mother.

She took them with tears in her eyes. "Thank you both so much. We're on our way to the rehearsal for the Christmas program this evening. If I had to change the tire myself, we'd be out here half the night." She opened the driver's door and reached for her purse. "What do I owe you?"

"Nothing, ma'am. Just pass on a little joy to someone else today, and we'll call it even," Carter said, nodding to her, then waving at the two little girls, who had their faces pressed against the glass of the back seat window.

"Merry Christmas!" the woman called as he and Ace walked to their vehicle.

"Merry Christmas!" they both answered, then got back into the warmth of the truck.

"That was great," Ace said, rubbing his chilled hands together, then holding them in front of the heating vent. "Kinda puts you in the spirit of the season, doesn't it, doing nice things for others?"

"Sure does. Those little girls looked cute in their frilly dresses." He tossed Ace a sly grin. "How long before you and Maddie decide to start a family? If you do that, you might seriously need to learn to cook."

"That's up to Maddie. According to her, she needs to work another year and a half to establish herself so some usurper won't steal her job while she's out on maternity leave."

Carter gave him a long look. "That wife of yours likes to plan ahead, doesn't she?"

"She does. If you ask her what outfit she's going to wear for Valentine's Day, she could tell you, in detail, what it'll look like." Ace sighed. "At least I don't have to worry about a lot of stuff anymore because Maddie has it all figured out before the thought even enters my mind."

"That's not a bad thing," Carter mused, then slowed as they took an exit and headed toward the St. Johns Bridge. Apparently, word had gotten around to avoid the area because there were few cars compared to the backed-up traffic that had been there earlier.

Carter waved at the officer manning the barricade blocking the bridge's entrance, drove around it and up the bridge, parking a handful of yards behind his wrecker. He and Ace had just gotten out of the truck when he felt something cold land on the exposed skin of his hands as he pulled on his glove. He glanced upward and felt icy pellets sting his face. Sleet. It was unwelcome but not entirely unexpected. The heavy, dark clouds that had hovered overhead all day were bound to drop something on them at some point.

"Perfect," Carter muttered as he finished yanking on his second glove and then turned his coat collar up since he'd left his scarf in the wrecker earlier. He and Ace started toward the officers they could see standing outside the damaged pickup. They'd reached the bed of the wrecker when they heard shouting.

"Gun! He's got a gun. Get back!" one of the young officers hollered to Carter, motioning for him and Ace to get out of sight.

Carter grabbed Ace's arm and jerked him behind the wrecker. He pushed the younger man out of sight, then peered around the edge. The suicidal guy who'd caused the wreck was now shouting and brandishing a gun.

"Can't the officers shoot him or something?" Ace asked quietly.

"No. It won't be necessary. Give him a minute, and Sergeant Raines will have the situation under control."

"What makes you say that?" Ace asked, trying to look beneath the truck's bed to see what was going on.

"I've seen him do it before. He's one of the best at talking people down when they're a threat to themselves or others." Carter glanced back at Ace. "I'm sorry about this, man. I had no idea what we'd be walking into."

"No one can say working for you is ever boring." Ace grinned, although Carter could see fear in his eyes. He often forgot that the young man was only a year older than his son. Ace was mature for his age and seemed to have his life figured out, while Carter's son was still getting his ducks in a row.

Ace interrupted Carter's thoughts. "Tell me more about Sergeant Raines. Have you seen him in action?"

Carter knew Ace needed something to distract him from what might happen if the situation headed south. "I got called to tow a vehicle from outside a bank. Seems two guys had walked in and decided to rob the place in broad daylight. They took everyone inside hostage. The PPB brought in a negotiator, but after hours of getting nowhere, they called in Sergeant Raines. Within an hour, the hostages were released, and the two guys surrendered. No one was hurt, and that's what I call success."

"Let's hope today ends well, then," Ace said, trying to get a glimpse of the guy with the gun.

Carter motioned for him to stop. He turned so his back was braced against one of the dually tires, then looked over at Ace. If it came right down to it, he'd step between the young man and a bullet. Ace had his whole life ahead of him, and Carter had lived more than half of his.

"You remember the first time we met?" he asked, keeping his voice quiet.

"Sure. I was stealing a hubcap, and you came out of nowhere. Scared the stuffing right out of me." Ace grinned. "Then you offered me a job. I thought you were nuts."

"I probably was to give you a chance, being a delinquent in the making and all." Carter smiled at him. "I don't think I've ever told you this, Ace, but you're like another son to me, and I'm so grateful I've had the privilege of watching you grow up this last decade. You mean a lot to me."

"Well, shoot, boss, I love you, too, but don't go getting all teary-eyed on me. While we're venting our emotions, I'll tell you right now I'm glad you couldn't get in touch with your son earlier to come with you. I'd hate to think of him being here in this situation."

"Me, too. If I had to drag someone into this mess, I'm glad it's you."

"Aw, gee. You keep that up, and I'll start to think you really like me." Ace jokingly batted his eyelashes at Carter. "Does that mean I get a raise after this?"

"Maybe. Talk to me in January." Carter sighed and propped his hands on his bent knees. "Seriously, Ace, you make my job easier, and it's great to work with you. You've grown into an impressive young man."

"You're not too bad yourself, old man, but remember when you offered to send me to college, and I told you I could learn what I needed to from you?"

Carter offered him a questioning look. "I do vividly recall that conversation. Why?"

"I'm starting to think I should have listened to your words of wisdom. If I had, I'd be sitting in some cushy office, drinking hot coffee my secretary brought me, and counting the minutes until I could leave for a week off to enjoy the holiday. Actually, I'd probably already be on my way to some tropical locale with Maddie where she can bask in the sun on the beach while I dip myself in a bucket of sunscreen to keep from turning into a burnt crisp."

A soft chuckle flowed out of Carter. "The picture that brought to mind will make me laugh the rest of the day. Thanks for that, Ace."

"Anytime. I'm always willing to bite the bullet for you. Take a hit to make you laugh."

Carter scowled at him.

"Too soon for gun humor?"

Carter nodded in affirmation.

"I'm working on my timing. Maddie tells me I'm improving and makes it perfectly clear when I'm not."

The dynamo Ace had married would have no qualms about setting him on his ear when he said something she deemed inappropriate.

"You always were quick to make a joke at your own expense. Why is that?" Carter asked the question he'd wondered about for years.

"If you're laughing at yourself first, it makes it harder for others to poke fun at you. When you're fourteen and the poor kid wearing cast-offs that come from the church donation box and carrying a My Little Pony backpack you found in the trash because you can't afford anything better, you learn to put up a few defenses."

Carter patted Ace's shoulder. "I'm truly sorry you had such a rough start in life, Ace. You should be proud of how far you've come."

"Maddie tells me life is a journey, and some of us have a steeper path than others."

"That's a good way to think of it." Maybe Maddie was the one who should be writing greeting cards.

Ace tried to look under the wrecker again and expelled a frustrated breath. "I can't see a blooming thing. I haven't heard a gunshot, so that's good, right?"

"Very good. The yelling has stopped. Could you hear what was being shouted?"

"Something about he did it, not me, and leaving his stuff alone." Ace shrugged. "The guy sounds like his brain went on a holiday vacation."

"I think it's a lot more than that, Ace." Carter edged close to the tire and peered around it. Sergeant Raines was holding out his hand toward the suicidal guy, clearly trying to talk him into giving up the gun. The madman was still holding onto the railing with one hand and the gun with the other, but he was no longer pointing it at anyone as it dangled from his fingers.

Carter shifted back so he was hidden behind the tire. "What are you and Maddie doing this evening?"

"We were supposed to spend it with her sister's family, but she texted a while ago that the whole lot of them are sick, and I refuse to go over there. The last time we did that, when her sister assured us it was *just a touch of something*—" Ace made air quotes with his fingers "—we ended up with a nasty stomach flu that lasted for three days. I told Maddie if her sister's kids even so much as look like they might sniffle or puke, I'm out of there. Anyway, it'll be nice to stay home. Have a quiet evening."

"Why don't you come to our house? We're just going to chill and watch some movies, but you and Maddie would be more than welcome. I ordered food from that Brazilian place we all love. Hopefully, someone will be at the house when it arrives." Carter checked his watch. Before long, it would be dark, and he detested loading the wrecker when he couldn't see what he was doing. There was lighting on the bridge, but it wasn't that great.

"Are you serious, boss? You'd open your home to us on Christmas Eve?"

Carter looked at Ace. "You're like family, you idiot. Of course, you're welcome. Send Maddie a text and see what she says."

Ace took out his phone and texted his wife. She sent a text back, and Ace smiled. "Maddie says we'll be there, and she'll bring a yule log cake. And don't worry, I know for a fact she bought it from the bakery, so it should be edible."

"Sounds great, Ace." Carter patted him on the shoulder again, then glanced up at one of the officers as he walked around the back of the truck.

"It's safe for the moment," the officer told them. "Sergeant Raines says to hustle and get the wreck out of here before anything else happens, though. We may need the vehicles for evidence. Can you haul them over for us?"

"Sure." Carter stood, and Ace hopped up beside him. He turned to the younger man. "You heard the officer. Let's hustle."

CHAPTER 15

IAN

"I'D FORGOTTEN WHAT AN excellent movie that is. So full of hope and reminders of how amazing life can be when we stop and look at the good things all around us." Ian smiled at Kate as they left the movie theater. He dumped the empty popcorn tub in the garbage can and took a last sip from his cup of soda, which was now mostly melted ice. "Thanks for suggesting this. It was great."

"Thanks for coming with me," Kate said. "Going to the movies alone isn't all that much fun."

"Agreed." Ian grabbed a few napkins from a dispenser and wiped his hands, then looked at Kate as she studied a sign advertising upcoming movies. A new movie that would be released in a few weeks caught his eye. He'd thought about going to see it, but now he wondered if Kate would go with him. The only way he'd know was if he worked up the courage to ask her.

Maybe they could do a whole dinner and movie evening. The pub had great food and a fun atmosphere, and she seemed to feel comfortable around him. She'd shared a tub of popcorn with him, and each time their fingers brushed as they dug into the buttery kernels, Ian felt like he'd been zapped with a jolt of electricity.

He'd only met Kate that morning. Yet, for reasons he couldn't begin to understand or unravel, he felt like he'd always known her. Like she was the one person he'd been created to find and spend his life loving.

That was beyond crazy, though. What did they really have in common, other than their taste in music, movies, food, books, and sense of humor?

However, there was so much he didn't know about her. Like her middle name. Or her hair color since she still had on that ridiculous slouchy hat that hid every strand of her hair. Did she always dress like that, as if she was waiting for a vampire lord to appear on her doorstep?

Ian rolled his eyes at his own absurd thoughts and took a step closer to Kate. "Have you seen the trailers for that one?" he asked, pointing to the movie of interest.

"I have. I thought it looked really good. Are you planning to see it?" Kate asked, turning to look at him.

Ian froze as his gaze connected with hers. Those incredible blue eyes drew him in until he could practically feel his brain cells dying one by one. He yanked his thoughts together and nodded. "I was thinking about it. I don't suppose you'd like to come with me, would you? We could have dinner here and then see the movie."

"I'd like that, Ian," she said softly, holding his gaze as something electric passed between them. "Should we make a reservation?"

"Yes. Let's do that while we're here."

Together, they picked a day and a time for their reservation and paid in advance for two movie tickets.

"I'm looking forward to seeing it with you," Kate said as Ian held the door and they walked outside.

Sleet pinged against cars and pounded the pavement.

"Where did this come from?" Kate asked as she sprinted toward her SUV.

Ian was right behind her. He would have offered to hold his coat over her to keep off the sleet, but she didn't give him the chance. Considering how fast she moved, he wondered if she'd ever participated in track events in school. Then again, maybe as an elementary school teacher, she had to move quickly to keep up with her energetic students.

"Tell me about the kids you teach," Ian said as she started the vehicle and they waited for warm air to blow through the vents.

"They're wonderful. Smart. Hilarious. Exhausting." Kate laughed. "They challenge me and make me think. The way their little minds work never ceases to amaze me. I love teaching them. There's this one little guy, Toby, who always looks so serious, but then he'll say something outrageous that makes me struggle not to laugh. They really are a great bunch of kids. I'll miss them while I'm on break for Christmas."

"If you get bored, I'll be around in the afternoons."

Kate frowned. "What is it you do for work right now? I'm not sure we covered that in all the things we discussed today."

"From seven until eleven in the morning, I work at Hotel Bradford as a valet. From five until closing in the evening, I wait tables at The Bricks."

Kate whistled. "Those are both pretty ritzy places in the downtown area. I hope you at least make good tips."

"I usually do, which is why I've been working both jobs. But I'm already looking forward to giving my notice and starting down my career path at Magra." Ian could hardly wait to begin the work he'd dreamed of doing as a mechanical engineer.

He wanted to work somewhere he could make a difference on a global level, not retrieving luxury cars for rich people or watching them waste more food than they ate because they could afford to live a decadent lifestyle.

"When will you give your notice?" Kate asked as she backed out of the parking space and pulled out onto the street.

"The day after Christmas. That gives them a little more than two weeks to find a replacement for me." Ian pointed to a house they drove past that was twinkling with Christmas lights. Dusk was fast approaching, and soon lights would glow through the darkness.

Ian's phone buzzed, and he took it from his pocket, read a message from his mom, then glanced over at Kate. "I know we talked about this earlier, but if you don't have anything better to do, would you hang out with me at my parents' place this evening? My mom wants me to grab a few things at the store, then pick her up from work in about two hours. Are you game?"

Kate grinned. "I think I can handle it. How's this for a plan? I'll drop you off at your place. If you can get your Jeep running, you can pick me up at mine in an hour and a half. We'll go do your shopping and then pick up your mom. If the Jeep won't start, call me. I'll come get you."

"That sounds great, but I'll need your number." Ian held up his phone.

Kate rattled off her number, and Ian sent her a text to make sure he'd entered it correctly. The phone she'd placed in the console holder buzzed, and she grinned at him. "Now you can't get away."

"I wasn't trying to," he said, tucking his phone back in his pocket.

Kate shifted from driving at a normal pace to speeding through traffic. Ian was sure he saw his life flash before his eyes at least three times before she pulled to a stop outside his place.

"Here's my address," she said, tapping out a message on her phone and texting it to him.

"Perfect. I'll see you soon," he said, hopping out. He grabbed the bag he'd set in the backseat, then waved as she pulled away from the curb.

Ian sprinted into the house, startling one of his roommates who'd been asleep on the couch.

"Dude, where ya been all day?"

"Falling in love," Ian answered honestly, then rushed into his room. He changed out of his suit into an old pair of jeans and a sweatshirt, yanked on a coat he didn't mind getting all dirty, and rushed back outside with his toolbox. He lifted the hood to find that one of the battery cables had loosened. It only took him a minute to tighten it, get in the Jeep, and sit there in shock as it started the first time he tried it.

"I don't believe it," he muttered to himself as he turned off the ignition and carried his tools inside. If he'd taken a minute to lift the hood that morning, he could easily have fixed the problem and driven himself to the interview. If he had, though, would he have been one of the cars that had plowed into the pickup on the bridge? Would he ever have met Kate?

He felt a tingle slide down his spine while goose bumps broke out on his arms. "What's meant to be, will be," he muttered as he set his tools inside the closet in his room, then rushed to take a shower and shave for a second time that day.

After pulling on a pair of newer jeans, he tugged a warm thermal Henley shirt over his head and shoved his feet into boots. Nervous, he glanced at the clock. He still had half an hour before he needed to head over to pick up Kate.

He retrieved the bracelet he'd made for her from his bag and quickly constructed a little box from a cardboard pizza box left on the counter. He searched the apartment for wrapping paper but ended up wrapping the box in a piece of computer paper, then cut pieces of paper into skinny strips he curled with a pair of scissors and taped to the top of the box.

The gift and the wrappings were anything but fancy, but he had a feeling Kate would like it just the same.

Maybe someday in the future, when he could afford to buy her a diamond bracelet, they'd look back and laugh about the year he gave her a paper clip bracelet in a pizza box.

Ian was getting way ahead of himself. He just needed to get through tonight without scaring her off, and then they could proceed from there. He would've asked for a date for New Year's Eve, but he was scheduled to work that night. Maybe they could do something when he got off work or the next day.

What if she'd grown tired of him by then? He'd be left nursing a broken heart before their relationship had time to blossom.

Annoyed with himself for his thoughts, Ian packed an overnight bag to take to his parents' house, along with their gifts, and slipped on his coat. He shoved his phone and wallet into his pockets, grabbed his car keys, and wished his roommate a Merry Christmas, although the guy was snoring when Ian turned off the television and turned on the kitchen light.

He tapped Kate's address into the map app on his phone and followed the directions to a nice section of homes not all that far from Pier Park. When he pulled up in front of a large home with a wide porch and a fence around the yard, he couldn't help but admire the curb appeal it offered. It was a far cry from the dump where he currently lived.

He'd already looked at a few apartments in the vicinity of Magra. Now, he could start searching in earnest for a better place to live.

Ian got out of the vehicle, taking the gift for Kate with him. He pushed open the gate and carefully closed it behind him, then hurried down the walk and up the steps. The sound of a dog barking reached him, followed by the sound of footsteps approaching the door before he had a chance to ring the bell.

The door swung open, and Ian thought for a moment he'd arrived at the wrong house. The woman smiling at him appeared nothing like the rideshare driver who'd captured his interest all day. This young woman looked like the epitome of the girl next door with a fresh face and wholesome appearance. His gaze traveled from the mass of shiny golden-brown hair curling around her shoulders down to her black flats with bows at the toes and then back up to her eyes.

The blue eyes were familiar, even if they were no longer framed by thick, dark makeup. Instead, a moderate application of mascara highlighted the length of the lashes.

Kate was beautiful, even more beautiful than he'd imagined she'd be without all the makeup on. He saw freckles on her nose. A natural blush of pink in her cheeks. Gone was the dragon earring, replaced by a simple pair of pearl earrings. The nose ring was also absent. So was the goth outfit. A pair of tailored black slacks and a berry red sweater with ruffles at the shoulders gave her a festive, stylish appearance.

"Wow, Kate! You look fantastic!" Ian leaned forward and kissed her cheek, breathing in her delicious fragrance. She smelled the same as she had earlier in the day when he'd first climbed into her SUV, and for that similarity, he was grateful. "Not that you didn't look great before, but you are gorgeous."

Her blush deepened, and she stepped back so he could move inside.

"You don't have to exaggerate, Ian. I dress all dark and brooding to keep people from bugging me. The majority of older people assume I'm a drug addict or belong to a cult. Most guys don't give me a second glance. Women are sometimes catty, but I don't care. They don't know the real me, and I want to keep it that way. I guess my costume, if you will, makes me feel like I can turn off the rideshare light and go back to being myself without any worry about someone recognizing me later and giving me trouble." Kate offered him a long look that started at his hair and traveled down to his boots. "You look pretty good yourself. You've got a hunky woodsman vibe going on for a somewhat homely, newly-employed-in-his-dream-job kind of guy."

Ian grinned, aware she was teasing him, and took a step closer to her.

The dog she'd been holding by the collar whined and wiggled her back end in greeting.

Ian set Kate's gift on a polished table by the door, then hunkered down to pet Jazzy. "Hi, Jazzy. Kate told me all about you. Aren't you a pretty girl? Yes, you are. Such a pretty girl."

The dog licked the hand he'd held out for her to sniff and rubbed against his leg.

"She's not usually this receptive to strangers. I guess you must be special," Kate said, leaning against the stair's newel post as Ian got acquainted with the dog.

When Jazzy rolled onto her back so he could scratch her belly, he was pretty sure he'd made a friend for life in the dog. "I can see why you love her so much."

Ian glanced around the house filled with expensive furnishings and art. "Will she be okay here by herself while we're gone or do you want to take her with us?"

"She'll be fine here. She has her own room and likes it in there." Kate pushed away from the post and motioned for him to follow. "Come on, I'll show you."

Ian grabbed Kate's gift and followed as she gave him a tour of the five-bedroom, three-bath house with a living room, family room, home office, and a sunroom that Kate had turned into Jazzy's domain. There was an old loveseat in it, along with a dog bed, dog toys, and a television mounted high on the wall.

"She likes to watch the old TV Land shows." Kate picked up the remote and turned on the television.

Jazzy barked, turned in two circles, and jumped onto the loveseat before she settled her chin on her paws and set her attention on the screen.

"She'll be content for hours," Kate said, patting Jazzy on the head, then making sure the dog had plenty of food and water before she walked out of the room. Ian followed, then Kate shut the door behind him. "It keeps her from tearing up anything while I'm gone. She has a doggy door into the backyard. If she wants out, she doesn't have to wait for me."

"It's a great setup for her and for you. It's nice that you can be gone and not have to worry if she's doing something she shouldn't be." Ian grinned. "Not that she would. She seems like a wonderful dog. So smart."

Kate gave him a playful shove. "You're just saying that because she clearly likes you. It's an honor of the highest degree and one you should not take lightly, sir. Jazzy has extremely particular and discerning taste when it comes to strangers, especially men."

"And mothers-in-law, right?"

Kate laughed and led the way to the front door. She noticed the box he'd carried in. "What have you got there?" she asked as she opened a coat closet and extracted a dark green wool coat with a matching scarf.

Now that the time had arrived to present the gift, Ian felt self-conscious. Was it a stupid thing to give a female he was trying to impress? A bracelet made of paper clips. Did it make him seem cheap? Tacky? Weird? All of the above?

Before he could change his mind, he held the box out to her. "It's something I made for you today while I was waiting for my interview."

Kate's eyes widened as she draped the coat and scarf over the stair banister, then took the box from him. "You made this? For me?"

"I did. I hoped I'd see you again but decided even if I didn't, it would remind me of an incredible person I met by chance, one strange Christmas Eve."

Kate grinned. "It has been an odd day, hasn't it?" She gave the box a light shake. "Did you wrap it yourself?"

"Guilty as charged." Ian felt so nervous that his palms began to sweat. "I couldn't find paper or ribbon at the house and had to get a little creative."

She fingered one of the curls made of paper and shook her head. "This is fabulous, Ian. I'm impressed."

Carefully, she slit the tape with her fingernail, pulled away the paper, and looked at the box. With a curious expression, she slowly opened the lid and lifted out the bracelet, holding it up to the light and turning it over in her fingers.

"A bracelet? It's wonderful, Ian! And you made this? How?" she asked, glancing at the Red Baron letters on the inside of the box and grinning before she set it and the paper on the table by the door, then returned her focus to the bracelet. "How could you make this in one morning?"

"It wasn't that hard," Ian said, taking the bracelet from her, opening the clasp and fastening it on her wrist. It looked nice if he did say so himself. Which he didn't. At least not aloud.

"I love it. It's so unique and feminine and perfect. I can't believe you made it for me. It's fantastic!" Kate threw her arms around his neck and gave him an impulsive hug. One that made his heart begin to race while a longing to hold her for the next fifty or so years settled over him.

Kate felt right in his arms. Like she belonged there. It was as though she was the one person who'd been created to fill an empty space in his life he hadn't even known existed until the moment they met. Ian figured someone would lock him up and throw away the key if the thoughts jumping through his head somehow made their way out through his lips. He knew it was beyond ludicrous to be thinking in terms of forever with a woman he'd just met, but he'd never felt like this about anyone. Deep in his heart, he knew he'd never feel like this again. There was something about Kate that was special, something that spoke to his soul, whispering, "She's the one."

Ian could have remained in the foyer for hours, returning her hug, but she eventually pulled back. He dropped the hands he'd held lightly against her waist and smiled at her. "Before you get too excited, I should probably tell you the bracelet is made of paper clips."

"What? No way, Ian! It looks like something from one of the trendy jewelry boutiques in the Alberta Arts District." Kate held out her wrist and slowly twisted it to better see the delicate swirls of the bracelet. "It's spectacular and even more special knowing you made it for me. Thank you, thank you."

"You're very welcome, Kate. I wanted to have something to give you. Something that was memorable. You don't have to wear it if you don't want to."

"No! I want to. It's perfect." She kissed his cheek, then spun around and grabbed her coat.

Ian took it from her and held it as she slid her arms in the sleeves. She wrapped the scarf around her neck, dug gloves from the pockets, picked up her purse, and walked outside when he opened the door for her. After checking to make sure it was locked, she settled her arm around his, and they walked out to where he'd parked his Jeep.

"I'm glad you got it running," she said, sliding onto the seat when he held open the front passenger door for her.

"Me, too. You'll laugh when I tell you all that was wrong was a loose battery cable."

She grinned. "That is pretty funny, but I'm glad you didn't take time to figure it out this morning. If you had, we wouldn't have met, and that would make me sad. You've been the best part of my day, Ian."

"I could say the same about you." He winked at her as he started the Jeep, and it roared to life.

"You could also say that about landing your dream job."

He shrugged as he pulled away from the curb. "There is that, but you're the reason today has been unforgettable."

Kate guided him out of the neighborhood, and soon, they were pulling up at a superstore. The only parking space Ian could find was at the far end of the lot, but at least the sleet had stopped.

After he opened Kate's door for her, she slid out and wrapped her arm around his. "Do you have your mom's shopping list?"

"Sure do. It isn't long, but I'll need your help figuring out what to buy."

"Happy to assist. Then you can give me some suggestions for something to take to your parents' house for dinner and a gift."

"You don't need to take anything, but if you want to, I can help with some ideas."

They searched for a shopping cart, but finding none, they each grabbed a plastic basket and with a glance at each other, braved the insane last-minute Christmas Eve shoppers.

Thirty minutes later, when they finally made it out of the store, they stopped, bags in hand, and stared up at the night sky as snow began to fall.

"No way. It never snows on Christmas Eve," Ian said, sticking out his tongue to catch a fluffy flake.

Kate laughed and bumped his side with her elbow. "Come on. Don't you know January snowflakes taste better?"

"I've heard that." He grinned and offered her his arm as they made their way back to his Jeep.

After they stored the bags in the back, they had to wait almost ten minutes just to get out of the parking lot. Ian glanced over at Kate and gave her a warm smile. "Mom is going to go nuts over what you picked out."

"I can't wait to meet her and your dad, Ian. I just hope they aren't too shocked you're bringing me along."

"Trust me. They're going to love you." Ian knew they would because, as crazy as it seemed, he already loved Kate.

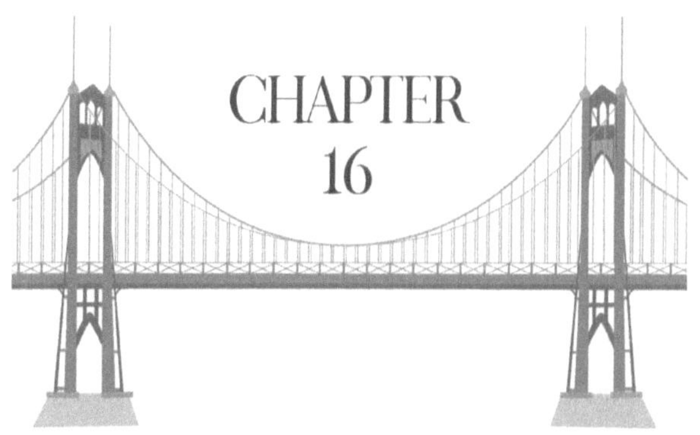

CHAPTER 16

ARCHER

ARCHER LOOKED LEON IN the eye, pinning him in place with a steely glare, although he kept his tone peaceful and pleasant. "You need to give me the gun, Leon. If you don't, things are not going to end well. Do you want your kids to know you died in a shoot-out on the bridge on Christmas Eve? Do you want them to find their picture covered in blood in your coat pocket? Is that the legacy you want to leave them? Is that the last memory you want them to have of you?"

"No!" Leon shouted, shaking his head so hard, his stocking cap slipped down over one eye. He pushed it up with the back of his wrist, using the hand holding the gun while the other remained wrapped around the railing.

"Don't you want Christmas to be a holiday they love instead of dread because it will always remind them of the way you killed yourself, Leon? It's a rough burden to give Emma and Aiden to bear. Are you sure that's what you want to do?"

"No!" He looked at the gun in his hand, then at Archer. "You leave my kids out of this."

"I want to, Leon, but you've made them part of this." Archer's tone was light, but it held a hint of accusation. "Why do you want to hurt them this way?"

"I don't want to hurt them. I never wanted to hurt them. *He* does. He's the one out to ruin everything."

Archer wanted to grab Leon by the collar and shake him until some sense rattled loose, but it was pointless and useless to even think about it. A physical altercation with Leon would not help the situation or bring about the desired result. However, after hours and hours of trying to talk Leon down, Archer was at the end of his rope.

He held up his hands in a placating motion and took a step closer to the lunatic brandishing the gun. "Who is *he*, Leon? Is it his blood in the camper and on the knife in your pickup? Did you hurt someone?"

"I'll hurt everyone!" Leon roared, lifting the gun and pointing it straight at Archer.

"Put the gun down, Leon. Put it down. Emma and Aiden wouldn't want you to do this." Archer pressed the one point he knew would get to Leon. "Don't you love them enough to try to fix this?"

"I love them. So much." Leon lowered the gun again. "They're my whole world."

"Then don't put them through the agony of knowing their father tried to kill someone, or himself. Especially not on Christmas Eve. Don't do that to them. Do you want them to carry those scars with them their whole life?"

"No!" Leon yelled, and then his voice quieted. "No."

"Then give me the gun, Leon. Just hand it to me." Archer took a step closer. Close enough that when he reached out with his left hand, Leon slowly extended the gun toward him. When Leon paused, Archer's right hand automatically settled on the weapon he had hidden beneath his coat. "Give me the gun, Leon. If you give it to me, I promise we'll figure this out. We'll fix this for Emma and Aiden."

"For Emma and Aiden," Leon repeated, stretching out his hand until Archer took the gun from him. He passed it to Officer Garcia, who was standing the closest, then motioned toward Leon, encouraging him to do the right thing. "Why don't you come on this side of the railing, Leon? It's cold. It's getting dark. You're so tired. Wouldn't it be nice to sit down somewhere warm and have a hot meal? Wouldn't you like that, Leon?"

"Yes," Leon whispered, then shook his head again. "But I'm not ready."

"Well, what can I do to help you get ready, Leon? How can I help you? How can I help fix this so you can see Emma and Aiden?"

Leon shifted so he was facing the water. "Don't know how to fix it. *He* ruins everything."

A name. That was all Archer needed. A name for the mystery man whom Leon clearly despised. "Where is he, Leon? All you have to do is tell me his name. We'll find him and make sure he never bothers you again. What do you say to that? We'll find him and fix this for you."

"No. You can't. They can't." He waved one mitten-covered hand at the other officers on the bridge. "No one can."

Archer took a step back, needing a moment to tamp down his emotions. He was angry at Leon. Angry at himself. Angry at the whole blasted situation that had dragged on the entire day.

He should've realized the man had a weapon on him, but Leon had done a good job of keeping it hidden beneath his coat. Archer had no idea how he'd managed to pull it out so smoothly with the fuzzy mittens on his hands, but he had. In truth, Archer figured the gun was more for show and bluster than an intention to do any of them harm.

Suicide-by-cop would have ended Leon's life and left the police looking like the bad guy. Thankful he'd been able to talk Leon into handing over the gun, Archer knew he had to get him off the edge of the bridge. This ordeal had gone on far too long. Everyone wanted to be somewhere else. Tempers, along with patience, were growing short.

It was time to end this thing. The question was how. Archer had tried every trick he'd been taught, and a few he improvised to reach Leon, but nothing had worked. Several times, he'd seemed like he was ready to give up and step onto the bridge, then he'd change his mind and act as if Archer had been trying to trick him into doing something against his will.

Aware the tow truck owner had returned, Archer stepped over to Officer Kennedy and told him to have Carter load the wreck and get it out of there as quickly as possible. If they needed to go through the vehicles again for more evidence, they could do it somewhere Leon wasn't observing their every move and freaking out.

With the sound of Carter and his helper loading the pickup and camper on the wrecker in the background, Archer studied Leon. The man looked even paler than he had earlier. He seemed to weave when he moved as though he was lightheaded. If he lost his grip on the railing, Archer had no doubt whatsoever the guy would fall to a certain death in the cold water of the Willamette River.

Nothing Archer had said or tried had gotten Leon to climb back over the railing. As far as Archer was concerned, they had to bring things to a head soon. Sleet stung and chilled every inch of his exposed skin. The sky was growing darker by the minute. Archer was tired, hungry, irritated, colder than he'd ever been, and worried about his wife. The last time he'd spoken to the captain, he'd said he was still tracking Lena down. She should've been home hours ago. Then again, she might have hit some last-minute sales or decided to hang out with friends when she'd finished work for the day.

Archer's phone buzzed in his pocket, and he took it out, knowing it would be the captain.

"You got the gun away from him?" Captain Cohen asked.

Archer moved out of Leon's range of hearing. "Yes. However, something has to give soon, sir. He's getting weaker by the second. I'm afraid he'll lose his grasp on the railing and fall before we can get to him."

"Agreed." The captain sighed heavily. "Archer, I located your wife. If you want to leave right now, that's fine with me. I'll put Officer Yeung in charge, and you can call it a day. Heaven knows, you've done more than anyone could expect of you. Leon has been the toughest nut to crack I've ever come across in all my years at the PPB."

Archer felt his heart skid to a stop. If the captain was offering to pull him out of such a complex negotiation, something was wrong with Lena. Exceedingly wrong. "Is she hurt? Is she somewhere safe? Does she need me with her?"

"No. She's not hurt. She's safe. She's just ..." The captain hesitated, then cleared his throat. "I can give you the details, or you can finish this mess with Leon. Totally up to you. Your decision. I'll support you one hundred percent in whatever you want to do. Once I give you the details, though, you're going to lose your focus on Leon. I know you, Archer, and the way you operate. Again, this is your decision. If you want to walk away, I'll have someone take you straight to your wife. To reiterate, she's not hurt, and she's safe."

Archer didn't answer right away. He needed a minute to think about what was best for everyone. Every cell of his entire being screamed at him to go to Lena. What in the world had happened to her? Where on earth could she be? The captain had said she was safe and not hurt, so she couldn't be in the hospital or anything along those lines. Maybe her car had broken down somewhere, although it was fairly new. What if she'd gone shopping and someone had stolen her vehicle or backed into it? That would shake her up, but she'd be safe and unharmed. Archer's need to go to his wife was nearly overpowering. He had no desire to be anywhere except with Lena. A vision of the Christmas Eve service, her smiling beside him while singing "O Little Town of Bethlehem," made him long to turn around and rush to her.

But he wouldn't.

Not if she was unharmed and somewhere safe. Not when he knew he was needed right where he was. He'd been tasked with getting Leon off the bridge, and he wasn't giving up. Not yet. He just hoped his wife would understand, as she always did, and forgive him for not being with her on Christmas Eve.

"I'll finish this up, but if Leon isn't on this side of the railing in the next hour, I'm walking away," Archer said, staring at the man who had altered so many plans and lives today. It boggled the mind to think how far-reaching one person's choice could be. Archer blew out a long breath. "It's not fair to Lena for me to be absent from wherever she is. Should I be worried? Do I need to find someone to sit with her, like one of her girlfriends?"

"No. Not worried. Like I said, she's safe. She's got a friend with her, and the message relayed to me was that you needed to finish the job you started. When you get to her, she'll be overjoyed to see you, though. I'll have one of the officers take your motorcycle home for you and someone ready to transport you to your wife."

"Thanks, sir. I'm going to do everything I can to end this as quickly as possible. Did Leon's ex-wife agree to talk to me?"

"She did. I just sent her number to you. She said she'd be ready for your call."

"Great. I'll get in touch with her right now."

The captain's voice sounded like he was speaking to someone in the distance, then he came back on the line. "Keep nudging his guilt about doing lasting damage to his children. That seems to be getting to him more than anything else we've tried today."

"Okay. Will do." Archer disconnected and called Leon's ex-wife from the warmth of the patrol car.

"Is this Tiffany?" he asked when a woman answered the phone on the second ring.

"Yes."

"Tiffany, my name is Sergeant Raines with the PPB. I've been here on the bridge all day with Leon, trying to talk him down. Leon keeps referring to someone he only identifies as *he*, saying the man ruined everything. Do you have any idea what or whom he's talking about?"

"No, I don't. I loved Leon with all my heart. He was such a sweet guy, so different from the dumb jocks I usually dated in college. We had so many good years together. There were days when our life was so rich and content, it almost didn't seem real. Everything was great until his mom passed away last year. She lived in Roseburg. It's where Leon was raised. After the funeral, Leon stayed there for a few weeks to settle his mother's affairs, sort through the belongings in the house, and get it ready to sell. When he came home, it was like he'd turned into a totally different person." The woman's frustrated sigh carried over the connection.

"A different person?" Archer repeated. "How so?"

"Leon had always been so gentle with me, but after she passed, he snapped at me constantly and became rough and demanding. He seemed paranoid. Started accusing me of cheating on him, which I wasn't. He yelled at the kids about the silliest little things. He insulted our friends to the point none of them wanted to be around him. He terrorized the neighbors, doing horrible things like dumping garbage on their porches and cutting holes in their hedges. Leon didn't want me to leave the house, ever. If I dared to defy him, he threatened me. He never actually hit me, but several times, I was scared he would. Leon became impossible to live with. It just got to be too much, so I kicked him out, got a restraining order, and filed for a divorce. Of course, the judge granted me full custody of the children. Leon started drinking. Lost his job, and the spiral got worse from there. The other day, when I found out that he'd lost his apartment and was living in that rust-bucket camper that looks like a disease waiting to happen, I refused to let him have Emma and Aiden for

Christmas. I think it pushed him over the edge. I'm sorry. I didn't mean to make things worse, but I have to keep my kids safe. Leon is not safe right now."

Archer wholeheartedly agreed with her but kept his thoughts to himself. "Has Leon ever been treated for mental health issues or had a psychological evaluation?"

"No, although I suggested several times before I filed for divorce that he needed to see a shrink. There were days it was like I was dealing with two completely different versions of Leon."

Archer digested that bit of information. Could Leon suffer from something like a dissociative identity disorder? Trying to make sense of it all, Archer kept an eye on Leon out the car window and continued his conversation with Tiffany. "Tell me more about Leon's mother. Was he close to her?"

"He was. Once, not long after we were married and he'd had too much to drink, he told me his father had been abusive, both verbally and physically, to him and his mom. He didn't go into detail, but Leon has scars all over his back and legs. Most of them are little round burn marks. I've often wondered if his father burned him with a cigarette as punishment. His dad died when Leon was fifteen. Leon said things were so much better with his father gone. Every time I attempted to pry details of his past out of him, though, he'd become quite upset, so I stopped trying. Leon's mother was even more tight-lipped about his childhood. Although Leon adored his mother, we didn't see her often. She tended to want to hide at home, and the kids were always too noisy for what Leon referred to as her delicate sensibilities. Leon usually went to visit her for her birthday each June and would spend a day or two with her, doing projects around the house, that sort of thing. He'd always return home sad and withdrawn, like seeing her resurrected painful memories from his past."

"That's a big help, Tiffany. Thank you." Archer watched Leon sink into a sitting position on top of the railing, as though he was too tired to continue standing. "Did Leon or his mother ever mention how his father died?"

"His heart stopped one morning when he was at work."

Archer's mind started racing. If Leon's father was as abusive as Tiffany implied, would Leon or his mother have killed him? There were poisons that could affect the heart, poisons that were nearly untraceable. Maybe his imagination was running away with him, but he was desperate to finish this and spend what was left of the holiday with his wife. If something had happened in Leon's past, something he never wanted to remember, and some event had triggered that memory, it could be part of the reason for his mental break today.

With nothing left to ask Tiffany, Archer ended the call. "Despite all this, I hope you and your children have a nice Christmas."

"We're trying. We came back from the ski trip so they could be here if Leon needed them. They both love their dad, but this isn't something they should have to deal with. No one should."

"Agreed. Thanks again, Tiffany. Someone will let you know if anything changes."

"Thank you, Sergeant Raines."

Archer sent the captain a text, tucked his phone in his pocket, sent up a prayer for Lena to remain safe and to feel wrapped in love, then got out of the patrol car. He tugged on his gloves and walked back over to where Leon had turned his shoulder so he wouldn't have to look at any of them.

He motioned for the other officers to stay ready for whatever Leon might do next, then went to lean against the railing where he'd stood when he'd first started talking to him that morning.

For several long moments, Archer didn't say anything as he studied Leon. The man was freezing, huddled into his inadequate coat for warmth. The hand not clinging to the railing shook with tremors that were visible even through the fuzzy mittens. Leon looked weak. So weak Archer wasn't certain he could have done battle with a kitten and won.

The fact that Leon was still on the bridge and not already in the morgue reassured Archer that he wanted to live. Something in Leon was clinging to every last shred of hope that someone would give him a reason to cross the railing and come off the bridge.

Archer just needed to identify the one thing that was serving as Leon's lifeline. And he needed to do it quickly. If the thoughts tumbling through his head had any basis in fact, Archer knew where to begin.

"You love Emma and Aiden more than anything, don't you, Leon?"

The man nodded slowly.

"And you'd never do anything to intentionally hurt them, would you?"

A slow shake of his head.

"That's how things were with your mom, right, Leon? She would never have done anything to intentionally hurt you, would she, Leon? Why don't you tell me about her? Tell me about your mother." Archer spoke in a friendly, casual tone, the kind one might use while chatting with a new acquaintance at a social gathering. "What was she like?"

"Don't talk about her," Leon growled, then turned to glower at Archer. He looked angry. Defiant.

"I bet she was a nice woman. Did she bake cookies for you to enjoy after school? What was your favorite kind? Maybe peanut butter?" Archer already knew from the details gleaned earlier from Tiffany that Leon loved peanut butter cookies because it was what his mother had always made for him. "Mmm. I can almost taste the peanut butter cookies my mom used to make. There was nothing like them when I came home hungry from school. They'd still be warm from the oven, while their scent filled the house. I'd drink a big glass of milk and eat those delicious cookies. They were so good, weren't they, Leon?"

Leon nodded, looking like he was suffering from acute pain.

"If you come on over here, Leon, I'll get you a peanut butter cookie. We can take you somewhere you can have a warm one. What do you say to that?"

"I ..." Leon shook his head. "No! No, no, no!"

"You loved your mom, didn't you, Leon? She took care of you, didn't she?"

"My mother was a saint. Don't you talk about her." Leon jabbed his hand in Archer's direction. "You don't get to talk about her."

"Talk about her?" Archer relaxed his pose, leaning one foot back against the railing as though he had nothing better to do than shoot the breeze. He took his phone from his pocket when it buzzed, read a message from the captain and sent one in return, then looked back at Leon. "Let's talk about Dorothy Mumford. Mother to Leon Mumford. Member of the First Congregational Church for fifty years, although she didn't often attend. Is that where you held her funeral?"

Leon gave Archer a hate-filled glare. "Stupid church. Wretched minister. Never did a thing to help her, only pointed fingers of shame in her direction."

"Shame?" Archer asked, his voice curious. "Why?"

"Shame because of him, what he did."

"Because of him? Who? Your father? Howard Mumford?"

"No! We don't talk about him." Leon moved the hand not holding the railing as if he was swatting at mosquitoes, batting away the questions. "Don't talk about him."

"Okay, okay. That's cool, Leon. Did you have any brothers or sisters?"

"Nope. Just me."

Archer nodded. "Let's talk about your mom. Was she a good cook?"

"The best." Leon dragged in a shuddering breath, then seemed to calm slightly.

"What was your favorite thing she made?"

"Potpie. She put leftover roast in it and carrots and peas with little chunks of potato. Mama had a garden and raised all our vegetables."

"She did? It sounds like she was a good mother, Leon."

"She was. She tried to do her best. She tried." His voice faded and he looked out over the water again as though he was assailed by memories better left forgotten.

Archer felt he was finally making some progress. "What kind of vegetables did your mother raise in her garden?"

Leon shrugged. "Tomatoes, zucchini, potatoes, peas, radishes, carrots, cucumbers, lettuce, and beans. She tried and tried to get melons to grow, but they just never seemed to do well. One year, we had sweet corn. It was so good, with butter dripping off it."

"That sounds great, Leon." Archer paused and took out his phone when it vibrated in his pocket. "Excuse me just a moment."

Archer backed away far enough that he could speak to the captain without Leon overhearing the conversation.

"You were right, Arch," Captain Cohen said. "The Roseburg PD had a file on Howard Mumford. Calls for domestic abuse seemed to be common, usually phoned in by neighbors. Complaints of violence at work. He frequently changed jobs. Dorothy Mumford had a few hospital visits to treat broken bones. Then there was Leon. The kid was constantly in trouble from the time he was about ten until his father died. According to juvie records, he'd been picked up for theft, assault, breaking and entering. After his father died, it all stopped. From that point on, Leon became a model citizen—until his mother died."

"Any record of what Dorothy did before she married Howard?" Archer asked quietly.

"No. The only thing I could find out about her was that she was a master gardener and took great pride in her flowers."

"Hmm. Any photos turn up of her flowers?"

"I'll have the team keep digging. What is it you're looking for?"

Archer glanced at Leon. "Something poisonous that could kill her husband. What was the flower tied to Van Gogh?"

"Foxglove." The sound of the captain riffling through papers carried across the connection. "You might be on to something. You think you'll get any info out of Leon?"

"That's the plan." Archer tucked the phone back in his pocket and resumed his post near Leon. This time, when he leaned against the rail, he moved a little closer than he'd been before.

"We were talking about your mother's garden, Leon. About that tasty sweet corn she used to grow. Did she ever make creamed potatoes and peas?"

"She did. Sometimes, when he wasn't there, we'd eat ripe tomatoes right off the vine like they were apples. The juice would run down my chin and arms." Leon sighed. "You can't buy tomatoes like that in a store, that taste of summertime and sunshine."

"No, you can't. It's a shame, isn't it? Did you enjoy summertime and sunshine?"

Leon nodded. "Yes. I liked to ride my bike with my friend, Donny. He was like the brother I always wanted. I used to stay at his house when my father ..."

"When your father what, Leon?"

Leon remained quiet for a few minutes, then glanced at Archer. "Donny moved away when I was ten. His father got a job in Tacoma, Washington. I never saw him again."

"You never saw him again? That must have made you sad. Maybe a little angry?"

"Sad he was gone and angry I had to stay. Mama needed me."

"She needed you there to protect her, didn't she, Leon? To protect her from your father. Is that right?"

Leon's face hardened. "You don't know anything. Nothing!"

Archer gave Leon a moment to calm down. At some point, the sleet had stopped, but if he wasn't mistaken, it was trying to snow. "Did your mother plant flowers or just vegetables?"

"Both. She loved flowers. Had the prettiest flowers in town until he tore them out. She still planted them, hidden in the vegetables. He never went back there to the garden." Leon giggled. "She was so clever. So very clever."

"Clever?"

"Yes, Mama was clever, so much smarter than him. He thought he was the smartest of all, but she showed him. She put it in his tea."

Archer was pretty sure Leon had just informed him his mother had committed murder. If he didn't know better, he would have proclaimed the man to be both simple and innocent, but Leon Mumford was neither of those things. Half a dozen people in the hospital tonight could verify he'd purposely caused the wreck on the bridge that had left them injured.

To hear Leon speak of his father's murder with something that bordered on glee left Archer unsettled. What kind of monster was this man?

"Put it in his tea?" Archer asked, forcing his voice to sound inquisitive. "What did she put in his tea?"

"The flower juice. The purply flower juice. She pulled up the whole plant, smooshed the petals and stems, and stirred it into his thermos of sweet tea." Leon looked like a giddy child, eyes bright in the lights the officers had set up around them as dusk faded into night. "Mama was so clever. No one knew. He didn't know. He went to work, and that was that."

"What happened at work?"

Leon giggled again, an unnatural, frightening sound. "He died. Right there at his desk. They said his heart stopped, but you can't stop what you don't have."

"You don't think your father had a heart, Leon?"

Leon shook his head. "Nope. He was evil. He hurt Mama. Hurt me. Mama left him. She tried to stop him, and he hurt her so bad, she had to go to the hospital. That made him even angrier. He needed to go away."

As he sat on the railing, Leon swung his feet like a child sitting on a swing at the park. One wrong move, and he'd be in the water.

Archer had no idea if the crazed man was reliving his days as a child or what was tripping through his shattered mind.

Suddenly, the feet stopped swinging. Leon went from looking joyful to appearing irrationally angry. "I told you to be quiet."

"You did?" Archer asked, trying to process the abrupt change in Leon. One moment, his expression had been almost childlike. The next, he looked like a maniacal killer.

"Not you, *him*!"

Archer wanted to shout in frustration. They were back to *him* and *he*. He'd noticed Leon referred to his father in the same terms, but with his father gone all these years, to whom did Leon think he was speaking? A ghost? Or someone else?

Something Leon had said when Archer had first approached him that morning popped into his thoughts. "What do you say we find something warm to eat and drink? It's starting to snow. Emma and Aiden will be wanting to hear from you, to hear you wish them a Merry Christmas. How about you come over on this side of the railing, and we'll give them a call, Mr. Mumford?"

Leon's shoulders hunched and he made an inhumane growling sound in his throat. "I told you not to call me Mr. Mumford."

"Why is that, Mr. Mumford? That is your name, isn't it? Mr. Leon Mumford? Why shouldn't I call you by your name?"

"Because I'm not Leon," the man said in a creepy singsong voice that sent a shiver down Archer's spine.

CARTER

"THE BOSS SAID TO leave that mess there," an officer said, pointing to a spot near the gate as Carter pulled the wrecker into the police impound lot.

Ace had been thoroughly rattled after the incident on the bridge with a deranged loon waving a gun around, so Carter had sent him to close the office for the night, hoping it would give the young man time to gather his composure before he went home to his sweet wife.

Carter had been more than a little disturbed by the encounter, but he'd hidden it as best he could. He'd been more than happy to hastily load the pickup and camper and get away from the bridge and Leon Mumford. He prayed the officers there would be able to walk away from the bridge when all was said and done and spend the holiday with their loved ones. He even prayed for crazy Leon Mumford to get the help he obviously needed.

"You need anything?" the officer asked as Carter parked the wrecker and got out.

"If you don't mind telling me exactly where you'd like these placed, I'd sure appreciate it," he said, manning the controls.

It took longer than he would have liked to unload the camper, but it was in such a bad state, he was afraid one wrong move might completely cave in the whole thing, and that wouldn't be helpful if there was more evidence inside it the forensic team needed to gather.

Finally, the job was finished, and Carter breathed a sigh of relief.

"Have a great night, man," the officer called to him as Carter got back in the wrecker.

"You do the same. Merry Christmas!" Carter waved as he pulled back through the gate and drove to his towing company lot. He parked the wrecker, took the keys inside, then realized he had no way home. Ace had picked him up at his house earlier. Carter tried calling his son, but the kid was somewhere so noisy he gave up trying to talk to him and disconnected the call, then sent a text that he'd see him soon.

Carter thought about downloading a rideshare app, but he didn't really want one more app he never used on his phone. He could walk home, but it was five miles and would take more time than he wanted.

He was standing outside the office, trying to decide the best course of action, when it started snowing. Carter glanced up at the sky in disbelief.

"Snow?" He held up a hand and watched as a flake melted into his palm. "Snow for Christmas. How about that."

He took out his phone, just about ready to call Ace when a police vehicle pulled up at the curb, and the passenger side window rolled down.

He hurried over to the car and bent down so he could peer inside. He was shocked to see it was one of the police captains. "Captain Cohen. What are you doing out tonight?"

"I'm not going home until my team on the bridge does. That's where I'm headed, to check on them. I just wanted to stop by and thank you for your help with the mess that happened there and apologize for any distress you may have experienced when the person in crisis pulled out the gun."

"Not your fault, Captain. It's clear that poor man is in need of help."

"He certainly is." The captain smiled at him. "I don't want to keep you. I just happened to be driving this way to the bridge and saw you standing there. I promised Archer an officer would be ready to drive him straight to his wife, and I intend that person to be me."

"That's great, sir. I'm sure he'll appreciate the ride." Carter knew he shouldn't ask, but he couldn't stop himself. "As it turns out, I've somehow managed to leave myself without a vehicle to drive unless I want to take one of my service rigs, which I really don't. Not tonight. I don't suppose you could give me a ride, could you?"

The captain unlocked the door. "Get in."

Carter had always wanted to ride in a police car and folded himself into the front seat, then fastened his seat belt. It took a lot of restraint not to ask the captain to turn on the siren and ride with the lights flashing.

"Where to, Carter?" the captain asked as he pulled away from the curb.

Carter grinned at him. "My destination is part of a long story, Captain. How about I tell it to you on the way to the bridge?"

CHAPTER 18

"**I**'M NOT READY. CAN we wait? Please? Pretty please? I want to wait. I need my husband to be here." Rosalee tried to hold back her tears, but they trailed down her cheeks. "I don't want to have this baby without him."

"I know, Rosalee, but your baby is ready to make an appearance, and no amount of trying to push the pause button on this is going to work," Dr. Stoakes said as she snapped on a pair of gloves and walked over to the bed.

Rosalee wanted to turn her face into the pillow and sob or maybe scream. She couldn't believe this was happening. Not just the baby coming early but Rob's disappearance. He'd always been there when she needed him. She couldn't think of a single time in their eight years together that she'd needed him more, yet he wasn't there. He hadn't called. Texted. Nothing.

Her gut reaction to his absence was that something was terribly, horribly wrong. Maybe hormones were rampaging through her body, wreaking havoc in their wake, but she'd never felt this strongly that Rob was not in a good place or situation. She knew he wasn't. Knew it just as certainly as she hated being at the hospital, about to give birth to their child, without him by her side.

Rosalee thought back to the day she'd met Rob. She'd been jogging and was watching a puppy across the street gnawing on his leash instead of paying attention to where she was going. Rob had been working and had just stepped out of his vehicle when she'd plowed right into the door, knocking them both down.

It wasn't her most graceful moment, but Rob had been attentive and sweet, concerned about any injuries she might have sustained. When she assured him she was fine, he gave her both his work and cell numbers and told her to call him if she felt lightheaded or dizzy. He volunteered to drive her to the hospital, but she'd declined, although she had given him her cell number.

That evening, he'd called to check on her, and the next thing she knew, she'd agreed to go on a date with him. Six months later, they were engaged, and three months after that, they got married. They'd put off having children as they had both advanced in their careers. Then, time began to get away from them. Rob had taken her for a romantic weekend to the coast for Valentine's Day and suggested they get busy making a baby. She'd wholeheartedly agreed, and a few months later, she was pregnant.

As eager as she was to meet her baby, to hold the tiny miracle in her arms, she didn't want to do this without her husband there.

"It's going to be okay, Rosalee." Nova spoke softly, gently blotting at the tears on her cheeks, then giving her a tissue to blow her nose. "Everything is okay. You need to let your worries go and focus on what's happening right now, which is the arrival of your baby."

"I know, Nova. I'm just so concerned about Rob. It's not like him to be out of touch like this."

"He's fine. You're fine. This baby is healthy, and we're all going to have a Merry Christmas." Nova handed her another tissue. "So, how about we get this little one delivered? You'll be ready to show off the baby when your husband arrives."

"Are you sure crossing my legs and holding it in until Rob gets here is not an option?" Rosalee asked, trying to regain her sense of humor.

"That's so far off the table, it's in storage down in the basement." Nova grinned, then offered Rosalee a motherly look. "You've got this, Rosalee, and I'll be right here with you."

"Okay." Rosalee watched as her feet were positioned at the end of the bed and leaned back as the doctor took a look.

"This baby is ready to rock and roll," Dr. Stoakes excitedly proclaimed. "How about you, Rosalee? Do you think you can push?"

"Definitely," she said. She'd been holding back the urge to do that very thing for the past twenty-five minutes as she stalled, hoping Rob would suddenly appear in her room. "Maybe instead of my playlist, Nova, we could jam to some Christmas tunes."

"Anything you want, little mama." Nova soon had upbeat holiday songs playing on her phone as Rosalee got down to the painful work of delivering her child.

CHAPTER
19

I T TOOK EVERY BIT of training and experience Archer possessed to keep his shock at the words Leon had just spoken from showing on his face. "If you aren't Leon, then to whom am I speaking?"

"Kyle. Kyle King," Leon said, his eyes glittering with hatred through the evening darkness.

"Okay, Mr. King. Do you know where I can find Leon Mumford?"

The man shrugged, then a slow sneer spread across his face. "Here and there. There and here."

Archer wondered how a person's features could appear so vastly different with just a shift in expression. He did his best to ignore Leon's frightening face, which looked like it belonged in a third-rate slasher film, and focused on getting answers out of him. "How long have you known Leon, Mr. King?"

"Forever."

"Forever?" Archer looked at the man who had such lifeless eyes. He could practically see evil lurking beneath the surface, shrouding his soul in darkness. The force of it felt tangible, like something tainted that would leave a mark on anyone who dared get too close to it.

There were times today when he'd been speaking to Leon that Archer could see the joy on his face while talking about his children. From what he could surmise, Leon genuinely loved Emma and Aiden. He was fiercely protective of them, wanting them safe and sheltered from harm. During their many conversations about the children that afternoon, Leon had even asked Archer to keep his kids safe from him.

At the time, it hadn't made much sense, but now it did. Everything made sense as the puzzling pieces of Leon Mumford's life slid into place.

Archer couldn't believe it had taken him so long to figure it all out, but now that he had, he knew exactly what he needed to do.

"Mr. King, could you remind me how long you were married to Tiffany?"

Leon scoffed, then spit off the bridge. "That she-devil kicked me out of my house. Mine! I paid for it, and the cars and the clothes and the activities for the kids. Don't get me started on the cost of braces. How can two kids have such crooked teeth? The girl's mouth, which runs as often as her mother's, looked like she had fence pickets instead of teeth. And the boy, well, he might as well have been a gopher for those big ol' things hanging out of his mouth." Leon curled his upper lip and stuck out his teeth. "Looked more like a beaver than a kid. He's still got another year of his mouth full of metal before they get him straightened out. How am I supposed to pay for that? Should've just tossed them in the camper and ended it all."

"Ended it all? Are you saying you would willingly hurt your children, Mr. King?"

"Why should I care about those brats? They're his, not mine. Tiffany was his too." Leon shook his head. "He took everything from me, so I'm going to take it all from him. That's how it works."

"How what works?"

Leon looked at Archer as though he was the stupidest human he'd ever encountered. "I don't have to tell you nothing, fancy boy."

"Fancy boy?" Archer repeated.

"Sure. You're some fancy-pants cop who thinks he has everyone figured out. Maybe I'd be that way too if I looked like you with your magazine-model face. Ever thought about where you'd be if someone messed that up for you?"

"Are you threatening me, Mr. King?"

Leon held up the hand that wasn't clinging to the railing. "Nope. Not at all."

Archer noticed something dripping from the mitten as Leon lowered it back down. Archer motioned for Officer Kennedy to shine his flashlight on the mitten. It was dark and wet.

"What's on your mitten, Mr. King?"

"Snow, probably, genius. In case you missed it, it's falling down at a pretty good clip."

"I did happen to notice that, but your mitten is leaking something dark."

Leon glanced at his hand and made a dismissive motion with it, slinging droplets in his wake. Drops which, as they landed on the snow, looked like blood. "Oh, that. It's nothing. Just a little something to remember Leon by."

"What do you remember of Leon?" Archer asked, shifting slightly as he kept a steady gaze on the crazed man.

"He's a weakling. A coward. An idiot. Him and that bloated cow of a mother of his. Always was that way. Always will be. He caught me off guard this morning. That's all."

Archer was sliding more mental puzzle pieces together. "Okay, Mr. King. Perhaps you could shed some light on the blood that's all over the camper. Is it yours?"

Leon nodded. "It's mine. That spineless fool tried to kill me this morning while I was taking a shower.

I stopped him good by threatening to shoot Emma and Aiden if he didn't leave me alone. Then he got loose and tried to drive off the bridge, but I stopped him again. Slammed on the brakes at the last second. It was a bonus that it caused such a mess today. How many other people got hurt?"

Archer wanted to lie and tell him no one was injured, since the person claiming to be Kyle King seemed to be taking great pleasure in the notion that he'd hurt someone, or multiple people. "A few," he said, then redirected the conversation.

"Has Leon been here on the bridge today?" Archer asked, certain that Leon's personality had been there for part of the day.

Leon nodded. "Yes. Sometimes. He likes you. Thinks you're a good listener. Personally, I think I should've shot you when I had a chance."

Archer kept his tone modulated. Smooth. "That would have been difficult since the gun wasn't loaded."

"Leon did that when I wasn't watching." The man took three bullets out of his coat pocket and dropped them on the ground, watching as they rolled off the bridge to the water below.

Archer turned away from Leon and spoke into his radio. "We're going to need an ambulance and a psychiatrist standing by."

"Confirmed and available," a voice replied.

Behind him, Archer saw an ambulance waiting at the bottom of the bridge. On the other side of the bridge, he could see a police car slowly approaching.

If Leon had stabbed himself and cut his wrist, it was a wonder he hadn't already passed out from losing blood. He knew the man had been growing progressively weaker as the day went on, but Leon had hidden his injuries well.

"Let me get this straight, Mr. King. Leon tried to kill you, you refused to die, and that's why you've been clinging so tightly to the railing all day." Archer inched closer to him. "Is that it?"

"In a nutshell." Leon smirked at him. "Took you long enough to figure it out. I thought I was going to have to borrow that dork's tablet and spell it all out for you." Leon gestured toward Officer Kennedy.

"Let's go over this again, Mr. King. You can tell me if I'm right. Howard Mumford was a terrible man who took out his frustrations on his wife and son. Leon was too weak to defend himself or his mother, so he created you, Kyle King. A force to be reckoned with. How am I doing so far?"

"So far, so good," Leon jeered.

"The more Howard beat Leon, the more Leon let you out to play. Then Mrs. Mumford decided to take matters into her own hands, mixed up a batch of poison from a flower in her garden, added it to her husband's thermos of tea, and let everyone think he'd had a heart attack."

"Wow, you're good," Leon taunted. "Then what happened?"

"This is the part you don't like. With Howard out of the picture and Leon no longer getting beaten and burned all the time, he didn't need you anymore, did he? No, he didn't. Leon shoved you back into the dark hole you crawled out of and sealed it shut. He cleaned up the messes you'd made in his life, finished high school with honors, and went to college. Leon met Tiffany, got a great job, and had two beautiful children. He was as happy as he could be until his mother died."

"Boo-hoo." Leon made a show of rubbing his eyes, unwittingly smearing blood from the mitten across his face, adding to his grisly appearance. "Poor little Leon. The whiny wimp."

"Leon went back to the house where he'd grown up, the place that had represented all the darkest, most terrible moments of his life, when his mother passed away. Somehow, through his grief, you found a way to creep out of that hole and back into his life, didn't you, Mr. King?"

"Of course I did. It didn't take much. Leon was cleaning out the attic and found the belt his father used to beat him with. You know what he did with it? He wrapped it around his hand and smashed every single thing up there that had belonged to his father. That rage is what feeds me, you know. It's what breathes life into me. Without it, he'd just be plain ol' sorry-as-can-be Leon."

Archer nodded, as though he was commiserating with the deranged man. "Leon finished packing up the house, gave the keys to a realtor, and drove home—only you were the one behind the wheel, weren't you, Mr. King?"

"That's right. I'm the one who came back from Roseburg. I thought I'd see how Leon liked being locked away, buried so deep it's nearly impossible to get out, while I set his life and wife straight. Only Tiffany wasn't as easy to manipulate as I expected. And those kids have minds of their own. Why, if Leon had sassed his dad like they do him, he'd have ended up in the hospital by the time the old man got done teaching him a lesson. Ingrates. That's what they all are. Leon was busting his hump to take care of them, working for a company that didn't appreciate him, and for what? So Tiffany could have a newer car, or Emma could have another pair of shoes, or Aiden could buy another techie gadget he didn't need? Nope. I set them all straight. Let them know who was in charge."

"And how did that work out for you?" Archer questioned.

"She threw me out, told the bunch of you I was violent and unstable, and then she divorced me—well, Leon—but still. She took over the house

I paid for. Took away the kids, just because she could. So yeah, I started drinking a little too much. Those morons at Magra didn't give me the credit I was due, so I didn't see the need to keep working like a slave for them. I showed up when I wanted, left when I decided to. When I threatened a dimwit with a knife, they acted like I'd tried to murder old man Jackson. That snippy little Taylor Jackson called me into her office and fired me. Me! If not for me—Leon—and his work, her old man wouldn't have had a company to expand. Leon worked there for sixteen years, and for thirteen of them, he was the lead mechanical engineer. I might not be able to do what he does, but even I can admit he's brilliant when it comes to that stuff. After all his years of dedication and service, they walked me—I mean him—out the door like he was a piece of trash."

Archer nodded again. "Then you lost the apartment you were renting and traded your car for that pickup and camper so you'd have a place to live. Tiffany didn't approve of that, did she?"

"Are you kidding? She went ballistic when she found out I planned to make the kids sleep in it tonight and tomorrow. That's when she told me she wasn't going to allow me to see the kids until I got my act together." Leon scoffed. "Like she's doing so well. Ha! She'd be living on the street, thankful for the camper, if it wasn't for that Mr. Moneybags she's been dating and the money she wrings out of me every month for the kids. They're all worthless. The whole lot of them!"

"Is that what pushed Leon back into the light, Mr. King? The fact that you messed things up so badly, he wasn't going to get to see his kids again?" Archer's tone was friendly, but Leon scowled at him. "I bet Leon didn't appreciate that, did he? Because the one thing more important to Leon than anything else in the world is his kids. He loves them and would do anything for them. Isn't that right?"

"Think you know it all, don't you? I'll tell you what pushed ol' Leon into action. Me. I did. I decided I was going to drive over to Tiffany's house this morning and teach them all who was in charge. Only Leon surprised me when I was in the shower in the camper. One minute, I was plotting how I'd make Tiffany suffer, and the next, I felt a knife against my ribs. When that didn't do much damage, Leon slashed my wrist, but I managed to bandage it up and stop the bleeding. It took a while to clean up the bathroom, but I did. Smelled clean, just like his old house used to after his father would go off on one of his tantrums, and the old lady would spend hours scrubbing and polishing to wash away the filth of the old man's anger." Leon drew in a deep breath. "I sure do love the smell of bleach. It always meant Leon was about to release me for a while."

"What about the writing in the camper?"

Leon shrugged. "I was just getting ready to go when Leon sliced open my finger and wrote that in there. I grabbed the knife, hopped into the pickup, and was on my way to pay Tiffany and the brats a visit when Leon fought free again. He grabbed the wheel on the bridge. I think he planned to drive over the railing and kill us both, but I couldn't have that."

"I see," Archer said, trying to wrap his mind around the two opposing personalities of Leon Mumford. "Which one of you wanted to jump off the bridge?"

"That would be Leon. He still wants to go over the side. He thinks if we die, I'll leave his family alone and not cause anyone else any pain. But you know what? I like causing people pain. I like watching them suffer. I like being in control and seeing their fear. It's so ... invigorating."

Repulsed, Archer hid it well behind a modulated, easy tone. "If you could walk away from this right now, Mr. King, what would you do?"

Leon giggled again, that eerie, high-pitched sound that made Archer want to cover his ears. "I'd get rid of Leon. Just to make sure he won't ever come back, I'd go take care of Tiffany and those rotten kids of hers. Without his family, Leon doesn't care if he lives or dies. If they're dead, I can at least have the house and cars and all his stuff. All those electronics are worth a pretty penny, you know. I wouldn't need to go back to work if I was careful. I could be a man of leisure."

In a lightning-fast change, the look of evil on Leon's face morphed into one of indignant fury. "You won't touch my children or my wife! I won't let you! I'll stop you for good this time, Kyle! I'll stop you!"

"Grab him!" Archer shouted as Leon let go of the railing and leaned forward. Before he could fall, Archer seized his left wrist, and Officer Garcia caught his right arm. Leon screamed a primal cry of pain that Archer knew would haunt his worst nightmares.

Together, he and Garcia pulled the man up over the railing and pushed him down to his knees on the snow-covered surface of the bridge.

Leon sobbed, great gulping, racking sobs, as he bent forward, head bowed. "I didn't want to hurt anyone. I didn't mean for the wreck to happen. I'm sorry if anyone got hurt. I just needed to stop him before he got to Tiffany or my kids. I tried so hard to stop him."

Archer settled his hand on Leon's back. "It's okay, Leon. It's okay. Everything will be okay now. Everything is going to be just fine. You'll see. Everything will be okay."

Leon looked up at him with a glimmer of hope in his eyes and mouthed "thank you" before two paramedics approached. Archer stayed just long enough to see Leon settled, in restraints, in the back of the ambulance before he collected his backpack from the patrol car and sprinted to the car driving toward him from the other side of the bridge.

"Need a ride?" Captain Cohen called through the open window.

"I sure do," Archer said as he piled into the back of the car, then did a double take to see Carter, the towing guy, in the front seat with the captain. "What are you doing here, Carter?"

"In a strange turn of events, you and I are heading to the same location. I'll explain while the captain gets us to where we both need to go."

Archer offered the two men a confused look as the captain turned on the sirens and sped down the bridge, then headed southeast on Highway 30. "Where, exactly, are we going?"

"The hospital."

The air whooshed out of Archer. When he had enough breath to speak, he glared at the back of the captain's head. "I thought you said you'd have someone take me directly to Lena. If this is about Leon, I really don't want to go."

The captain looked at him in the rearview mirror, one eyebrow raised higher than the other. "It's not about Leon, it's about your wife."

Archer scowled. "You assured me she was safe and wasn't injured."

"True. She is safe. She isn't injured, and I'll add that she's in great company at the moment." The captain grinned at Archer over his shoulder. "I decided I'm the one doing the driving. Now, sit back and listen to what Carter has to say. Our ETA is in about thirteen minutes, so talk fast, Carter."

CHAPTER 20

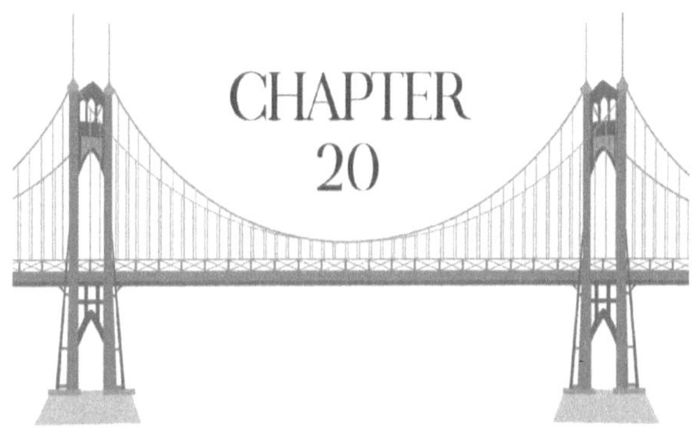

CARTER

"THANKS FOR THE RIDE," Carter said as he and Archer hopped out of the police car the moment Captain Cohen pulled up to the curb at Lennox Medical Center. "Merry Christmas!"

"The same to both of you. Raines, I expect to see photos of that little Christmas miracle soon. Call me the day after Christmas, and we'll figure out the paperwork from this whole mess with Leon Mumford."

"Yes, sir," Archer said, backing toward the entry. "Merry Christmas!"

Archer was already halfway to the door before Carter turned around. He raced after him, following him inside to the main lobby, which was surprisingly empty.

"Which way?" Archer asked, appearing frantic to get to his wife. Carter couldn't blame him. He'd been the same way when his daughter was born and again with his son.

"Over here." Carter led the way to the nearby elevators and pushed a button. Thankfully, they didn't have to wait. A minute later, they reached the maternity ward. Carter stopped short at the sight of his son with a lovely young woman standing at the desk outside the ward. Judging by their body language, they seemed to be upset with the guard-dog nurse who ruled over the door to the ward and decided who gained access and who was denied entry. The woman looked old enough to be a great-grandmother. If Carter wasn't mistaken, she'd been working at the hospital when his own children were born.

"But, ma'am, we just want to go in to see my mother. Nurse Nova Alexander. She's expecting us," Ian said in a pleading tone with a hint of exasperation. "Please? May we go in?"

"I know for a fact that Nova is not expecting a baby, and neither is this young lady. Now, you two get out of here. It's ridiculous, the pranks young people try to pull these days. Just shameful," the woman huffed, then flapped an arthritis-gnarled hand at them. "Go on. Shoo!"

Carter strode up to the desk, pasting on his friendliest smile. "Nurse Lynch, it's Carter

Alexander, Nova's husband." Carter patted a hand to his chest. "She's with a patient, Rosalee Raines." He motioned to Archer, who looked like he might try to storm through the doors in his need to get to his wife. Nurse Lynch gave them a panicky look, as though she sensed Archer's intentions. Carter placed a restraining hand on Archer's shoulder. "This is Sergeant Raines, Rosalee's husband, and he needs to get in there right away. His wife is about to deliver their first child."

The nurse nodded, then glared at Ian. "Why didn't you say that in the first place, young man?" She pushed a button, and the big double doors slowly opened.

Archer was in such a rush, Carter thought he might try to barrel through them before they opened far enough for a human to squeeze inside.

"Hey, kid, nice to see you. Congrats again on the job. We're so proud of you," Carter said, settling a hand on Ian's back and smiling at the young woman who stayed close to his side. "Since you're here to give your mom a ride, think I can come along?"

Ian nodded as they followed Archer inside. "Sure. How did you get here?"

"I caught a ride with a police captain." At Ian's wide-eyed expression, Carter grinned. "I'll fill you in later."

"I'll look forward to hearing that story, but it looks like your friend is about to self-destruct. Maybe you should give him a hand."

Carter hurried to the nurse's desk, where Archer was trying to simultaneously ask questions and answer them while his gaze darted around, as though they might land on his wife, the woman he called Lena, but everyone else knew as Rosalee.

"His wife is the one Nova's assisting. He needs to get suited up so he can be there for the big moment," Carter said, recognizing the nurse from the years he'd attended the annual hospital picnics and Christmas parties with Nova. "Can you help him out, Jacqui?"

"Yes, but you'd better hustle. See that monitor?" She pointed to one of several small screens on the wall above her desk. "That's showing how things are progressing. Another big push or two, and that baby's going to be here." She motioned to a nurse as she came out of one of the other delivery rooms. "Susan! Grab a gown for this daddy, and I'll get the rest."

In a whirlwind of activity, Archer was divested of his backpack, coat, and duty belt, then "suited up" as Carter called the hospital gown, a mask, gloves, and coverings for his shoes. In a rush, he was taken to a room down the hall.

The nurse opened the door. "One more big push!" floated into the hall as Archer rushed into the room.

CHAPTER 21

ROSALEE

"**I** CAN DO THIS. I can do this," Rosalee chanted under her breath. She was in pain beyond anything she'd ever imagined, but hope and excitement and anticipation all mingled together in the tide of emotions flooding through her.

She'd been pushing for the past hour and had never felt so weary in her entire life, but the doctor and Nova had encouraged her to give one more big push.

"There's a head full of hair," Dr. Stoakes said with a smile Rosalee couldn't see behind the woman's mask, but it was evident in her voice and her eyes. "One more big push!"

Rosalee took a deep breath as the door swung open, and a man in a hospital gown hustled into the room. It took only a second for one thought to enter her mind.

Her husband had made it! He'd finally made it.

"Rob," she whispered and held out a hand to him. He hurried past the doctor and nurses, stepping around the equipment and monitors, taking the place next to the head of the bed where Nova had been standing. "You came."

"Of course, I came," he said, his eyes full of love. "I only found out where you were less than half an hour ago. Captain Cohen dropped me off."

"I'm so glad." Rosalee squeezed his hand. "I tried so hard to wait for you, but this baby seems to be in a big hurry to spend Christmas with us."

"Okay, Rosalee. Time to push," the doctor said, drawing Rosalee's attention away from Archer and back to the hard, painful business of birthing a child.

With Archer's gloved hand holding hers, Rosalee felt his strength flowing into her, giving her depleted store a much-needed boost.

"You can do it, Lena, my love. I know you can," Archer whispered in her ear, then kissed her temple through the mask he wore.

It was then she realized how cold he was. It was like he'd brought the temperature in the room down five degrees. She intended to find out later why he felt like a human Popsicle. Right now, her baby needed her to push. She clasped Archer's hand tightly in hers, bore down with a grunt, and, with strength waning, flopped back against the pillows as the baby entered the world.

"Look at him! A picture of health," the doctor said, then a loud, lusty cry filled the room. "A beautiful boy!"

Rosalee couldn't stop the tears from trailing down her cheeks. She knew it! They had a son! Her head turned, and she watched as Archer brushed at his eyes with the sleeve of the gown he wore. It was the first time she'd ever seen him in such a tearful, emotional state.

Nova, who'd moved to the other side of the bed at the head, looked at her with joy in her expression, eyes lit with wonder. "Good job, little mama. He's beautiful and so perfect."

The doctor held up the baby for Rosalee to see. He was perfect and beautiful, just as Nova had said.

The next several moments passed in a blur, but it wasn't long before the baby was being cradled on Rosalee's chest, skin to skin, absorbing her warmth and making his first out-in-the-world bond with her. Archer leaned over them both, looking awed as he repeatedly kissed Rosalee's cheek.

"I'm so sorry I wasn't here sooner, Lena. Had I known this little one was making his appearance today, I would have done anything to be here."

Rosalee pulled her gaze away from their baby and smiled at her husband. "I know you would have,

Rob. It was you, wasn't it? On the bridge with the man who caused the wreck and tried to jump. You were the one who talked him down."

Archer nodded and drew in a shuddering breath. "It was me. It was one of the toughest cases I've ever dealt with, Rosalee."

The use of her given name by her husband meant that he was rattled. He didn't often say it. Not long after they'd begun dating, he'd discovered her full name was Rosalee Natalia. He'd shortened the two names to Lena, and she'd loved it. Because his name was Archer, and he thrived on helping people, she'd started calling him Rob, short for Robin Hood. The nicknames, silly as they might be, were something special they shared.

"You didn't know, Rob. You had no way of knowing I was here. When you do check your cell phone, you'll find a dozen texts and voicemails from Nova's phone. She let me borrow it."

"Where's your phone?" Archer asked, his brow furrowing. "You mean you never got the message I sent about getting called into work?"

"Nope. I forgot my phone. Left it at home this morning, along with a client file. I was on my way to get them when the wreck happened on the bridge."

His face paled, and for a moment, he looked woozy. He gripped the edge of the bed to steady himself. "You were on the St. Johns Bridge during the collision? Is that what sent you into labor?" His gaze roved her, as though he was searching for gaping wounds.

"I guess I've technically been in labor since yesterday. I had a backache and didn't feel well all night. I thought it was something I ate." She glanced down at their son and gently rubbed her index finger over his round cheek. Despite arriving early, the doctor had declared him in great health. He weighed just an ounce under six pounds and measured nineteen inches long. Not bad for a baby who came three weeks early. "Anyway, I had time between appointments, so I decided to run home for the file and retrieve my phone. I was about half a dozen vehicles back from the ones that plowed into the pickup. Nova was a few cars behind me. It wasn't long after the wreck happened that I realized I was in labor. Stupidly, I thought I could postpone the inevitable, so I got out of the SUV. Then my water broke, and Nova ran over to help me. She left her car on the bridge, Rob, left everything to drive me to the hospital because she thought it would take an ambulance too long to get there, and I absolutely refused to give birth on the bridge next to that horrible man who caused so much grief and trouble today. If I'd stayed a little longer, or looked around, I likely would have seen you."

"I'm so grateful Nova was there to help you. Carter said she was supposed to be at home sleeping instead of working." Archer kissed the top of her head. "I'm so glad you had someone you trusted beside you all day."

"She's wonderful, Rob, but I feel so selfish. Nova worked all night and was going to stop by the store to get groceries, then go home and sleep. Instead, she helped me and gave up both her rest and her holiday. I know it's going to sound crazy, but I feel like Nova and I became really close today. She's like the big sister I always wanted or perhaps even more, like the mom I used to wish I had. If you don't object, I'd like to thank her for her sacrifice and friendship in a more lasting way than a thank you note and a vase of flowers."

Archer nodded. "Whatever you want, Lena. I've known Carter for years. He's a great person, and from what I've heard, so is Nova."

Alone in the room, they spoke about Rosalee's plans for a few more minutes, then Nova returned to check on them.

"Isn't it about time you went home? Rob said Carter and your son are waiting for you." Rosalee smiled at the woman who was now closer to her than a friend. "I can't begin to express my gratitude for what you did today."

"It was my pleasure, Rosalee. Being here with you reminded me how much I used to love working in the maternity ward. Thank you for sharing the opportunity to be here to witness a miracle today." Nova bent down and tenderly brushed her fingers along the baby's back. "Did you decide on his name so we can get his birth certificate filled out?"

Rosalee glanced at her husband, then at Nova. "We were just discussing it. If you have no objection, we'd like to name him Ryder Alexander Raines. Ryder is a name we both liked and had agreed to a while back, but we hadn't settled on a middle name. We'd also like to ask you to be Ryder's godmother. Would you be willing?"

Tears sprang into Nova's eyes and a few dripped down her cheeks as she nodded her head. "I would be more than willing, and thank you. What a gift for this precious little one to have our last name. You didn't need to do that."

"Perhaps not, but we wanted to." Archer held out a hand to Nova. "Thank you for being here with my wife when I couldn't and for taking such good care of the two most important people in my life."

"My pleasure, Archer. Thank you for the work you do. It can't be easy having to make the choice between helping the greater good or your loved one."

"It is never easy, but if I'd known Ryder was in a rush to get here, I would definitely have chosen to walk away from the bridge and be here with my wife." Archer smiled at Rosalee with such warmth and devotion, she felt her heart melting. It was simple to forgive his absence when she realized what he'd been through all day.

"Thank you again for the sacrifice of your time, Nova," Archer said. "And for helping Rosalee."

"Anytime." Nova smiled at them, then left the room to add the baby's name to his birth certificate.

"Did you say your SUV is here, Lena?" Archer asked, his gaze roving over their son as he nestled close against her.

"Yes. Nova had an orderly park it somewhere. The keys are in my purse. There's a note attached with the exact row and location in the parking lot."

Archer glanced down at the gloves and gown he still wore. "The last thing I want to do is leave you, but I don't want to touch you or the baby until I can clean up. Would you hate me if I dashed home and took a quick shower? I can bring the bag you packed and your phone when I come back. If I hurry, it'll take less than an hour."

"I could never hate you, Rob, and I know you need to clean up. There's a shower in the bathroom here, but you wouldn't have anything to wear unless you borrowed a set of scrubs. Go do what you need to. Ryder and I aren't going anywhere."

Archer kissed her temple, her cheek, and her lips, then gave her a look so full of love it almost hurt to see the depth of it. "I don't know what I ever did to deserve you, but I love you so much, Rosalee Natalia, and I love this perfect son you've brought into the world. There is no gift that will ever be as precious or mean as much to me. Thank you."

"Thank you, Rob, for loving both of us. Now go. On your way out, would you ask Nova to come in? I'm about to fall asleep."

"You rest, sweet mama, and I'll be back before you know it." Archer stepped into the hallway and returned with Nova and another nurse.

"Ready for some rest?" Nova asked as she brushed the hair back from Rosalee's face with a hand that had become familiar to her. More familiar than her own mother's hand had ever felt.

"I am. Rob is going to run home and clean up. Would it be okay if the baby stayed right here with me like this for a while?"

"Of course, he can." Nova looked to the nurse Rosalee recognized from when she'd walked up and down the hall earlier. "Jacqui will get you settled into a maternity suite while Rob's gone, then the three of you will be all set for the night. How does that sound?"

"Perfect," Rosalee said, glancing at Archer. Despite her fears, Rob hadn't let her down. He'd arrived at just the right moment. She knew he needed time to shift from his police officer mindset into a doting new daddy.

"Are you sure it's okay if I go clean up?" he asked. "I feel like I've wrestled with pure filth today and don't want to pass anything on to you or the baby."

"It'll be fine, Archer," Nova assured him. "You were here for the big moment."

Rosalee smiled at her friend before her eyes grew too heavy to keep open. "I'm just going to rest a minute." As her eyes drifted shut, the last thing she saw was her husband's warm smile, and then she heard him whisper, "I love you," in her ear.

CHAPTER 22

CARTER

CARTER POINTED TO THE small waiting room they'd walked past, and Ian led the way inside. No one else was there at the moment, which was nice. They could wait there until Nova was ready to go. From the way it sounded, Archer had arrived just in time to witness the birth of his first child.

After the day the poor guy had endured, Carter was glad Archer could be there for the baby's arrival. The thought of missing the birth of his children sent a wave of sadness through Carter. He couldn't imagine how bad he would have felt and knew Archer would have experienced a lifetime of regret if he'd missed being there for Rosalee and their son.

Archer had to be freezing, in need of a hot shower and a warm meal, but his only thought had been to get to his wife. That one thing—his determination to reach her—assured Carter of what he already knew. Archer Raines was one of the good guys.

As Carter slipped off his coat, he watched as his son helped the young woman with him remove hers. She unwound a scarf from around her neck and draped both the coat and scarf over the back of a chair, then took a seat. Ian settled next to her without a word of explanation about who she was and why they were together.

Carter chose a seat across from them, so he could watch how they interacted, tossing his coat in an empty chair. When it became evident his son wasn't going to make an introduction, Carter stepped forward with his hand extended.

"May I meet your friend, Ian?" he asked with a friendly smile, hoping his son hadn't forgotten all the manners he and Nova had taught him. "I'm Carter Alexander, Ian's dad. And you are?"

Ian jumped up. "Sorry. Dad, this is Kate Gifford."

The young woman stood, took Carter's hand, and shook it with a firm grip before she resumed her seat.

She was tall. Pretty, with a wholesome, girl-next-door appearance enhanced by her fresh face and the freckles on her nose. She was conservatively and tastefully dressed, looking festive in a red sweater with her green coat and scarf. A glance at her made the word classy come to mind.

Considering some of the girls Ian had dated in the past, Carter thought she was a vast improvement. Most often, his son seemed to gravitate toward beautiful blondes who made up for their lack of brains with their curvy shapes.

Over the years, Carter had acquired the ability to size people up, and he thought Kate Gifford was most likely a person worth knowing. She seemed intelligent but not stuffy. There was a kindness about her, making him curious as to what she did for a living.

"It's good to meet you, Kate. Will you be joining us for dinner?" Carter asked, glad he'd called the restaurant earlier and asked them to triple his order. He wouldn't think about the hole that was going to dig in his wallet. It would be worth it to arrive home to a hot meal none of them had to prepare. At last count, unless Nova found a stray to bring to dinner, their quiet evening for three was now a dinner party for eight.

Kate looked at Ian and smiled, then nodded at Carter. "If it isn't any imposition, Mr. Alexander, I'd like that very much. Ian has spoken so highly of you and your wife, and I'd enjoy the opportunity to spend time getting to know both of you."

"We'd love to get to know you too." He leaned back in the chair, bent his leg, and rested his right ankle over his left knee. He draped his arms over the backs of the chairs on either side of him. "How long have you and Ian known each other?"

Ian glanced at his watch. "About nine hours, Dad. I couldn't get the Jeep to start this morning and didn't have time to waste figuring out the problem. Kate was the rideshare driver who got me to my interview."

"What?" Carter couldn't hide his surprise. "You two just met this morning? I assumed ..." Ian had broken up with his last girlfriend, a snobbish little thing neither he nor Nova had liked, back in September. Or was it August? The timing was irrelevant. The point was that Carter had presumed, due to the way Ian and Kate looked at each other and seemed so attuned, that they'd been together for a while, and his son had just failed to mention a new woman in his life.

"Yeah, Dad. It kind of caught us by surprise too. Kate took me to Magra. Ms. Jackson was on the phone all morning. Turns out it was with the police. It had something to do with the guy who was on the bridge, the one who caused the wreck. He used to work there. At Magra, I mean. I heard a couple of the employees mention it when I was in the restroom. He'd worked there a long time before Ms. Jackson fired him."

Carter's eyebrows inched upward. "I did not know that. Interesting. So, the person interviewing you was on the phone ... and?"

"Oh, yeah. Ms. Jackson kept having the receptionist ask me to wait. To pass the time, I made Kate a bracelet."

She held up her arm, and Carter leaned forward to admire a bracelet fashioned out of what he knew to be paper clips. Nova and his daughter, Macie, had several of Ian's unique creations. "Nice, kid. You did a good job with that."

"Thanks. Anyway, the receptionist seemed interested in what I was doing, so I made a snowflake ornament for her. When I first got there, I thought she was kind of a mean ol' biddy, like the nurse out front here, but after I gave her the snowflake, she disappeared and came back with an amazing lunch. She's the one I invited to join us for dinner."

"Tipton, right? Ms. Tipton?"

"Yep. Anyway, Ms. Jackson had to leave to meet her family at the airport, so she invited me to ride with her and do the interview in the car. I thought it was going well, but then it seemed like I was about to blow it. In a panic, I pulled out one of the magnet trees I first made back in like, what, third grade?"

Carter nodded. "Sounds about right."

"She seemed more impressed by that simple thing than anything I'd said. By the time we got to the airport, she'd offered me the job."

"And how does Kate figure in to all that?" Carter asked, trying to steer Ian back on track. When his son got excited about something, he tended to ramble.

"Right. I got out with Ms. Jackson and offered to carry her suitcase in for her. She declined, but said her driver would take me home or wherever I needed to go. I turned around, and Kate was pulling up to the curb, dropping off an old dude right behind us. Can you believe it? It's like we were meant to connect today."

Carter couldn't help but grin. "Certainly sounds that way. Then what happened?"

"We ended up going to the movies at the pub down on Ivanhoe, the one with the domed roof. Did you know that building was moved down the river on a barge after the Lewis & Clark Exposition?"

"Really? I was not aware of that." He looked at Kate. "I see you're already educating him. What do you do for a living, or is it just the rideshare service?"

"Rideshare is a side hustle. I teach first graders." Kate looked over at Ian with more adoration on her face than Carter had ever seen in any of Ian's past girlfriends.

"That's fantastic. I loved my first-grade teacher. She had this cardboard trunk, like a pirate's chest, full of cheap toys and candy. When we did well in class, we got to go up and choose something out of the trunk. She was the nicest teacher I had in school."

"I think it's our duty as teachers of the primary grades to give children a solid foundation for the rest of their school years. It's a balance between educating, encouraging, and entertaining them. Keeping them engaged and interested in learning."

"Exactly. Ian always liked the teachers who held his attention with hands-on projects better than the ones who just lectured and assigned tons of homework." Carter glanced over at his son, smirking at his frown. Obviously, the kid wasn't yet ready for him to share stories from his childhood. What did he expect, though, bringing a girl home for Christmas Eve? "You went to the movies. What was playing?"

"*It's a Wonderful Life.* I decided it *is* a wonderful life, Dad. We really are so blessed with everything, you know, especially our family." Ian took Kate's hand in his as he turned to look at her. "Kate doesn't have any family, so I didn't want her to be alone for the holiday. And she's got the best dog. Jazzy is a ..." He paused and glanced at Kate, as though he hoped she'd fill in the details he obviously couldn't remember.

"An Appenzeller Sennenhund."

Ian grinned. "Bless you."

Kate giggled and leaned her head against his shoulder before looking at Carter. "That's the breed. Appenzeller Sennenhund. They're herding and mountain dogs from Switzerland."

"I've never heard of that breed," Carter said. "What did you two do after the movie?"

"Went home. It took me five minutes to get the Jeep running. It was just a loose battery cable, but if I'd taken the time to figure that out this morning, I wouldn't have met Kate. I don't feel like that was an accident, more like it was—"

"Meant to be," Nova said as she walked into the room and plopped down next to Carter, leaning against his chest.

He wrapped his arm around her and kissed the top of her head. "Hey, babe. You've got to be completely exhausted. You've been awake for at least twenty-seven hours."

"Closer to twenty-nine, but I wouldn't change a thing. I feel so blessed to have been part of Rosalee's birth experience. You won't believe this, but she and Archer asked if they could give the baby the middle name of Alexander."

"That's so sweet," Kate said, pressing her hand to her throat. "What's the rest of his name?"

"Ryder Alexander Raines. Has a nice ring to it." Nova dabbed at her eyes with a tissue she took from the pocket of her scrubs and leaned closer to Carter. He patted her shoulder, waiting, knowing she had more to say.

"They also asked me to be the baby's godmother. No one's ever asked me that before. I know it sounds ridiculous, but I feel so close to Rosalee, almost like she could be a younger sister or even a daughter. We just ... connected."

Ian looked at Kate, then kissed the back of the hand he still held. "Doesn't sound crazy at all, Mom. I totally get what you're saying. It has been an unforgettable day."

Nova nodded. "It's such an honor and truly touched my heart. Being with Rosalee through Ryder's arrival reminded me how much I loved working in the maternity ward years ago."

"Things have changed a lot since then, haven't they?" Carter asked, motioning to their surroundings. "Would you go back to it?"

"Maybe. There's an opening coming up in February, so I'll think about it."

"Why did you quit in the first place, Mom?" Ian questioned.

"Well, you and your sister were starting to get active in sports and after-school activities, so I moved to a nursing spot with day-only hours so I could be home in the evenings to attend your events."

Ian looked thoroughly surprised. "I had no idea, Mom. If you loved being around the babies, you should go back to it."

"I might do that. I'll definitely give it some thought." She blew out a long breath, one that hinted at her exhaustion.

Carter glanced down at her and smiled the private smile the two of them had always shared. "I'm proud of you, babe. You did great today."

"Thank you. I just couldn't leave Rosalee on the bridge to deal with things alone. Had we known Archer was the one negotiating with that lunatic, we could have let him know what was happening. It's almost more than I can wrap my brain around to think Archer and Rosalee were only—what? Maybe fifteen yards away from each other?"

"Probably closer to ten, based on where I found your car parked. Wasn't she just a few vehicles ahead of you?"

Nova nodded. "You said you got my car home for me?"

"Sure did. It's in the garage, all safe and sound." Carter glanced at his watch. "Do we need to stay, or can we head out? We've got company coming, and dinner will arrive at seven."

"I still can't believe you took care of everything. Thank you for handling the meal, Carter. It wouldn't have been easy to pull something together at this hour on Christmas Eve." Nova patted his cheek, then kissed it. She leaned forward and held out a hand to Ian. "Is that the gift for Rosalee?"

"Yes. Kate picked it out. It's a good thing she was along for the ride, because I would've had no idea what to get." Ian handed Nova a Santa-themed gift bag.

Nova carefully removed the tissue paper and pulled out an impossibly tiny red outfit, the kind with the feet connected to the pajamas. It had a little reindeer on the front that made Carter think of art from the 1950s, along with the words "Baby's First Christmas." Attached to the hanger was a red and white striped cap that looked like an old-fashioned sleeping cap. The outfit was adorable.

"That's cute," Carter said, touching the soft fabric of the sleeve. "It's hard to think of our kids being that little once upon a time."

"Macie was a butterball and never that tiny, but Ian was." Nova lifted her index finger and pointed it at Ian. "You will not tell your sister I said she was a butterball."

Ian gave them an exaggerated look of innocence. "I would never," he said with feigned sincerity, causing everyone to laugh.

"Seriously, this outfit is perfect. Rosalee was so upset that she didn't have the bag she'd packed to bring to the hospital and nothing to dress the baby in other than a blanket one of her clients made for her. Anyway, I wanted her to have an outfit to take him home in tomorrow. This is so perfect. Thank you for choosing it, Kate." Nova grinned at the young woman, then at Ian. "And you, too, son."

Nova tucked the outfit and tissue back into the bag and stood. "I shouldn't be much longer. I just want to make sure Rosalee is settled, then I'll be ready to leave."

"We'll go down and get the Jeep," Ian offered. "I'll park close to the main exit, so you won't have to trek all the way across the parking lot, Mom."

"Thanks, sweetie. I appreciate that." Nova hurried from the room.

Ian and Kate rose to their feet. Carter watched as his son helped the young woman with her coat, being very gentlemanly in his behavior. "We'll be down as soon as your mom wraps things up."

"Sure, Dad. No rush. We'll get the Jeep warmed up and the windows defrosted," Ian said, winking at Kate.

She blushed, and Carter had to bite his cheek to keep from laughing.

"I meant so Mom doesn't have to sit in a cold vehicle half the way home."

Kate's blush deepened as she and Ian stepped into the hall. Carter heard her say, "Do you have any idea how that must have sounded to your dad? He probably thinks we'll be sitting out there slobbering all over each other while we wait, and I hardly even know you, Ian Alexander!"

A soft chuckle rolled out of Carter. He definitely liked Kate. She'd keep Ian on his toes and in line.

Nova was only gone about five minutes before she reappeared, shrugging into her coat while her purse dangled from one wrist. Carter stepped behind her and helped with her coat, then held out his arm after she adjusted the purse strap over her shoulder. "You gonna be able to stay awake long enough to eat dinner?"

"Absolutely. I'm starving. Rosalee chased me off to the cafeteria earlier, but I don't even remember what time that was. I didn't eat much during my shift last night, thinking I'd have a nice breakfast at home this morning before I got some sleep." Nova looked up at him as they made their way out of the maternity ward and over to the elevator. "It's been the oddest, strangest day, hasn't it? But something about it seems almost magical."

"It's been different, for sure." Carter had never experienced a Christmas Eve like this one, but being at the hospital as a new life entered the world made it seem special indeed.

He took Nova's hand in his as they moved into the elevator and pushed the button for the first floor.

"You do realize Ian's in love," Nova said as the elevator doors opened, and they stepped out into the main lobby. "I've never, not once, seen him look at a girl like he looks at Kate."

Carter nodded. "I thought the exact same thing. But how can that kid be in love after only meeting her today? Then again, like you said, it's been the oddest, strangest day."

They walked outside just as Ian pulled up in his Jeep. Carter opened the door to the backseat for Nova and waited until she was inside to stride around the vehicle and climb in behind Ian.

"This is kind of nice," Carter said, fastening his seat belt. "I don't usually get to ride around in the backseat like royalty."

Ian guffawed. "If this old Jeep is the royal transportation, I'd hate to see what the paupers are driving."

Carter winked at Nova. "It's been a good rig for you, kid. I suppose now that you landed your dream job, it won't be long until you're buying an upgrade."

"I've had my eye on a few options for a while and have been saving up, but I wanted to wait until I was sure I had more financial security before I spent my money. Same with the housing situation. I figure once I make it through my ninety-day trial period at Magra, I can get some better wheels and an apartment that doesn't smell like a gym locker."

Carter could see Kate wrinkle her nose. "Do you have to put up with roommates, Kate?" he asked.

"No, sir," she said, turning to look over the seat at him. "I'm house-sitting. It's something I did through college to save on housing expenses. The family I'm house-sitting for now is out of the country for another year and a half. After they come back, I'll have to figure out something else, but for now, it's a sweet deal."

"They even pay the utilities, Dad." Ian looked at him in the rearview mirror.

"That's great. So how does one get into the house-sitting business?" Carter was genuinely interested, and his voice reflected that.

"I started out pet sitting for people I met at school, then it segued into house-sitting and dog walking. I love animals, and kids, obviously, but when I moved here to take the teaching job, I asked around to see if anyone needed someone to watch their house. Usually, I'm only there for a few weeks to a few months, so landing a long-term gig was unexpected but much appreciated."

"She loves kids," Nova whispered to Carter, and grinned as Ian took the freeway exit nearest to their house.

Surprisingly, the streets weren't as busy as Carter had anticipated. In no time, Ian was pulling into their driveway.

They all sat in the Jeep for a moment, looking at the Christmas lights around the house and the yard twinkling through the freshly fallen snow.

"Ian, you're in charge of taking some photos of that, because I don't think we're apt to get too many Christmas Eve snows." Carter patted his son's shoulder, then got out and walked around the vehicle, opening Nova's door. "I don't know about you, but I am so glad to finally be home."

"Me, too, honey. Me, too. The lights sure are a lovely welcome. Thank you for turning them on for me." Nova kissed his cheek, then led the way to the front door and opened it while Carter helped Ian carry in a few shopping bags from the back of the Jeep.

"Welcome to our home, Kate," Carter said, standing back as he motioned for their guest to go ahead of him into the warmth of the house.

CHAPTER 23

NOVA

N OVA WALKED THROUGH THE house, turning on lights. She stopped in the living room to plug in the Christmas tree, surprised to see several boxes beneath it that hadn't been there when she'd left the house yesterday.

It was hard to think she'd been awake and on her feet for so many hours, but the idea of company coming soon and celebrating Christmas Eve with them kept her going. However, she doubted that even a triple shot espresso could keep her from immediately falling asleep when her head finally hit the pillow tonight.

She walked through the kitchen and put her coat and purse in the hall closet near the garage. She snagged her cell phone, sure it needed to be charged, and saw a text message from Archer Raines, a man she'd spent all day thinking of as Rob. The nickname Rosalee had given him was cute, like the way he called his wife Lena. They seemed like a loving, solid couple, and Nova couldn't be happier for them about Ryder's birth. Even if the baby was early, he was healthy and had no issues they'd need to worry about.

Both Archer and Rosalee had been so pleased with the little outfit Kate and Ian had brought. When she'd taken the gift bag to Rosalee's room and given it to Archer to open, he'd seemed taken aback. Rosalee had encouraged him to open it. Slowly, he'd removed the red and white tissue paper, then lifted out the onesie, holding it reverently before he showed it to Rosalee.

"It's so tiny," Archer had said in a quiet voice as he'd looked from the size of the outfit to the newborn baby lying on Rosalee's chest.

Rosalee had blinked away tears and smiled at Nova in gratitude. "You knew how much I wanted him to have an outfit to go home in. This is perfect, Nova. Thank you."

Nova would have to remember to thank Kate again for choosing such a perfect outfit for the newest member of the Raines family.

It boggled her mind how all of them had been on the St. Johns Bridge today. According to Ian, even he and Kate had been on the bridge but had managed to turn around just as the collision was happening. It was a miracle that they'd all walked away unharmed. Other than the injuries during the wreck, none of which were fatal, thank goodness, things could have been so much worse.

Archer had said something earlier about how it was a good day when he and his team could walk away whole and unharmed at the end of it.

Today had been an exceptionally good day, at least in Nova's opinion.

She read the text from Archer and felt tears welling in her eyes.

Words don't exist to express the depth of my gratitude to you, Nova. You were there for my girl when I couldn't be and gave her the confidence and strength to give birth to our son. Anything I can ever do for you, just ask.

Thank you!

From Rosalee's Rob

Sleep deprivation, coupled with the emotional roller coaster of the last several hours, was really starting to get to her. She blinked away her tears and sent him a brief message.

Being beside your sweet Lena was my honor and pleasure. If I had to do it all over again, I would in a blink. May the two of you always feel as blessed and loved as you do today. Congratulations on the birth of a beautiful baby boy who will fill your hearts with

*joy beyond measure and your home with more love
than you can imagine.*

Merry Christmas!

Nova

Nova plugged her phone into the charger she kept by the coffee pot in the kitchen, peeked in the refrigerator to see that Carter had stocked it well, then returned to the living room, where Ian was helping Kate out of her coat.

She stood in the doorway and smiled as she watched them, wondering if this was the first of a lifetime of holidays they would spend with Kate. Although she'd just met the young woman, she liked her immensely. "My apologies in advance for being rude, but I really, really need a shower. I'll hurry."

"Take all the time you need, Mom. If the food and guests arrive while you're cleaning up, we can handle it," Ian said, shrugging out of his coat as he looked her way.

"Thanks, sweetie. I won't be long."

Carter followed her into the hallway, settled an arm around her waist, and kissed her neck in the spot she liked just below her ear. "Need any help with that shower?"

She rolled her eyes at him. "You've got to be kidding me."

"I am. Mostly. I could use a shower myself. I'll grab my things and use the guest bathroom."

"How long will it take you to shower?"

"Less than five. Why?"

"Go ahead and get cleaned up while I figure out what I want to wear."

Carter flicked on the overhead light as they walked into the bedroom that had been their own special haven for the twenty-some years that they'd lived in the house. They'd been terrified of not being able to meet the payments when they'd bought the house all those years ago, but it was in a good neighborhood and had three bedrooms and two bathrooms, perfect for their family. Now, the house was paid for, and they'd been working on updates and renovations. Carter had insisted on doing their bedroom and bathroom first. They'd extended an exterior wall, making the side yard a few feet smaller, but that extra space had made a huge difference in both the bathroom and the bedroom. Now they had a big soaking tub, a walk-in shower, a walk-in closet, and enough room on either side of their king-sized bed that both of them could move around it without bumping into furniture in the middle of the night.

"You sure?" he asked, removing his work boots and dropping them in the closet.

"I'm sure. You'll be faster than I will and can get out there to welcome our guests. Remind me who all has been invited?" Nova pulled the clip from her hair and shook it out.

Carter took off his shirt and lobbed it into the hamper by the bathroom door. "Ian invited the widow woman from Magra, who fed him lunch. Apparently, you need to make Easter ham more often because he's raved about how the sandwich he ate tasted just like the ham you always make for Easter."

"Noted." Nova kicked off her work shoes and set them neatly inside the closet, then moved Carter's boots to the rack that held his footwear.

Carter threw his pants and socks into the hamper, and for a fleeting moment Nova considered taking him up on his offer of helping with her shower. She loved Carter Alexander with all her heart and had for three decades. To the world, he might look like a solemn giant, but to her, he would always and forever be her loveable bear.

She leaned a shoulder against the bathroom's doorjamb as he walked across the tile floor and turned on the shower so the water would warm. It didn't hurt her feelings any that he was still as physically fit as the day they'd met. She'd always been entranced by his muscular physique.

He waggled his eyebrows suggestively. "See something you like, babe?"

She grinned. "Yeah. That hot shower."

Carter scowled and lunged for her. She pretended to be in a hurry to get away from him while casting flirtatious glances over her shoulder.

He wrapped his arms around her when he caught her halfway across the bedroom, lifted her off her feet, and kissed her neck again. "I love you."

"Love you, too. Now, hurry up. We don't have time for your shenanigans this evening."

"Does that mean you'll have time for them later?"

Nova leaned to the side so she could kiss his cheek. "Maybe. If I'm still awake and semi-coherent."

"I'll hurry, babe." Carter disappeared back into the bathroom while Nova dug through the closet, trying to decide what to wear to the impromptu dinner party they were hosting.

She realized she and Carter had gotten distracted, and she still had no idea who had been invited to dinner. She stepped back into the bathroom. "Who else is coming besides Ian's new grandmother and girlfriend?"

"Ace and Maddie. They were supposed to go to her sister's house, but the whole bunch of them are sick, so they had nowhere else to go. I don't think Ace is terribly disappointed. He's not a fan of his brother-in-law." Carter peeked over the frosted glass of the shower door. "I also invited Mr. Werner from down the street."

"Mr. Werner? He hardly ever speaks to anyone since his wife died. Was that four years ago?" Nova rubbed a facial mask into her skin, one she could rinse off in the shower. It would make her face glow, and she could avoid spending time on makeup. "Why would he agree to come to our house for Christmas Eve?"

"I think it's because he's lonely. He was out in his yard earlier, so I stopped to talk for a minute. He just sounded sad about not having anyone to spend the holiday with, so I invited him for dinner. Maybe he'll hit it off with Ian's ham-baking grandma."

"Maybe." Nova stuffed her scrubs into the hamper and dashed into the shower the second Carter opened the door.

He started to say something, but she shook her head. "Don't even go there, hon. People coming. Christmas Eve. Starving for dinner. Focus, husband of mine. Focus."

Carter laughed as he toweled off, then went into the bedroom to dress. When Nova stepped out of the shower five minutes later, he'd already left the room. She dried off, hastily blow-dried her hair, and gave her lashes a few quick swipes of mascara before she slipped into a deep hunter-green maxi dress with red and cream roses splashed across it. She shoved her feet into a pair of green velvet flats, then added a few chunky curls to her hair with a flat iron before she put on a paper clip necklace Ian had made for her a few years ago. It curled around her neck with what appeared to be Scottish thistles on the ends of two swirled wires. Every time she wore it, she received compliments on it, and some of her friends had wanted to know where they could buy something similar.

If Ian ever needed extra money, he could have a successful side career making jewelry. The bracelet Kate wore that he'd made today was gorgeous with its intricate swirls that looped together.

Kate and Ian.

Nova didn't mind the sound of that. She was already having to adjust to Macie and Ben. Granted, Ben was a great guy and made Macie happy, which was the important thing, but Nova missed her daughter. Thoughts of her stayed with Nova as she walked into the living room just as the doorbell rang.

Ian hopped up from his seat near the fireplace to answer it while Kate remained seated, looking at the collection of unmatched ornaments on their Christmas tree. Nova knew they'd never win any awards for their holiday decorations, but the things they set out each year were loaded with sentimental value. Most of the ornaments on the tree were made by either Ian or Macie, or had been a special gift from Nova's siblings or Carter.

"This one," Nova said, stepping over to the tree and removing a small tree-shaped ornament made of twisted silver wire with a tiny gold jingle bell fastened to the top. She held it out to Kate. "This was the first ornament Ian ever made."

"It's incredible. How old was he?" Kate asked with interest, holding up the little tree and studying it in the firelight.

"Seven. He worked on that thing for three days before he got it just how he wanted it. Ian isn't one to give up easily when his mind is set on something. He's also pretty good at following things through."

"Those are good traits, Mrs. Alexander." Kate held the ornament out to her, and Nova hung it back on the tree.

"Call me Nova, please. We truly are so glad you could join us this evening, Kate."

"I'm glad to be here, Mrs... Nova." Kate stood and grinned at her. "It's been a long time since I've been part of a family holiday."

Nova slid an arm around Kate's shoulders. "Then I hope this will be a special one for you. Come to the kitchen. You can help me get out plates and silverware. Do you think we should set the table or eat buffet style?"

"After the day you had, buffet style." Kate studied her a moment. "You probably hear this all the time, but there is no way on earth you look old enough to be Ian's mom. Maybe his sister, but definitely not his mother."

Nova laughed and gave Kate a one-armed hug. "You are now my favorite person in the world."

Kate grinned, and they busied themselves setting out plates, cutlery, glasses, mugs, and napkins.

While Ian introduced Kate to Ace and Maddie, Nova rushed down the hallway to Macie's former room, which they'd converted into a guest room. She flicked on the closet light and opened a large plastic tote where she kept what she called emergency gifts. Whenever she found a great bargain on a potential gift, she bought it and tucked it away for a day when she needed one at the last minute.

Nova chose a velvet yarn throw blanket in a beautiful shade of soft peach for Kate. A wooden puzzle brainteaser would be perfect for Mr. Werner. Ms. Tipton, whom Nova had yet to meet, might appreciate a basket with soaps and lotions in a delicate scent called Nectar. For Ace and Maddie, she selected a date night cookbook with menus and activities she'd bought for the next bridal shower she was invited to attend. Since Maddie had next to zero cooking skills but was trying to learn, maybe she and Ace could learn to cook together.

Nova had set up a table in the room with wrapping paper, tape, ribbons and bows, gift tags, and gift bags. She didn't have time to wrap the gifts, so she stuffed them into gift bags, added tissue and tags, then carried them out to the Christmas tree, where an attractive older woman in a dark red cashmere sweater that matched the red and black plaid wool skirt she wore visited with Mr. Werner by the fireplace. It was the most animated she'd seen their elderly neighbor since his wife passed away. Maybe Carter had known what he was doing after all. Nova would wait to introduce herself to Ms. Tipton, not wanting to disturb the older couple as they got acquainted.

Ace and Maddie stood by the tree with Ian and Kate, laughing at something one of them had said. It was wonderful to see the young people enjoying each other's company.

Carter lingered in the kitchen doorway and lifted the glass he held in his hand to her in a toast. Nova blew him a kiss, then hurried to the door as the doorbell rang.

A delivery driver handed her bags packed with what seemed like enough food to feed a small army. The smells emanating from the containers made her stomach growl with hunger.

"Who's ready to eat?" she asked as Ace and Ian took the bags from her, carrying them into the kitchen.

After plates were filled and everyone was seated at the dining room table, Carter enveloped Nova's hand in his, and she took Ian's in her other.

"Shall we give thanks?" her husband asked, then bowed his head. He offered a humble and humbling prayer of thanksgiving for those gathered around the table, for those who couldn't be there, and for the precious gift of a baby boy, a gift that filled their lives and hearts with love.

Nova dabbed at the tears in her eyes with her napkin, then noticed Kate, Maddie, and Ms. Tipton doing the same.

"I sure hope there's enough food," Carter quipped in a voice dripping with mock concern, making everyone laugh as they dug into the delicious meal.

When they'd all eaten as much as they could hold, no one seemed in a rush to leave the table.

"Mom, can we wait a little while for dessert?" Ian asked, leaning back in his chair, patting his flat stomach. "I'm so full I'll explode if I eat more right now, and I really want some of that peppermint stuff you made."

"Peppermint stuff?" Kate asked, looking from Ian to Nova.

"It's something I make for Christmas Eve and have for probably a dozen years. Ian loves it. I'll share the recipe with you if you'd like." Nova smiled at Kate, wondering if she'd be passing on many of Ian's favorite things to this impressive young woman in the days to come.

"Why don't we play a game or two while we wait for the meal to settle?" Carter suggested as he rose from the table. "You all go on. I'll handle the dishes."

"I'll help, boss. It won't take long," Ace said, kissing Maddie before he hopped up and began carrying plates into the kitchen.

Nova didn't protest since she felt full, warm, and relaxed for the first time in more than twenty-four hours.

"Come on, Mom," Ian said as he stood and motioned to her. "Maybe you can show off your skills at charades."

It wasn't a secret to anyone who knew Nova that she was terrible at the game. But it was still fun to play.

"Make it a Christmas version, and I'm in," she said, rising to her feet and following as Ian led their guests to the living room. It didn't take Carter and Ace long to deal with the dishes and store the leftovers in the refrigerator. When they joined the others, they divided into four teams to play the game.

Ace and Maddie won the first round, while Ian and Kate won the next two. Ms. Tipton and Mr. Werner won the last round and were both laughing at their unexpected victory.

"There are a few gifts under the tree you could pass out, Ian," Nova suggested as she rose from her seat next to Carter. "Would anyone like coffee or hot chocolate?"

"We're all fine for the moment, dear. Sit down and rest. Ian told us about your interesting day. You must be exhausted," Ms. Tipton said, reaching over to pat Nova's hand. "It's so kind of you to open your home to us."

"I'm grateful to have you all here to celebrate the holiday with us. We were dreading our first Christmas Eve without our daughter, so this has brought us unexpected joy. Thank you." Nova settled next to Carter once again and watched as Ian passed out the gifts she'd hastily assembled.

When he continued to pass out gifts, she realized their guests had brought things for her and Carter, as well. She watched as they opened the gifts she'd selected and realized they all seemed to like what they received. Kate especially seemed to love her throw blanket. She kept rubbing it against her cheek as though she'd never touched something that soft and rich. Nova would have to go back to the high-end department store where she'd discovered it on sale last January to see if she could find more of them for future gifting.

Once their guests had finished with their gifts, they all looked at her and Carter expectantly, so Nova began opening their presents. Mr. Werner had brought them one of his hand-crafted birdhouses, shaped like an English cottage. Ace and Maddie had given them a gift certificate for dinner at one of Carter's favorite barbecue restaurants. Ms. Tipton gave them a basket full of gourmet hot chocolate mixes with packages of marshmallows shaped like snowmen and snowflakes. There were exquisite peppermint bark bars and two gorgeous poinsettia toile latte mugs included in the decorative wooden basket.

"These mugs are beautiful, Ms. Tipton. Thank you." Nova smiled at the older woman.

"You're welcome, dear. I have some similar to that and love them for serving hot chocolate. There's lots of room for the marshmallows."

Nova opened Kate's gift last. It was in a large gift bag, indicating she, too, had been short on time for wrapping. Nova lifted out a smaller gift bag from inside it, and Ian pointed to his father. "That's for Dad."

Carter took the bag and pulled out several packages of his favorite jerky. It was a snack he often took with him when he didn't have time to eat lunch while he was working. "This is perfect, Kate. Thank you."

"You're welcome. Ian told me which ones you liked the best." Kate smiled at him, then shifted her attention to Nova. She studied her with a hopeful look on her face, betraying the fact that she so badly wanted Nova to like her gift.

Even if she hated it, Nova intended to act as if the gift was the best thing she'd ever received. She slid out a wooden box with a clear glass inset in the lid. "Oh, I've always wanted one of these," she said—and it was true. She brushed her fingers across the top before opening the lid to reveal compartments for tea bags. The spaces were filled with all her favorite teas, including the spice tea she could only ever find at the hospital cafeteria.

Nova looked over at Kate with a happy, sincerely grateful smile. "This is fabulous, Kate. I love tea, and this holiday spice blend is my absolute favorite. I've been meaning for years to get a tea box and just never got around to it. Thank you for this thoughtful gift."

Kate beamed. "Ian mentioned you like tea, so I hoped this might be something you'll enjoy."

"Like Carter said, it's perfect. Thank you." Nova stood and motioned in the direction of the kitchen. "Is anyone ready for dessert?"

"Yes!" Ian and Ace said in unison, making everyone chuckle.

Carter got out the pumpkin pie and canned whipping cream he'd purchased at the store. Ms. Tipton had brought an eggnog Bundt cake. Kate contributed gourmet seven-layer bars she'd picked up at the store when she and Ian had stopped to get the baby gift for Rosalee and the gifts for Nova and Carter. Ian took a huge serving of the peppermint dessert Nova had made sure to assemble the previous afternoon before she'd headed off to work. It was something that needed to chill overnight, so it worked out perfectly.

"I need the recipe for this," Ms. Tipton said as she took a bite of the peppermint-laced dessert.

"Nova will give it to you if you share this cake recipe," Carter said, helping himself to another slice of Bundt cake. "It's wonderful, Ms. Tipton."

"Thank you. I'm happy to share."

Nova smiled at Carter and listened as the conversation flowed around them. Ace and Maddie invited Ian and Kate to join them for a double date to try a new food truck that had been getting rave reviews. Mr. Werner suggested Ms. Tipton meet him for an afternoon of perusing an exhibit at the art museum.

By the time everyone left, Nova felt the strangers who'd arrived at her door had become an extension of her family.

Carter helped her clean up the dessert dishes, made a cup of the holiday tea for her to enjoy, and then the two of them settled onto the couch by the fire to wait for Ian to return from taking Kate home. With the fire adding a warm glow to the cozy atmosphere created by the glimmering tree lights and Christmas music playing quietly in the background, Nova snuggled contentedly against her husband.

"I had such a great evening," he said in a quiet, mellow voice. "When this day began so badly, I had no idea it would end so ..."

"Perfectly," Nova whispered, then tilted her head to look at Carter. Even if his hair was a little thinner and he had craggy lines around his eyes, in her opinion, he continued to improve with age.

"I thought this was going to be one of the worst Christmas Eves ever, especially when Ace and I were hiding behind the wrecker hoping we wouldn't get shot, but—"

"Shot!" Nova bolted upright and glared at her husband. "What on earth happened?"

"Calm down, babe. It wasn't loaded, but we didn't know that at the time. Not until Archer talked that crazy guy into handing it over. If you ever get in a pickle, Archer is someone you'd want on your side."

"Good to know." Nova resumed her comfortable position leaning against Carter's chest. As she rested her ear against the soft fabric of his flannel shirt, she could hear the steady thump of his heart. That was her man. Steady and true. Always there for her and their children. Always thinking of her.

She tilted her head back a second time and studied him until he glanced down and caught her gaze.

"I have pie on my chin?" he asked, playfully brushing his chin over the top of her head.

"No. I was just thinking about how glad I am to be married to you. You're a good man, Carter Alexander, and a marvelous husband. Thank you."

"I'm the one who should be thanking you, Nova. You're the glue that keeps everything together around here. Ask Ian. He'll agree. We would all be so lost without you, but I'd be devastated if we weren't together. You make every day so much better just by being part of it. The greatest gift of my life is being married to you, Nova."

"I would say the exact same thing about you." Nova sighed and let her gaze drift to the tree and the presents beneath it they would exchange with each other and Ian in the morning. Nova still needed to hang up the stockings, but thankfully, they were already filled. At least Carter's and Ian's were. Carter always took care of filling hers. Just like he took care of so many details she was sure she took for granted.

Nova decided she'd be more mindful of her blessings, particularly the blessing of her family.

"Do you think we'll have two weddings next year?" Carter asked as a log popped in the fireplace and sent sparks dancing up the chimney.

"I don't know." Nova shrugged. "It seems ludicrous to ponder Ian and Kate's future after one day together, but when she was helping me in the kitchen, I had the oddest feeling of déjà vu. It was like we'd worked together many times before. I could so clearly picture the two of us in the kitchen, laughing together on future holidays. Is that insane?"

"No." Carter shook his head. "At least with Kate, we won't have to share Ian with in-laws. She has no family."

"She does now." Nova smiled up at him. "Having everyone here tonight was a delight, even if I wish Macie and Ben could have joined us."

Carter smirked. "You wish Macie was here and that she'd never met Ben because that young man has stolen your little girl."

"You're the one who started it, whining about him shoving you out as her favorite guy." Nova sighed. "It would be so easy to dislike him if he weren't such a good kid, sweet, thoughtful, and kind. And he's not bad to look at either."

Carter chuckled. "I believe when Macie first introduced him, you called him the campus hottie. Our kids are growing up, and we have to let them, babe."

"I know, but it's hard not to want them to stay young. I am so proud of Ian, though. This job sounds like everything he's been searching for since he graduated last year."

"I agree. I hope it's something that will launch his career. According to Ms. Tipton, Magra is a great company to work for. She should know. It sounds like she's been there longer than Ian's been alive."

Nova nodded, then grew quiet as she thought back over their day. "Do you really think Ian is going to fall for Kate?"

"I think he already has. From the way she kept watching his every move, I'd say it was a mutual falling." Carter nestled back on the couch, wrapping his arms a little tighter around Nova as he drew her closer. "I knew the first time we met that I was going to marry you. It just took you a few months to catch up."

Nova turned her head and stared at him. "How can you possibly expect me to believe you fell in love with me when I was sitting in my car with watering eyes after nailing myself with pepper spray? I was a red-faced mess."

"A beautiful red-faced mess who still had enough of her sense of humor to make a joke about the situation. That's one of the first things that attracted me to you. Your laugh. Your smile. Your ability to see the humor in something where others would only see the disaster. You're smart, Nova, and interesting to talk to. You're fun and kind and caring. Your generosity often catches me completely off guard, like today." He lifted her and settled her across his lap. "You could have left Rosalee on the bridge or even at the hospital. Instead, you stayed with her because you have this remarkable capacity for love and couldn't leave her all by herself when you knew she needed someone beside her. By the way, Archer sent me a text letting me know how grateful he is for what you did."

"He texted me too. I truly feel like I'm the one who received something special by spending that time with Rosalee. It's impossible to explain, but I felt such a deep bond with her. I have a feeling we'll continue to keep in touch, especially since they asked me to be the baby's godmother. Isn't that an incredible honor, Carter?"

"Absolutely. Rosalee must think highly of you to not only ask you to fill that important role, but also to name the baby after us—after you."

"He is so precious and already so loved. Being there for Ryder's birth just made me even more grateful for this special time of year, and it reminded me that the first and best gift was and will always be love."

Carter bent his head down and tipped her chin up until their lips were just a breath of space apart. "Speaking of love, I do love you, Nova. So much it overwhelms me sometimes."

"I love you too, Carter. Always, with all my heart. Merry Christmas."

"Merry Christmas, babe," he whispered just before he captured her lips in a tender kiss and she surrendered to the magnificent man who would always hold her heart.

CHAPTER 24

IAN

“T HAT WAS GREAT, IAN. Thank you for inviting me.” Kate smiled at him across the Jeep as he parked in front of her house. The lights she’d left on glowed in the dark and glistened against the blanket of snow that covered everything in a soft layer of white.

“Thank you for coming with me, braving the crowds at the store, and for hanging out with my parents.”

“Your parents are incredible. You didn’t say your dad looked like he should have his own wrestling show or that your mom could be a model, though.”

Ian shrugged. He’d never thought of his parents in those terms. “They’re just Mom and Dad.”

"Just Mom and Dad," she mimicked, then grinned at him again. "Ms. Tipton certainly sang your praises. It was fun to watch her and Mr. Werner together. I think they made a date to get coffee and visit a museum next week."

"I picked up on that too. I think they have a lot in common. Mr. Werner used to be friendly, but he closed himself off after his wife passed away. I'm glad Dad invited him tonight."

"It was great your dad also invited Ace and Maddie. They're a neat couple. I'm looking forward to getting together with them again."

"Really?"

Kate nodded. "Really. I enjoyed meeting everyone, Ian. You and Ace joke around like you are brothers. How long has he worked for your dad?"

"Ace is kinda like an adopted brother. He started working for Dad in high school, and now he's the assistant manager. Ace didn't have much of a home life, so, of course, Mom and Dad included him in ours."

Ian hopped out and ran around the Jeep to open Kate's door.

"Did it bother you, including Ace in family stuff?" she asked, taking his hand and holding onto it as they walked toward the door. She held the throw his mom had given her clutched against her with her other hand.

"Nope. Ace and I like a lot of the same things, and he was always just so grateful to be included. He's also pretty funny and keeps things entertaining. I've never felt jealous of him or anything like that. Over the years, he's become part of the family."

"I think you're accepting of him because your parents are that way. Accepting. Welcoming. Caring." Kate took out her keys and unlocked the door. "I can't believe your mom, though. I mean ... Wow! She gave up her Christmas Eve to help Mrs. Raines. How cool is that? Who does that?"

Ian grinned. "My mom. She's awesome, but don't tell her I said that."

"Come in for a minute while I go check on Jazzy." Kate motioned him inside, set her purse on the table by the door, draped the throw over the stair banister, and rushed down the hall.

Ian stepped inside and shut the door behind him, carefully wiping his feet on the mat.

He heard Jazzy before he saw her racing toward him. He hunkered down and held out his hand. Tail wagging, she slid to a stop in front of him, licking his fingers, then landing one on his cheek before he turned his face away to avoid a slobbery lick on the lips.

"Hey, girl. Good to see you, too," he said, giving the dog some scratches behind her ears and along her back. She licked his fingers again, then loped off toward the back of the house.

"She has to check on everything when I let her in from the sunroom," Kate said, carrying her coat over her arm as she returned. She hung it up in the closet with her scarf, then picked up the throw and brushed it against her cheek. "This is the softest, coziest thing I've ever touched. Tell your mom again how much I love it. There was no way she could possibly have known, but this is my favorite color."

Ian tucked that detail away for future reference, then smiled at Kate. "Tell her yourself. Both Mom and Dad said to invite you to join us tomorrow. We're going to church, then we'll eat whatever we can find in the fridge for lunch and spend the rest of the day playing games and watching Christmas movies. You're welcome to join us for church, lunch, movies, games, or dinner. Whatever you want, or all of it. We'd all be so happy to spend more time with you, but I'd be especially elated if you wanted to hang out with us tomorrow. Ace and Maddie might drop by later in the afternoon."

Kate gave him a speculative glance. "Are you sure I won't be imposing? I don't want to stomp all over your holiday family time. I feel like I've already intruded enough on your life."

"Intruded? On my life? Don't talk crazy, Kate. I enjoyed every second we spent together today. And my parents adore you. Mom told me, like, five times how much you impressed her. Dad said, to quote him, 'It's nice to meet a sweet girl with both beauty and brains instead of your usual, kid. I hope she'll be back tomorrow. Make sure you invite her.' See, they think you're great, and so do I. Truly, Kate, we would love to have you join us, but only if you want to. No pressure at all. It's totally up to you, and we'll all understand if you have something you'd rather do."

"Are you kidding? Of course, I want to spend Christmas with you and your family. Your parents are beyond fabulous, and their son, homely thing that he is, has somehow managed to capture my interest despite my plan to remain uninterested."

"I'm more concerned about capturing your heart than just your unattainable interest," Ian teased, but the words were spoken with blunt honesty.

Kate blinked three times, as if she had to digest what he'd said. She draped the throw on the banister again and walked over to him. "Don't you think it's a little soon for that?"

"Nope. I think when you meet the person you can't bear the thought of never seeing again, you should do everything in your power to make sure they stick around."

Kate took a step closer, sliding her hands up the arms of his coat until they circled the back of his neck. "What drastic measures are you willing to take to get me to stick around?"

"You mean offering you my parents isn't enough?"

She shook her head. "They're lovely, lovely people, Ian, but I need a little more than that."

"How about this?" Ian lowered his head to hers and kissed her softly, then more intently. Passion exploded between them when Kate made a soft noise in her throat and pressed closer to him. Ian deepened the kiss, so lost in the wonder of Kate, the rich taste of her, he could have remained rooted to the floor in the foyer, kissing her all night.

Only Jazzy had other plans.

The dog ran between them, nearly knocking them over, and woofed, as though voicing her disapproval of their fervent kisses.

Ian chuckled and took a step back as he released his hold on Kate's waist. "I see you have a built-in chaperone."

Kate stroked her fingers over the dog's head. "I do. That might not be such a bad thing."

Considering the eager kisses they'd exchanged, he had to agree with Kate. "What do you say? Christmas with the Alexander family?"

"I'd love to spend the day with you. What time should I be ready for church?"

"How about nine-thirty? I'll come pick you up."

"I'll be waiting, Ian. Is there anything I can bring over tomorrow for lunch or snacks?"

"Nothing I can think of. You saw how much food was left from dinner, and Dad bought a bunch of stuff at the store. You're welcome to bring something if you want, but you don't need to." He gave Jazzy another scratch along her back, then reached for the door. Before his fingers connected with the knob, Kate grabbed the lapels of his coat and pulled him to her, kissing him with heat and longing.

"Thank you for tonight," she whispered when she let him go.

"It's been the best Christmas Eve I've ever had, Kate, and a big part of that is thanks to you. Merry Christmas, Goth girl."

"Merry Christmas, Ian. Good night."

Ian whistled all the way back to his Jeep. It was going to be the merriest Christmas ever. One full of hope, possibilities, and love.

ARCHER

"I 'M A FATHER," ARCHER said to the image in the mirror as he hastily ran an electric razor over his face. He didn't want his stubble, which seemed to grow in double time, scratching Rosalee or little Ryder.

The baby they'd been so excited to welcome into their home and their hearts had arrived, and Archer was struggling to get his brain to process the fact that the wait was over. Maybe part of it was because he was still amped up on adrenaline from dealing with Leon Mumford. He'd been thrust from that high-stress situation into one of an entirely different variety when Carter had shared the news about Rosalee going into labor on the bridge and his wife staying with her all day.

If only Archer had looked at the cars on the far side of the bridge when he'd arrived, he might even have seen Rosalee when she'd gotten out of her SUV. He'd been so intently focused on Leon, on doing what he could to end the situation quickly and safely, he'd blocked everything else. What kind of person did that make him, beyond one who was good at his job?

Archer knew that unless he left the force or took a desk job, there were times he was going to have to focus like he had today. But how would that affect Rosalee or Ryder, especially as his son grew older? He never, ever wanted them to feel they took second place to his work. They were, and would always be, the most important people in his life. In all the years they'd been married, Rosalee had never, not even once, complained about his job, which sometimes kept him late or rousted him out of bed in the middle of the night. There were times he'd been tied up at work, and they'd had to cancel plans that were important to both of them. She'd always been incredibly understanding and supportive.

With the arrival of Ryder, would she continue to be?

Although he'd hated to leave Rosalee and the baby at the hospital, Archer had needed to come home and take a shower. He felt filthy after being on the bridge all day, and especially after dealing with

Leon. Now he needed a few minutes to decompress and pull himself together, to step out of his role as negotiator and into the role of doting husband and new father.

When the captain had dropped him and Carter off at the hospital, the enormity of what was about to happen hit Archer all at once. If he hadn't been in such a panic to reach Rosalee, he wasn't sure his legs would have carried him inside the hospital, let alone up to the maternity ward. Thank goodness for Carter. He knew the nurses, where to go, what to say. Because of his quick action, Archer had made it into the delivery room just in time to witness his son's birth.

His son.

The notion that he was a father with a son to raise left him simultaneously thrilled, anxious, terrified, excited, and humbled. He wondered if Joseph had experienced similar emotions when Jesus was born.

As Archer stepped into a hot shower, he couldn't help but consider what it would have been like to watch the woman he loved more than life itself give birth in a stable—a place that seemed crude and primitive compared to the comforts of the delivery room at the hospital.

Despite his body's longing to remain in the hot water, chasing away a chill he was sure would take days to get over, Archer didn't stay long under the warming spray. Instead, he rushed so much, he dropped the bar of soap twice and banged his head on the shower faucet once.

"Get it together, man," he cautioned himself as he rinsed off and got out of the shower, briskly scrubbing his skin before he pulled on jeans, a thermal shirt with a heavy sweater over top, wool socks, and warm boots. He quickly stuffed a pair of lounge pants and a change of clothes into a bag, tossed in his toiletry kit, grabbed Rosalee's bag from the closet, then hurried to the living room. He dug around in the packages under the tree until he found the one he wanted, tucked it into his bag, and pulled Rosalee's cell phone off the charger. When he saw there were more than thirty missed text messages and nearly that many voicemails, he considered leaving it at home, but she'd want to be able to text Mac, her best friend, and her parents, even if they'd probably send an indifferent reply like, "Isn't that nice, dear."

His in-laws were the most hands-off parents he'd ever encountered. It was their loss because Rosalee was an impressive, marvelous person. Anyone who didn't realize that after getting to know her was just an idiot.

Archer rushed through the house, making sure everything was turned off and locked up, then grabbed a throw blanket off the couch and headed out to Rosalee's SUV.

His total time in the house had been less than twenty minutes, but he was anxious to get back to the hospital and his family.

His family.

Those words pierced his heart in a way that was new to him. Before, when it was just Rosalee and him, he'd felt a strong, primal urge to protect her. Now that they had a son, the urge to turn into a rampaging cavedweller if anyone even thought of bothering them multiplied a hundredfold.

The feelings he experienced helped him better understand the lengths Leon Mumford had been willing to go to in an effort to keep his family safe from himself. Archer didn't know whether to feel sorry for the guy or just be glad the ordeal was over and that Leon would get the psychiatric help he desperately needed.

On his way back to the hospital, Archer swung by a restaurant that still had an open sign lit in the front window. The diner wasn't one he'd frequented because it was out of the way from the route he normally traveled. However, he and Rosalee had eaten there a few times, and the food had been good. He ordered three of their evening specials, along with a side salad and two slices of pumpkin pie to go. After he paid for the meal and waited for them to box his order, a tiny red plush Christmas stocking by the cash register caught his eye.

"Excuse me, ma'am. Is that little stocking for sale?"

The woman who'd taken his order shook her head as she slid the slices of pie he'd ordered into a take-out container. "Sorry, hon, it's just a decoration."

"I know it's rude of me to even ask to buy it, and I hate to put you out, but would you consider selling it to me? My wife and I were expecting our baby to come in the middle of January, but he decided to arrive today. I'm heading back to the hospital now and would really like our son to have a stocking tonight. Are you sure you wouldn't be willing to sell it?"

"I won't sell it to you, handsome, but I will give it to you. What's the baby's name?" she asked.

"Ryder. Ryder Alexander."

"That's a good, strong name. Congratulations." The woman winked at him, then tucked the little stocking inside the bag of food before she handed it to him. "Merry Christmas to you and your family."

"Thank you so much. Merry Christmas!"

Archer set the food into an insulated tote bag to keep everything warm, then rushed back to the hospital. He'd expected the roads to be slick, but the snow was wet, and the temperature hovered a degree above freezing. They'd be a mess in the morning, of that he had no doubt. He left the SUV parked closer to the door now that the lot had emptied significantly and hastened to the maternity ward. The cranky woman who'd guarded the entry doors had been replaced by someone younger who didn't feel the need to interrogate him before entry.

As soon as he said, "My wife, Rosalee Raines, is in—"

"Room 305. They moved her about ten minutes ago." The woman smiled at him as she pushed the button for the doors to open. "Have a nice evening, sir."

"Thank you. Happy Holidays to you."

Inside the ward, Archer looked at the numbers posted outside each room until he found 305. He tapped once on the door that was open just a crack, then toed it open and stepped around the curtain that blocked his view into the room from the door. Inside, Rosalee was propped up in a bed big enough for two, nursing Ryder while a nurse guided her through the process.

Not only had she been moved to a bigger, much more comfortable room, but someone had helped her shower and change into a clean hospital gown. The only reason Archer knew that was because the gown she'd had on earlier was blue, and this one was pink. There was also evidence of a shower in Rosalee's hair. It was a wild, thick mass that was getting wilder and thicker as it dried. He loved it when she left her hair down and didn't straighten or do anything to it. For work, she told him she looked more like a homeless degenerate than a partner in the accounting firm if she didn't make an effort to control it. So she straightened it or contained it in a knot at the back of her head.

But the wild-haired girl he'd fallen in love with years ago was the one who still held his heart in her lovely hands, just like she now held their son.

"You're back," Rosalee said when she saw him standing with the insulated bag in his hands. Her beaming smile warmed him far more than the shower he'd taken or the wool socks on his feet. "Isn't this room nice?"

"It's great," Archer agreed, walking across the room and depositing the food on a small table in the corner next to a tiny Christmas tree, then setting the two duffle bags beneath it. He removed his coat and washed his hands in the small bathroom before returning to stand on the opposite side of the bed from the nurse. He watched his son's little cheeks puff in and out as he nursed.

"He's a quick learner. Some babies take a while to catch on, but this one is hungry." The nurse adjusted the baby's position slightly, then smiled at Archer. "He's a strong, healthy boy."

"He must take after his daddy," Rosalee said, giving Archer a teasing grin. "Whatever you brought for dinner smells incredible. They gave me a tray of food before I had a shower. I hate to admit it, but I ate every bite, and I'm still hungry."

"It's chicken dumpling soup from that old-fashioned diner down by the garden supply store. I thought soup might be an easy thing to digest."

The nurse offered him an approving look. "That's a great choice. Good job, new daddy."

Archer pulled one of the two chairs in the room over beside the bed and sat down, mesmerized by the simple act of Rosalee feeding their son.

While Ryder nursed, Archer counted every one of the baby's fingers twice and studied the thick brown hair on his head that had just the tiniest bit of curl on the ends. Their son would have the same cowlick right in the back that Archer fought on a daily basis, as well as Rosalee's brown, wild hair.

Archer had been so amped up earlier, he hadn't really been able to focus long enough to look—really look—at this little miracle he and Rosalee had created, other than to admire what a handsome baby their love had made.

Now, though, Archer took in his son's creamy unblemished skin. When the baby stopped nursing, the nurse showed Rosalee how to burp him. After promising to check back in on them in a while, she left them alone with Ryder cuddled against Rosalee's chest.

"Can you eat with him like that, or do you want me to hold him while you eat?" Archer asked as he leaned forward, his forearms braced on the mattress as he drank in the sight of his wife and child.

"Have you had anything to eat all day, Rob?"

Archer shrugged. "I had three bites of my cereal this morning and a sandwich this afternoon, although I don't recall what time it was. I also had some hot chocolate."

Rosalee grinned. "You eat, then you can hold him." She pointed to a table by the bathroom door. "I think you can push that over here, and it'll come over the bed. That way, I can do my best to avoid spilling on him. We're going to have to get into the practice of eating one-handed. Now's a good time to get started."

"Probably." Archer retrieved the bed table and slid it into place. He was glad to see that the tray extended out far enough so Rosalee could easily reach it. Archer set out a foam carton of soup for her, a spoon, and a napkin, then filled a glass with water from the pitcher by the bed. He started to offer thanks for their meal, but got so choked up with emotion, Rosalee finished the sincere prayer. When they'd both said amen, she gave him a long, observant glance.

"How are you?" she asked once she'd dipped a spoonful of soup. "You look as exhausted as I feel."

Archer shook his head as he dug into his salad. "I'm the one who should be asking how you're feeling. You just pushed a bundle the size of a watermelon out of your body after a very unsettling day. Are you doing okay, Lena? Am I going to be in the doghouse forever for not being here with you sooner?"

Rosalee tasted the soup on her spoon and nodded with approval. "This is wonderful, Rob. Thank you. To answer your question, you aren't in the doghouse. It wasn't your fault. It was just how things went today. Did I want you here with me? Of course. Did I miss you all day? Definitely. Was I terrified something had happened to you when you didn't return my calls and texts, even though I had to send them from Nova's phone? Absolutely. I've never felt so strongly before that something was wrong. That something terrible was happening to you. I saw a news clip this afternoon with that man on the bridge. I didn't see you on the news, but I was certain you were the one trying to talk him down. He was evil, wasn't he?"

Archer wiped his mouth on a napkin. "Want a bite of my salad?"

"No, but thanks." She took another bite, then pointed her spoon at him. "Are you going to answer my question or keep dodging it?"

"I'll answer, but after this, I'd prefer not to talk about that man again. Leon Mumford had a split personality. He was physically and verbally abused as a child and created an alter personality to deal with it. It wasn't Leon who was evil, but the alter ego, someone who called himself Kyle King. I've never had a case like this before, Lena. One minute, I'd feel like I was making progress, which was when I was talking to Leon, and the next, I'd feel like I was banging my head on a brick wall that wanted to fall on top of me, and that was Kyle. We had no idea about the two personalities until later in the afternoon. Once all the puzzle pieces slid into place, I was able to make progress, but it was a rough, rough road to get there."

Archer took a few bites of his salad, then looked at her again. "About an hour before things reached the boiling point, Captain Cohen told me he'd found you and asked if I wanted to know the details. I'd been worried about you all day too. You know I don't keep my personal cell phone on me during a negotiation, but I just had this feeling something was wrong. I'd asked the captain to have someone check on you, but they couldn't find you. You didn't answer your phone. You weren't at the office. You weren't at home. When the captain said you were safe and uninjured, I had visions of you stopping by the mall and someone stealing the car with your phone in it. I promise you, Lena, if I'd known you were here, I wouldn't have hesitated even a second to get to you as quickly as I could."

"I know, Rob. I know. It's why, when the captain called, I had Nova ask him not to say anything to you. You needed to get that man off the bridge so he could get the help he needed. The only thing you're at fault for is being too good at your job." She smiled at him. "I've always understood that your job, and what you do to help people, is sometimes bigger than we'd prefer. That will never change. I'll always support what you need to do, Rob, even if there are times I don't necessarily like it."

Archer set aside his empty salad bowl and stood. He leaned over the bed and kissed Rosalee tenderly. "I am the luckiest guy in the world having you for a wife, and now this adorable little one too. Thank you, Lena, for filling my life with so much love and happiness."

"Thank you for doing the same for me." Rosalee motioned to the two foam soup containers on the table. "Are both of those more soup?"

"Sure are. You still hungry?"

She grinned. "Famished. Did you bring dessert?"

"Pumpkin pie."

"You really are the best husband ever." She winked at him and returned to her soup.

Once they'd finished eating, Archer showed her the tiny stocking and told her about the waitress giving it to him when he asked to buy it.

"Every year, let's hang it on the tree for Ryder," she said, watching as Archer looped it onto one of the small tabletop tree's branches.

He washed his hands again, then carefully lifted his son into his arms. He was so tiny, so perfect, his heart felt like it might burst with the love that flooded through him for his child. Archer hadn't held many babies in his lifetime, and never any this small. He'd expected to feel intimidated or petrified by the thought of dropping him, but all he felt in that moment was love.

He'd memorized nearly every word of the books Rosalee had purchased to help them know what they needed to do through her pregnancy and the first months after the baby's arrival. But applying what he'd read to his cherished son was something very different.

"See outside, Ryder? It's snowing. That's kind of a miracle around here, snow for Christmas. Just like you've become our Christmas miracle." Archer brushed a feather-light kiss across Ryder's forehead, inhaling the wonderful, heavenly scent of his newborn son. "Someday, you'll be all grown up with children of your own, but I hope you'll always know how much Mommy and Daddy love you, and how happy we are that you're our baby boy."

He turned back to see tears filling Rosalee's eyes. Evidently, he wasn't the only one feeling overly emotional tonight.

Before he could say anything, the nurse breezed back into the room.

"Let's get this sweet baby settled in his bassinet for a bit." She took Ryder, then showed Archer how to swaddle him and gently place him in the tiny bed. "Nothing to it, right?"

Archer shook his head. "I think it takes a lot of practice on your part to make it look so easy. I'm terrified I'll wrap the blanket too tight and mummify my son or leave it too loose."

"You'll do fine, new daddy." She patted his back, checked on Rosalee, then sailed back out of the room.

"She's ..." Archer searched for the right word, "efficient."

Rosalee laughed softly. "That she is, but she's sweet. She's the one who brought that in." She pointed to the little tabletop tree. The lights twinkled and reflected in the window, where Archer could see it was still snowing outside.

"Honestly, Rob, everyone here has been so kind and helpful and made me feel well taken care of. I almost panicked at the thought of our doctor being out of town, but Dr. Stoakes is outstanding. Nova said she's one of the best obstetricians in the state."

"I'm so glad they took good care of you and that Nova was here. I have a feeling that things might have gone far differently if she hadn't been beside you every step of the way. We should do something nice for her and Carter once we get home and our heads back on straight."

"That would be great, Rob. Thanks for thinking of it. Speaking of thinking of things we should do, I decided we need a code word. We used to have one, and I can't even remember what it was. If something happens and either of us needs the other to come immediately, we should have a word we use to let the other know it's a don't-stop-for-anything-except-backup situation."

"Agreed. Wasn't our old word *sassafras*?"

"It could have been *snickerdoodle* for all I remember," Rosalee said, pushing her hair away from her face. "But we do need a new code word. How about *anchovy*?"

"Anchovy?" Archer frowned. "We both hate them. Why would you choose that word?"

"Because it's a word neither of us would ever use unless we had to."

"Okay. Anchovy it is. So, if you ever need me, just text *anchovy,* and I'll do everything but bend time to get to you."

"Same goes for you, Rob. If you ever need me, need help, you send that word to me, and I'll show up with every officer you know at my side."

He nodded in agreement, then moved close to the bed, burying his hands in the thick strands of her wavy hair.

"I've always loved your hair best just like this," he said in a soft tone. Although he wasn't deft at the task, he braided her hair so it would be out of her face. One of her hairbands was on the bedside table, so he looped it around the end of the braid, then let it fall against her back. "You are too beautiful for words, Lena."

She rolled her eyes at him. "You really need some rest, Rob. Obviously, you're hallucinating. I'm the size of a hippo. I feel like my body came out of a tube of silly putty, and I hate these stupid hospital gowns." She tugged at the front of the shapeless gown to emphasize her point.

"Here. Open this," Archer said, pulling out the wrapped gift he'd grabbed from beneath the tree at home.

"What is it?" she asked, eagerly accepting the package. "I don't have anything here to give you."

Archer smiled tenderly and looked at the bassinet where Ryder slept. "The best gift you've ever given to me is your love, and the second best is right there sleeping peacefully. Beyond you two, I don't need anything else."

"You really do say the nicest things, Archer Raines. Thank you." Without a moment of hesitation, Rosalee untied the ribbon, ripped open the festive red paper with white snowflakes, and lifted the lid on a box to reveal a pair of silky maternity pajamas and a matching robe in a pale shade of green with pink roses. "Oh, wow! These are gorgeous."

"The lady at the store said the waist is adjustable as you lose baby weight, and the top is a nursing one."

Rosalee lifted the top and held it against her. "Do you think anyone would care if I were to change?"

"No. I don't think they will. Do you need help?"

"Just getting up. I need to visit the little girl's room anyway."

After Archer helped her into the bathroom, he went to stand by Ryder's bassinet, enthralled as he watched the baby sleep.

With his heart feeling softer than warm butter, he turned at the sound of the bathroom door opening and helped Rosalee back to bed. After she was settled, he took his bag into the bathroom and changed into lounge pants, brushed his teeth, and debated removing his sweater, but he was still cold.

He pulled out the throw he'd brought along and eased into bed beside Rosalee. "If my being in here bothers you or causes any pain, I'll sleep in the chair," he said, spreading the throw over his legs and feet.

"No. I want you right here, beside me."

He placed an arm around her, and she snuggled against him. She felt so warm and smelled fresh from her shower. He breathed in the scent of her and let himself relax for the first time since the captain had called that morning.

"You're like an ice cube. You can put those cold feet on my shin. I feel like I've been in an inferno since I was on the bridge."

"Just holding you close will help me warm up."

Archer smiled as Rosalee rubbed her hand on his arm. "I'm sorry it was such a rough day, but I'm proud of you for helping that man of whom we will never speak again."

He sighed and kissed the tip of Rosalee's nose as she looked up at him. "Thanks, Lena. I'm just glad the ordeal is over with and behind us." He abruptly switched the subject. "Will you text your parents tomorrow about Ryder?"

"Probably. It's not like they'll change their plans and come see us. If a grandbaby doesn't get them excited, I don't think there's any hope for them. What about your mom and dad? Did you get in touch with them?"

"I sent them a photo of Ryder and a text earlier. They are, as you can imagine, beyond excited. They're going to try to get a flight out tomorrow or the next day. They said they'd stay for a week and do whatever they can to help."

"That's much appreciated. As tired as I feel, it'll be great to have the extra hands when we get home." Rosalee yawned but looked up at him with love shining in her gorgeous brown eyes. From the first time they'd met, when she'd knocked them both down while watching a puppy play across the street, he'd thought her eyes sparked with life, matching what he viewed as her vibrant personality.

She yawned again. "What about you?"

"What about me?"

"Will you be able to start paternity leave now, or will you have to wait until you originally had it scheduled?"

Archer grinned. "After today, the captain won't have a problem with switching my time off. I'll need to go in and do the reports about what happened on the bridge, but that can wait until after Christmas. Other than that, my next two months are yours."

"I'm glad, Rob. I love you so much, and I still can't quite believe this has all happened. Despite everything, this has been a spectacular Christmas Eve."

"It sure has, Lena. I love you—and Ryder—with all my heart. I had no idea I'd feel so full of love for him the moment he came into the world, but I do."

"What do you think tomorrow will bring?" Rosalee asked in a hushed whisper as her fingers feathered through his hair.

Archer bent closer to her, his arms surrounding her with his love. "Another good day."

If you enjoyed *The Bridge*, I hope you'll check out *Moonlight Cove*, another story brimming with mystery, friendships, hope, and love.

Be sure you sign up for my newsletter to get the scoop on latest releases.

Or read about one spoiled Portland heiress who gets sent to the edge of nowhere to serve out her community service sentence in *Catching the Cowboy*.

Recipe

I have been a fan of lush desserts since the first time I tasted one. The name comes from the word LUSH, meaning something delicious and sumptuous. A lush dessert is essentially layers of bliss that begin with a graham cracker or cookie crust, a layer of no-bake cheesecake, pudding, and whipped cream. This peppermint version is perfect for the holidays. Enjoy!

Peppermint Lush

   1 package Oreos
   ⅓ cup butter, melted
   1 ¼ cup sugar, divided
   16 ounces cream cheese, softened
   3 teaspoons peppermint extract, divided
   2 packages instant white chocolate pudding mix (3.4-ounce size)
   3 ½ cups milk
   red food coloring
   2 cups heavy cream
   ½ cup powdered sugar
   1 teaspoon vanilla extract
   2 cups mini chocolate chips
   30 Peppermint Hershey Kisses, chopped
   Grease a 9x13 baking dish. Set aside.
   Crush Oreos in a food processor or by hand until they are fine crumbs. Add melted butter and ¼ cup

sugar. Stir until incorporated then press mixture into bottom of prepared pan, and place in the freezer for 30 minutes.

In a medium bowl, whip cream cheese until creamy. Add remaining sugar and 1 teaspoon of peppermint extract. Beat until combined. Evenly spread mixture on crust and refrigerate while you make the next layer.

In a large bowl, combine pudding mix and milk. Stir until thickened. Add in food coloring and 2 teaspoons of peppermint extract. Stir until blended. Set aside.

Mix heavy cream on high speed until it begins to thicken, then add in powdered sugar and vanilla, and continue mixing until thick.

Fold in half of sweetened whipped cream (or 1 cup frozen whipped topping) and chocolate chips into pudding mixture until blended.

Spread this mixture over the first layer. Top this layer with remaining whipped cream.

Cover with plastic wrap and refrigerate overnight (at least 5-6 hours) before serving. Garnish with chopped Peppermint Hershey Kisses when ready to serve.

Reader's Guide

1. Some of the characters in the story went through changes. Who do you think had the most life-altering day? Why?

2. If you were in Archer's position on the bridge, what would you do? How would it make you feel?

3. What's one thing you would have done differently if you were Rosalee? One thing similar?

4. Were you surprised by any decisions Archer made during the course of the story?

5. What did you think about Ian's blossoming relationship with Kate? How might it change in the future?

6. Near the end of the story, Nova considers a new direction for her future. Have you ever had a moment when you considered pivoting in your career or life? What led to the moment?

7. In one scene, Carter realizes he would take a bullet for Ace. What do you think this says about his character?

8. What do you think about Rosalee's relationship with her parents? How do you envision her future relationship with Nova and her family?

9. Why do you think it was hard to figure out Leon was suffering from a split personality disorder?

10. Which character do you most relate to? Why?

Author's Notes

The idea for this story started a few years ago when my husband, Captain Cavedweller, and I were traveling from Seattle to Portland. We were supposed to arrive at my cousin's house in time for dinner and thought we had plenty of time to make the trip.

About an hour out of Portland, the traffic on the freeway suddenly came to a standstill. Was it a wreck? Road construction? What was happening?

Of course, I began searching for news on my phone and finally found the cause of traffic coming to a halt. An armed man had carjacked multiple vehicles. When he attempted another carjacking on one of the main bridges crossing the Columbia River into Portland, deadly force was deployed by police. Traffic both ways was blocked, resulting in the delays.

After creeping along at a top speed of about fifteen miles an hour for close to two hours, we finally made it to an alternate bridge and to my cousin's home.

The whole time we were in that snarl of vehicles and irate drivers who just wanted to get to their destination, I kept thinking how one man's choice—one bad choice—rippled out to affect thousands of people that day.

My imagination kicked into high gear with "what-ifs," wondering what if there had been a woman who went into labor while she was stuck in traffic, or someone on their way to their dream job interview, or even just travelers eager to spend time with loved ones they hadn't seen for a while.

By the time we returned home, I knew I wanted to write this story, but I needed all the characters to fall into place before I began.

I hope you enjoyed meeting Archer (Rob) and Rosalee (Lena), Carter and Nova, as well as Ian (the kid), Kate, Ace, and the other characters in the story.

If you've never visited Portland, in the northwest area of the region, you'll find the St. Johns Bridge, one of the most famous in Oregon because of its beautiful design and historical significance.

Bridge engineer David Steinman, one of the most famous of the 20th century, specialized in designing suspension bridges. He and fellow engineer Holton D. Robinson turned their talents to creating the iconic green Gothic suspension bridge that spans the Willamette River between North Portland and the Linnton and Northwest industrial neighborhoods of Northwest Portland.

Construction began on the bridge in 1929, right before the stock market crash. When it was dedicated in 1931 during the annual June Rose Festival, it held the longest span of any suspension bridge west of Detroit. The concrete piers of the bridge are unusual for the period in which they were built because they contain solid steel frame reinforcement rather than rebar, which was common during this period.

The bridge carries US Route 30 bypass over the river on four lanes of traffic. There are sidewalks the length of the bridge for pedestrians to use for a great view of the river. The bridge, and neighborhood in the area, is named after pioneer James John.

Beneath the bridge on the St. Johns neighborhood side is Cathedral Park, named after the 408-foot-tall cathedral-like bridge towers. The park was constructed in the 1960s and is the site of many weddings and celebrations.

St. Johns Bridge has been featured in television series including *The Librarians* and *Grimm*, and even included in the 1943 comic book Captain Marvel Adventures #23.

If you ever find yourself in Portland, take a drive to the northwest side of town to view this bridge that has long been held as a favored spot in photographs from the region.

As for the pub and theater where Ian and Kate went to watch a movie, the old building really does exist as McMenamins St. Johns Theater & Pub. Just like in the story, the building was originally part of the National Cash Register Company's exhibit hall for the Lewis and Clark Exposition held in 1905 in Portland. The building was later barged down the river and established at its current location.

The scene where Carter reminisces about his first-grade teacher comes from my own experience. I adored my first-grade teacher. She was patient and kind and made learning fun. When we did well, she would take down a big cardboard pirate's chest she kept on a high shelf behind her desk. It was full of toys and individually wrapped pieces of candy, but I always felt like I'd struck gold when I got to choose a treasure from the chest.

When I was in my early twenties, our local newspaper put out a Women in Business publication every month. My aunt was one of the featured entrepreneurial women included in one of the editions. We were all so proud of her for her accomplishments. Recalling that inspired the idea for the business magazine Kate and Ian discuss.

The inspiration for Lennox Medical Center, particularly the maternity ward, came from an experience I had with my niece and her husband. I had the great honor and privilege of being with them when they welcomed their first son. The facility they chose was amazing with a wonderful delivery room and a fantastic recovery space where they could both be comfortable throughout the night they spent there with their newborn. I wanted Rosalee to have a similar experience. After the day she and Archer had, they deserved a little pampering.

Thank you for coming along on this reading journey with me.

May all your choices ripple out to bring joy and blessings, and may every day be a good day.

♥ *Shanna*

Thank You

Thank you for reading *The Bridge*. Now that you've finished the story, I would be so grateful if you'd leave a review.

If you enjoy contemporary romances with a little mystery, be sure to read *Moonlight Cove*. If historical stories are your favorite, check out *Aundy*.

If you haven't yet, I hope you'll sign up for my newsletter. When you do you'll receive:

* Free Books
* The Welcome Letters
* VIP notice of sales
* Recipes
* Exclusive giveaways and bonus content
* Sneak peeks at new titles

Join the newsletter today and check out all of my books on my website at shannahatfield.com

Acknowledgements

Without the help of my husband and his willingness to spend car trips brainstorming ideas with me, this book would not exist. Thank you, Captain Cavedweller!

Also, big thanks to Brad and Brenda for sharing your ideas and excitement about this story long before the first word was written. Thank you for driving us all around Portland, especially across the bridge – twice! I'm so grateful for both of you.

Special thanks and deep gratitude to the Portland Police Bureau, especially Lieutenant Chris Burley and Dr. Liesbeth Gerritsen, of the Portland Police Bureau's Behavioral Health Unit, for their helpful answers to my multitude of questions. Also, my heartfelt thanks to the PPB for the hard work they do that often goes unnoticed and unacknowledged.

I would be remiss if I didn't thank Paula Eykelhof and Allison Moore, my wonderful editors, as well as Alice, Linda, and my beta readers. Thank you for your help in adding polish to the story.

Also, many thanks to Sami, my incredible publicist from Roger Charlie, to Luke Andreen for narrating the book, to those who voted for their favorite cover, to my wonderful readers, and to everyone who offered encouragement. You are all appreciated!

About the Author

USA Today bestselling author Shanna Hatfield is a farm girl who loves to write. Her sweet historical and contemporary romances are filled with sarcasm, humor, hope, and hunky heroes. When Shanna isn't dreaming up unforgettable characters, twisting plots, or savoring dark, decadent chocolate, she hangs out with her beloved husband, Captain Cavedweller, at their home in the Pacific Northwest.

Connect with Shanna online:

Website: shannahatfield.com

Facebook: Shanna Hatfield's Hopeless Romantics

Email: shanna@shannahatfield.com